# JAGUAR PALOMA AND THE CAKETOWN BAR

Mirador Publishing
10 Greenbrook Terrace
Taunton
Somerset
UK
TA1 1UT

Visit our website at: www.jesswells.com

# JAGUAR PALOMA
## AND THE CAKETOWN
## BAR

*To Chris —*
*Best of life & love to you*

*Jess Wells*
*(Friendships 2022)*

## JESS WELLS

Praise for *Jaguar Paloma and the Caketown Bar*

"Author Jess Wells has crafted **a gorgeously unique work** that places women at the forefront of adventure and weaves seamlessly realistic fantasy elements into the piece with flair and panache. A novel with oodles of style, original ideas and the authoritative, confident narrative to back it up. **An absolute treasure to read**." – K.C. Finn, Readers' Favorite

"A story filled with unusual characters, and **a wonderful ride for readers who enjoy carefree laughter, quirky situations and dialogues, and magical realism**. Add the drama to these qualities and you have a rollicking ride in Jaguar Paloma and the Caketown Bar....The way Jess Wells describes the village gives it a soul of its own. This author takes readers to such a place and gives them the most enviable company of well-developed, likable, and fun-loving characters. It is a page-turner for fans of character-driven novels and stories that excel in humor and adventure. **You won't be able to put this book down**."—Divine Zape, Readers' Favorite

"I thoroughly enjoyed the vivid details throughout the whole book. The captivating characters played their parts well and kept my attention until the last page. This story has many twists and turns but in the end, **Wells does a fabulous job of weaving everything together and creating an ending that will stay with you for a long while.** I encourage you to check out this story and all of its wonderful people." – Joy Hannabass for Readers' Favorite

# Other Titles by Jess Wells

Dedicated to single mothers everywhere.

She had bolted. Again. Bolted from midnight mass that put her on a dark street and into the hands of her rapist. Bolted from her family after their betrayal. Suddenly diving from the barge into the Magdalena River in spite of the river's dangers that had plagued her dreams since she was a toddler. If she had just stayed put, she would be halfway to the lively cities on the coast where she had intended to ply her special skill with trading. She had paid for a ticket. All her clothing was still on board. Fortune favors the bold, she reassured herself, but a quieter voice told her the bold, not necessarily the bolter. No course now but to walk, she decided, picking the burs and seedlings from the folds of her skirt.

She spent three steadfast days on good trails that skirted a marsh, eating wild salad and digging for tubers, convinced that a village was just beyond the bend. Each evening, she set up a system to collect fresh water from the dew, and each morning she set out without hesitation, as if the resolution with which she marched might magically serve as a compass and present an easy route. It had seemed like a reasonable plan and surely the coast, with merchandise straight off the boats, was just on the other side of the marsh.

The fourth morning, however, she woke up to a foggy white-out, and she built a small fire to combat the chill, then spent the morning crouched on the ground with her arms around her shins like a little girl. After another full day of fog, she became increasingly spooked by the sound of animals in the underbrush.

Finally, the fog cleared but when she climbed a tree to get her bearings, she saw that she was surrounded by the *Cienaga Grande*, an enormous marsh that was devoid of track or trail, and that had swallowed every sign of her step. Retreat was not an option.

At the same time, though, as a citizen of Calexicobia, she had grown up on tales of the marsh and its magic, so progress seemed dangerous as well. Every child had heard of the sprites who lived on the lily pads, the snakes mistaken for tree branches that then swallowed men whole. The fog that had fingers, the bats the size of buses, the demons that lurked in the muck to suck reason out through your ears. North to the coast, she resolved. North.

The days became drier; birds hid from a blistering sun and lizards stayed in the shade. Paloma walked across land bridges in the direction of fresh water, only to discover it was another enclosed, drying pool circled with dying reeds. She headed toward cattle that were grazing on what was surely a plain but turned out to be a thin strip between newly exposed and deadly swamp mud. She thought of following gulls who might be heading toward the ocean, but they no longer ventured into the wicked heat. Further into the swamp it started to smell brackish and then she was surrounded by the stench of dead vegetation. The rust-colored mud gave way to the black and fetid, writhing with insects who struggled to bore their soft bodies through increasingly hardened mud. She climbed another tree in the hopes of seeing a sign of progress but frightened herself with the immensity of the marsh which was now different every day, as the heat dried it and exposed new land.

She persevered. Based on the sun she headed north but had to double back, head west. She calmed herself with two small goals: feed herself and keep heading north toward the coast.

After a month of privation, she looked like a feral woman. Her hair was matted but she had woven it with snail shells and caked her skin with black mud to protect her from the increasingly brutal sun. She talked to herself. She slept on a mat she had woven from the reeds and rolled it up to carry each morning, strapped to a frame she made from branches. She wove a larger one to serve as a roof to keep the dampness off while she slept. She whittled a fine point on a stick to skewer fish who flopped in ever-shrinking pools and used the other end to test the ground before stepping. She wove a net from reeds to catch birds, tore the bottom of her skirt to make a cloth bag for eggs that she found, and she tucked scores of loose bird feathers into her belt.

Her resolve broke, though, when it seemed that the sun would crack through her skin and boil her blood. She prayed every night for guidance. It was not given. Then she prayed for forgiveness. She prayed to forgive her mother and was met with drought that shriveled the trees, cracked the mud. Her siestas began with a frightened shudder and a long, plaintive cry.

Paloma was lost for three months.

2

THANKFULLY, THE CREST OF PALOMA'S head with its
black hair was seen above the rushes and drew the
attention of the neighborhood watch of a small floating
village, *Nueva Venecia*, that had traditionally bobbed at
the edge of the marsh.

For years, the village had been a conglomeration of
floating houses painted happy colors, tethered to a
maze of docks, piers and posts. Villagers had used
narrow, dug-out boats to fish, and glide between their
homes, the small bar, and the church. Esteban the
boatman delivered groceries to wives as they mopped
their decks; he shuttled children to the floating school
and jested with the old men who dangled their fishing
pole off the front of their house, certain of a catch. In

their village, dampness and the smell of vegetation had always been everywhere: it had been a struggle to cut back the jungle, to scrap off the moss, to keep potted plants from climbing up struts and blanketing their roofs. They lived surrounded by the glittering jewels of afternoon sun on the water, the gentle imperceptible movement of the tide, and any wave that rocked their buildings was from a ship long gone, not worth mentioning but in passing. Amid aquamarine mornings of bird song and delicious breezes, their village was quiet, serene, colorful, and flowers of brilliant hues grew in a tangle into their own bouquet on the decks and posts. Moonlit evenings threw diamond shards on the water, the silhouette of birds against the fading light, pulling sweet cold air off the ocean to cool them after even the hottest day. The villagers were poor in every way except beauty, living amid the colors of St. Tropez, the fragrances of the best beach resort, the languid tempo that would make a gloomy barrister in London stop in the street and wonder about his life.

However, the severe drought that was challenging Paloma, worse than any experienced by even the oldest of the elders, had transformed the village.

They had to paddle further to find food, so the village became eerily quiet during the day. The birds flew deeper into the jungle and were harder to catch. The drought had made the men's skin flaky and tight. Their lush landscape of riotous colors was now brown and brittle; beams in their homes had shrunk and were exposed to the sky. Dust blew, a substance they had never seen. Their dogs lay panting in the shade while old mothers spent all day in the dark church praying, at first nervously chatting among themselves, but by the second month of crushing heat, they were silent and frightened. Everyone was always thirsty. They were hungry. With no fish, no birds, the children had started sucking on their knuckles and their mothers hid their faces in their aprons to weep.

For months, the swamp shrank, becoming so shallow that three buildings nearest the land rested on the mud. Every morning another family found itself in peril and chose to cut through ropes that had held fast for decades so they could float further away, rather than rest cock-eyed in the mud. All the floating houses were soon unmoored and clustered in the center of the largest pool, but it was steadily shrinking, fraying everyone's nerves with houses bumping into one another, and a sudden intimacy of porches that had always faced the water now facing each other. They had lived with water, fog, and moist air their entire lives, so tempers flared from the heat, the worry, the unwelcome intimacy and shifting alliances.

There was no water over which to ply their boats, and the mud had become too deep and dangerous to cross on foot except with rickety planks they had assembled in confusion. They were surrounded by mud deep enough to swallow up knives and a bottle a young man threw out of the bar in frustration. A chicken fell off a porch and disappeared, and when an angry man drove his six-foot fishing spear into the mud after church, the whole village watched it sink straight down, swallowed without a trace. They started to panic. What if one of their children fell off the walkways? What was to stop their houses, barely eight feet tall, from sinking and drowning them all? It was one thing to sit on the mud. It was entirely another to be swallowed by it. Now they were frightened to their core. At the bar, men with several drinks in them considered abandoning their homes and moving inland, though it meant taking on a lifestyle that even ten generations had not experienced.

So, when the cadre of protectors from the village saw the top of Paloma's black head above the reeds they thought of jaguars and food. There was enough meat on a jaguar to feed them for a couple of days if they stewed it and shared the soup. Everyone knew there were jaguars in the swamp: the next inlet over was Cienaga del Tigre, swamp of the tiger. The question was how to catch it.

The cadre assigned to protect the village was made up of old men whose decrepitude was now more apparent that they had to get out of their boats and walk. Only two of them could stand up straight; one man's feet were so bad that every step was a journey on hot coals. Not one among them had perfect vision and

*Chapter 1*

1865, IN THE SOUTHERN COUNTRY OF CALEXICOBIA

1

After the government had burned it to the ground, it was hard to imagine the Caketown Bar surrounded by a raucous shanty town, home to cast-off mothers and unclaimed children, filled with lively mirth and mayhem together, where every day was a celebration even if not a holiday, where peacocks cawed from the backs of donkeys, and women's wigs and bunting were playthings for the monkeys in the trees when they stopped playing catch with the dogs. Flowers of unknown origin bloomed in the night and then flew away, and blue mist or green fog rolled in without warning. It was a town where morning was heralded by a rum cask being rolled across a dance floor, and the groggy question of who had arrived in the night; evening announced by the sizzle of lightbulbs in bent sockets and men slapping the dust off their pants with their hard-working hats, women putting a baby to the breast and finally sitting down. Tartatenango, Spanish slang for Caketown, hosted every traveling circus and any Romani family who wandered the southern country of Calexicobia, every soothsayer and shabby hawker of medicinal nonsense, any run-away from the army, convent, or hostile home. No one was turned away for being muddy or misshapen or ragged. Everyone was welcome until proven unworthy and it was just assumed that everyone was on their second chance: at the Caketown Bar, sharing stories of the past was much more intimate than nudity.

In the beginning, seekers from the north trekked through the jungle, veered off a minor mule-train road just after the third hollow acacia tree and followed a wide animal track to find it. Burdened with sadness and loss on top of their possessions, they trudged toward the little town whose name was whispered among the laundresses or spoken low by the cook after a glance over her shoulder. The midwives knew of it, the women of the theater troupes and Romani spoke of it late at night.

Those who used the snaking Magdalena river that was its western boundary had an easier time finding it.

The river was calm and narrow at this spot before growing wide and wild as it headed north toward the sea. Boaters set their sights on a beach between two enormous white boulders that were smooth and firm like the breasts of a new mother in the morning.

Its founding was more a protest than a selection. Paloma Marti, who was six foot five, at seventeen far younger than she looked because of her surprising height, saw the hungry glare and familiar danger from the boatmen and two male passengers on the barge she was riding. When the ringleader flashed a knife under the guise of cleaning his nails, she abandoned her small bag and dove off the side of the boat, swimming toward the inviting boulders.

She had taken to the road after having been raped by a man who then presented himself at her house and, despite her protests, was received by her family as if he was an appropriate suitor. After he had left their home with his belly filled with her mother's best sausages and the wine her father saved for Saints days, Paloma threw her clothing into a small leather bag and, after dark, slammed the door behind her with such force that it cracked both windows in the front of the house and sheared from the wall a shelf of her mother's prized china. It was the last time they would see her, her last commentary.

Paloma was gangly and thin, her height making her bend oddly to sit, and her legs were so long that they stuck out at odd angles from under a table. She had the hair of a raven and never cut it, wore it in a braid so long that by the time she was an adult she settled it like a lapdog when she sat. With full lips and a smile that circled her head when she deigned to show it, she had a presence that could fill a room from dust devils to cobwebs and all the space in between, though not always for the better. Her gaze was its own Inquisition. She saw inside you, her eyes a pool too deep with no escape that still made you want to dive in. Some men thought her exquisite, like juice from bruised fruit. Others merely shrugged their shoulders. "Too much tree, not enough flower."

ESCAPING THE MEN ON THE barge with nothing but a waterskin slung across her back, Paloma clambered onto the muddy shore and, fearful that the men might beach their craft and pursue her, she ran due east, her enormous strides propelling her forward and her long arms parting tall swamp grass like curtains.

After an hour of running full tilt, she stopped in a clearing, put her hands on her knees to catch her breath. When she stood and took a swig of water, she looked around her and listened in vain for the sounds of pursuit. While the silence was a relief, the noon sun gave her no indication of directions, the swamp grass had closed behind her and she had taken so many evasive turns that she had no idea where she was.

every night on patrol they inevitably argued over the broken hearts of their first communion class more than a half century ago, an old rivalry stopped only by communal narcolepsy.

For Esteban the boatman, however, there was no question, no debate: there was a jet-black jaguar, so large that the crest of its head could be seen above the tall reeds as it crisscrossed the marsh, with their (now barren but surviving) chickens and vulnerable young children its obvious destination. First the watchmen ignored Esteban. The next day the second-in-command fell asleep just as the jaguar appeared and rather than admit it, derided the boatman as drunk. But soon women washing clothes in what little water was left at the marsh's edge spotted it and set more men to the task: they double-teamed the watch, then resolved to bag the beast as perhaps the last hunt in their soon-to-be desert home.

They set out in the morning, seven of the village's most virile men including Esteban, lead by the elderly watchman who insisted on leading the way though he had not seen the jaguar and slowed their progress with his faltering step. They crept through the reeds, thought about splitting up to encircle the beast but were too timid.

WHEN THEY REACHED THEIR JAGUAR, Paloma was at the bottom of a steep, muddy embankment that she had climbed down to spear fish and had exhausted herself trying to ascend. She was skeletally thin, covered in black mud that had dried and cracked like elephant skin. She was splattered with the blood of small rodents and the feathers of common birds. Her black hair fell over her shoulders like a mane, obscuring her face. She was delirious, nearly comatose.

They pointed their spears at her, stunned by the enormity of this jaguar, but trembled, worried that they would all be torn apart if it survived their attack.

When she slowly raised her head to them, the man with the poorest eyesight lunged forward but Esteban held him back.

Paloma pushed matted locks of hair from her face.

"Thank God!" she said and started to cry for the first time in her ordeal.

The men were shocked, mouths gaping: a jaguar had transformed itself into a weeping woman. They hesitated, fearing bad magic, but Esteban dropped his spears and slid down the embankment, knelt beside her, offering her water from his waterskin. The youngest of cadre turned aside to cry for his children who would continue to be hungry, and for the indignity of wishing that this woman had been something to eat. Esteban dispatched the fastest of them to relay the news and to bring fruit and water.

They gently grasped her by the elbows to help her up but discovered that her right foot was caught in mud that had dried overnight, trapping it like cement. Esteban ordered them to scrape the mud with their spear tips. It was slow going.

"Where are you from?"

She was too delirious to say.

"How long have you been out here?"

Paloma shook her head, shrugged her shoulders, tried to compose herself.

Esteban was the first to see a rivulet of water trickle across the hardened mud, and when it reached the others, they were so newly accustomed to drought that it surprised them. At first Esteban was pleased when the water seemed to change course and fill the small scratches their spears had made. Softer mud was a good thing.

But the trickle of water soon became a torrent, as if flood gates had been opened, and Esteban realized that they were sitting below the low tide level of the marsh: this jaguar-turned-woman would drown if they couldn't free her.

He ordered them to pick up the pace and the young men pushed aside the old.

Still, the water continued to pour into the marsh. When it reached their calves, it was at Paloma's waist. It obscured their vision, so Esteban got on his knees with a knife and using his other hand on her ankle as a guide, scraped at the rim of the hole encircling her foot. The water rose to their chests. Paloma and

Esteban were face to face, both knowing the consequences. Paloma craned her neck upward to stay above the water and pulled on her foot. Esteban took a deep breath and laid on the marsh bottom, and just as he pulled the last clump of restricting mud and stood, lifting Paloma in his arms, lightening struck the horizon and a monsoon-force rain poured down in sheets.

The men made a chair with their arms to carry her, though she was so tall that a third man had to walk in front holding up her ankles. All looked up at the unexpected rain.

The relief among the group was palpable: Paloma over her rescue; Esteban that he had beaten the torrent and freed her; the rest of the posse that the water was finally returning, soaking their dusty clothing, gloriously dripping off the ends of their hair, their feet squishing into the thirsty, dry moss on the banks.

When they approached the village, everyone was already outside, jubilant over the rain, the women putting out buckets and uncovering rain barrels. Children spun in circles, laughing with their mouths open, their faces tipped back to the sky.

As Paloma pulled the hair away from her face with her forearm and looked the villagers in the eye, seeing the old women in their once-vibrant dresses, soft hair behind kerchiefs, she was so thankful that as she scraped the mud from her face she bent into her hands in supplication and gratitude. She panted thanks and kissed the old women's hands.

There was no extra food for a party, but the exuberance was irrepressible. Potted plants were moved from the shade into the rain. Men brought out the rum, and dogs barked with abandon. Pots and pan were set out on the deck to fill with water. Chickens released from their cages strode the decks flapping and fluffing their wings. Women brought out brooms to clean their decks, but they were smiling with relief, and, with much fanfare, the men and women of the village band scurried over the bouncing planking to retrieve their instruments and herald the blessing of the rain.

The watchman and his team crossed a gangplank over the muddy marsh to the village church and, as the rain pinged on the brass of the trumpets, set Paloma on a bench under a sheltering eaves. They had gone to kill a jaguar but had brought home a woman, odd though she was. The ancient women looked carefully to see if her eyes glowed: she had come from the marsh of the tiger, hadn't she? Whole cadres of jaguars could be heard on the full moon there singing in guttural harmony. Cienega del Tigre, home of the blue-black jaguar the size of a horse who leapt over trees, whose wife was the color of honey and spewed rubies into the water, challenging men to trade their blood for the jewels. It was well known that there was a Magdalena caiman who was half man, punishment for peering at women while they bathed. The black mud cracking on this one's skin might be the hide of the jaguar sloughing off. They resolved to lock up the chickens and children tonight, in case she went prowling. The men secretly hoped that she was dangerous and still untamed.

Esteban the boatman chuckled and pronounced her Jaguar Paloma.

# Chapter 2

1

Orietta Becerra sliced mango under the shelter of the local bar's eaves, peering through the pelting rain at an enormous, blackened woman shedding feathers as she was carried over the planks of the marsh city. Odd though it was, she turned back to her paring knife and fruit: she didn't need the particulars of the story, since women are always running away from something or desperately running toward something, and both most often involve tragedy and scar tissue. In this case feathers and mud. Best not to ask most times. Especially as Orietta had just arrived in the village yesterday as an oddity herself.

She had been run out of the village of her birth and

had hitched a ride with a yuca truck driver who kicked her out at the edge of the swamp without giving her a reason. She protested to the back of the truck as it turned sharply and sped away but her righteous indignation was short-lived: Orietta's predicament was her own fault, and she knew it. Even young girls know not to fall for a married man, so she had no excuse. The unholy trinity of the village priest, the man's wife and a cadre of her school mates had chased her out of town. She had had no idea where she was going but, unceremoniously dumped into the brutal, dry heat, she had seen the lights of the barely floating bar and hoped she might sweep the floor in exchange for water or maybe a meal. She had adjusted what she had always relied on for a disguise: a scarf low on her forehead, cinched over her hair and sometimes purposely worn askew to make her face look misshapen. Most times she wore a sun hat over it to further obscure her face. An old poncho hid her shape. Even in the heat here, when children laid listless and naked on their porches, it was best to not let people see her.

The problem was that Orietta was an extraordinarily beautiful woman, far more arresting than the sum of her parts: auburn hair that was thick and straight, a perfectly symmetrical face with smooth brows and flawless skin; breasts that were high, firm, and ample; narrow hips, shapely legs, enchanting lips. Despite her mother's vehement protests, this year Orietta, at 24, had abandoned her disguise and won every beauty pageant, had been crowned princess of every harvest festival within a day's walk of her village. But it had come at a price that she had been warned about: girls hated her; old women predicted a life of sin and treated her as if she already lived it; men claimed that her beauty released them from morality, that they couldn't help themselves for their lasciviousness; that somehow it had released the married man she loved from his vows.

Orietta understood that her beauty had ruined the marriage of her lover, her own path in life, and her family of origin. Even when she was a child, her mother had warned her, shielded her, taken precautions after recognizing the wonder of her daughter's beauty. She had carried her in her arms until Orietta was quite old to keep the hood of a cape hiding the toddler from the eyes of strangers. Washing her, her mother sat back on her heels and put her soapy hands on her apron. Every day it seemed the child's beauty increased. Naked in the suds, Orietta glowed, luminescent. So fragile and exquisite, she was frightening. Orietta became an arresting young girl whose beauty made her own grandfather jingle the change in his pocket. Men shifted nervously on every park bench she passed. They clustered around her mother in the market with the flimsiest excuses.

SOMETHING HAD TO BE DONE, her mother had resolved. When Orietta was of school age, her mother pinned tight braids to her head like an old woman and escorted Orietta home while other children ran together in packs. Orietta's mother grew nervous and fretful. By the time she was nine, her mother forbade her husband to get together with his friends in the yard because of the way they watched for Orietta. Her mother stopped inviting women over when their catty remarks began. The woman's sternness drove her husband from the house and since she had caught him staring in wonder at his daughter once, she decided that even he could not be trusted and never allowed them to be alone. Her father's heart drifted away, though he came home every night and dutifully cared for his family while avoiding his daughter so as to not upset his wife. The family became isolated.

THEN HER MOTHER REASONED THAT the braids were not enough. When Orietta was ten, her mother tied her into a big scarf and suddenly the woman's nervousness subsided. Orietta felt a sudden calmness wash over her mother. Harmony and happiness came with the scarf; safety flowed from invisibility, it seemed. They walked through the market, Orietta's beauty hidden, and her mother was relaxed and easy. They swung joined hands walking between the booths; they had ice cream at noon.

"The best things are private things," her mother said as she gave Orietta an extra cookie from her plate. "And you, my sweet, are the best there is."

Orietta started a new school year in her headscarf and the girls in her class assumed that she was disfigured in some way; they pitied her, and they protected her from the boys who tried to yank off her disguise.

The arrangement worked for a little girl, but as she entered her teenage years and her classmates became focused on boys, Orietta shrunk into the background. No parties, no graduation, no promenade on festival days. Dressed more like a nun than the nuns, she made lace with her mother, and resigned herself to a life in the shadows.

ONE EVENING WHEN SHE WAS 23, though, the arrangement with her mother fell apart. Orietta was walking home from the market wearing a white cowl and a kaftan when she passed a *quinceanera* spilling from the church into the square, all the girls in their voluminous dresses, plunging necklines off their shoulders, a riot of pastels and patterns, the air fragrant with champagne and strawberries, roast duck and rice. It was a festivity that she hadn't had for herself, nor had she been invited to one when she was 15. Now that she was considered an old maid, she stood motionless by a tree, her basket heavy on her arm as she watched the girls twirl and laugh, displaying more skin of their cleavage, shoulders, and arms than she had ever seen, and would ever show. Orietta was surprised that they reveled in their display, drawing attention to themselves while their parents applauded. No one was skulking here: it was the opposite of Orietta's sequestered life.

She ran home and threw the basket on a table and threw her cowl off beside it.

"Why are you doing this to me?" she challenged, grabbing at her braids to rip them off her head.

Her mother jumped to her feet as if Orietta was about to break a priceless vase.

Orietta dug her fingers into her hair to loosen the weave, finally shaking her head with a growl. Her auburn hair, thick and full, glinted in the candlelight as it framed her face. Though she was enraged, her skin was beautifully flushed, and her eyes flashed.

Her father set down his newspaper and drank in the sight of her, knowing that it might be the last glimpse before his wife wrapped her up again. "You're beautiful, my dear." Doeskin, honey cakes.

Her mother gasped in wonder at the sight of her, and then was horrified.

"Mother Mary, you're even more beautiful than I thought. This is going to be so much more difficult." She wrung her hands.

"You can't hide her forever," her father protested. "How will she find a husband if no one can see her?"

"I won't live like this anymore," Orietta said.

Her mother grabbed the cowl and moved toward her. "We will pick someone for you. So much safer than..."

"I won't wear it. Get away from me."

"Let her be," her father said, gently taking the cowl from his wife.

WITHIN DAYS OF ORIETTA'S FIRST outing with a naked face, the whole village was up in arms. Instantly, every man's wife was dog-ugly in comparison; suddenly every woman was wounded and enraged, intent on Orietta's banishment. The girls from school who had protected her (now mothers, tired and worn from childbirth) were furious: she had used them, they whispered among themselves, by making them think she was deformed, which now made them look both stupid and ugly. Her father came home bruised and angry from the bar where he had to defend Orietta's honor and explain his wife's oddity. Young men crowded around their front door, and her father periodically charged into the crowd with a cudgel to disperse them, but he was outnumbered and ineffective. They returned the following night, leaving globs of chewing tobacco and cigarette butts outside the door, beer bottles in the shrubbery.

Orietta gobbled up life as the belle of the ball, dancing until late at night, inviting boys in to meet her parents and then running out the door with them for moonlit buggy rides and fireside gatherings under palm trees, where she enchanted the young men and infuriated the women.

Most nights when she came home, her hat in her hand and some token of affection pinned to her collar or rattling in her purse, her mother was weeping on the sofa, and Orietta sailed by her with her nose in the air. Serves her right for keeping me penned up for so many years.

Orietta's demise, however, was quick in coming. A knot of admirers was visibly plotting among themselves to surround her in the market when an older man stepped to her elbow and spoke to her in low tones, directing her away. Unlike the boys who fell over themselves trying to find the right word, the right entertainment, he was confident, well-traveled, well-read, smooth in his approach. He wore dapper vests and had pocket watches. He didn't pant over her like the youths; he met her away from her house.

When Orietta came home before dawn, her hair down, without the ribbon belt on her new dress, her mother met her in the hallway and started to shout. Her father got involved in the argument; the man was dragged from his home with his wife weeping at his heels. The village priest, who had been alternating his sermons between the sin of jealousy and the demon of temptation, now exploded from the pulpit on the satanic bond of adultery and fornication. Jessabelle, he shouted, while the village women were relieved by her demise and the men wished they had been the cause of it. As Orietta was chased out of town, her mother ran beside the truck and gave her the kaftan and a scarf.

HER FIRST NIGHT AT THE swamp-village bar she had stayed swathed in her disguise while she washed dishes for a meal and slept in a chair on the bar's back porch with a knife under her thigh. With the arrival of Paloma and the astounding rain, maybe she could slip further into the village and find a legitimate place for herself. Upheaval brings opportunity, after all. She touched her head covering as if it was a talisman and, bent against the rain, walked the rickety planks toward the commotion.

2

WATCHING THE PROGRESS OF TWO odd women moving toward the village center, a nun named Sister Agnes tongued the empty space between her two front teeth, crossed her arms over her pendulous breasts and further straightened her ramrod back. The one in the scarf looked like a specter and this thing from the swamp on the arms of the posse was clearly not of this world. In the middle of a freakish rainstorm after months of freakish heat, two unknown women were converging on their blighted village which meant that evil was clearly approaching. She was an expert on evil, after all. Taking vows made some women kinder and more forgiving, but in understanding the devil, Sister Agnes had been given a name for evil and a belief in its perniciousness. Thrice daily she recited incantations against it, and she developed a hardened conviction that the devil lived in everyone like bacteria just waiting for a chilly night so it could occupy the body and soul. Even the tiny and inconsequential contained the seeds of destruction, the contagion of immorality and blight. Her prayers were not celebrations of a savior or entreaties to the power of his love, but were verbal battles against the devil, a skirmish in an incessant war she must wage against Satan. These two women were trouble, unquestionably.

However, she took the tenor of her congregation: the filthy feathery one was being heralded as a jaguar woman, and everyone was so jubilant over the sudden rain that she did not want to suppress their much-needed relief. As for the cloaked woman standing to the side, best not to poke a demon until you are certain of its power.


THE POSSE DEPOSITED JAGUAR PALOMA on the floor of the church and brought her fresh rainwater, cloths to wash her, the crowd pressing in to see her. Children knelt at her knees and collected the falling feathers; dogs tried to lick her clean. The elation over the rain turned the church into a carnival, women in each others' arms weeping with joy, children jumping with glee, men either standing together in the doorway chortling and prognosticating over the date the fish would return, or standing at Paloma's feet, excited by her. The cloaked woman stood quietly by the wall, watching.

Even bleak Sister Agnes had to concede that the rain was a blessing: with the homes clustered together in the center of the marsh, access and temptation had been heightened, she was certain. In a few months, the wages of sin would be visible in more than a few bellies. But she had a deeper, more personal relief, one that had to be kept secret at all costs.

First, she commanded the villagers, time for prayers of thanks.

After the last Hail Mary, Sister Agnes ordered the night's watch to carry Jaguar Paloma into a small room with one single bed at the far end of the church. She assigned Orietta to tend to the survivor. It would be best to keep them together so they could be watched, the nun reasoned, to make certain that these questionable women did not influence the children or tempt the men. Bad enough that one of them now carried the animistic label of Jaguar Paloma.

The torrential rain continued long after dark, after the children began shivering where they had been laid to sleep in the pews, after the women rose from their stiff knees and put away their rosaries, and the joyous sound of gratitude was replaced by a new anxiety. The rain barrels overflowed; eaves that had stiffened in the heat tore away from the roofs. Boats hauled onto porches to keep out of the mud were filling up and tilting the houses to one side. Every gap in every roof caused by the death of moss and shrinking lumber was a portal for the deluge. Water sluiced from all points of the marsh toward the central cluster of homes, and villagers rushed back on rickety planks before the slats fell as the buildings rode new, erratic waves, and slammed into fragile railings and scraped away rotted porches. The villagers whose houses were stuck in the mud near the shore faced a new challenge: how to free their houses before the rising water flooded the sterns and sunk them. Teams of boatmen worked through the night, their shouts and calls to each other were monitored by all, and the strain of broken timbers could be heard across the marsh. Even the ducks took shelter.

PALOMA SHOOK AND, IN HER nightmares, rolled from side to side on the bed. Her hair was still filthy and knotted around bits of twigs; her skin was grey where the dogs and old women had tried to wash her clean, dotted with patches of black mud.

Orietta sighed deeply and came from watching the rain at the window to kneel on the rug and stroke the girl's forehead with cloths from a bucket of water. "Calm yourself. You're safe now," Orietta whispered. Every few hours, she woke Paloma to drink water and before midnight, Esteban the boatman brought mango that Orietta slid into Paloma's mouth. As the rain continued violent hammering on the roof, Orietta sat back against the wall opposite the bed in the barren, cell-like room and slept.

IN THE MORNING TWO OLD women and Sister Agnes were up first, since sleeping at their age had become not so much a necessity as a social convention. They were glad for a reason to have a hot cup of *aromatica* earlier in the morning and to assess the damage of last night's rain. They huddled under the awning of the church with their stained cups and old rosaries.

Water was on their mind: the filling marsh was a comfort, but it wasn't drinking water: they were as reliant on a spring on the marsh's edge for water as they were on the marsh for fish and game. True, since every family had opened the lid of their rain barrel, there might be enough to withstand another drought, but they looked askance at each other because they had a secret: the spring on the far side of the marsh had dried up months ago and without it, they were little better off than before this rainstorm. The nun had been supplementing their water supply from the church's rain barrels and swearing the other women to secrecy: no need to alarm anyone. But this morning it was time for an inspection. Had the rain enticed the spring to flow again?

The nun rapped sharply on the door to Orietta and Paloma's room. Orietta quickly covered her head and cinched the scarf.

Sister Agnes was not about to leave two strangers of indeterminate morals alone in the church. "Get up. You're coming with us."

"She's still very weak," Orietta said.

"Then carry her." The nun held the door.

The absurdity of a woman Orietta's average size trying to carry the enormously tall Paloma did not change the nun's steely gaze. Nor did the prospect of braving the sheets of rain that had everyone else in the village inside or watching from the shelter of their porches.

Orietta helped Paloma to her feet and put her arm around her waist as the groggy girl struggled to comply.

Thankfully, just before they reached the door, the rain stopped, though the sky was dark and menacing. A few young men launched their canoes to find the edge of the now re-expanding swamp and returned later that afternoon with a pair of boots, a gaff, a rosary, and a small table with an upended tea set. The objects had been exposed when the swamp had dried but no one had braved the mud to claim them.

When Paloma saw that the nun and the old women were taking her in the direction of the marsh she froze, and then in panic strained against Orietta's support. She was not going back into the marsh. Shaking her head and muttering under her breath, Paloma peeled Orietta off her and stumbled back to the little room.

Sister Agnes pivoted and called to Orietta to retrieve her, but then relented, as perhaps the girl was still too sick and besides, it was this shrouded girl who concerned her most.

"Leave her," she said sternly, though there was no way to control the giant girl anyway. "You're with us."

THE NUN TENTATIVELY LED THE other three women over noisy walkways on pilings and pillars. They looked suspiciously at the sky. She called Orietta to the front and demanded that she haul boards out of the mud to reconstruct the walkway where they had fallen. "You're the youngest," she explained brusquely. Orietta adjusted her hood, especially unwilling to let the nun see her, and complied. Orietta scraped her knees, dirtied her hands and, at one point, Sister Agnes caught her by the hem of her poncho to save her from falling into the treacherous mud.

They reached the land, walked along a narrow berm with the confidence of women who had been marching the path for decades. But when they neared their destination, they slowed, turned to each other. The leaves of the enormous tree that sheltered their fresh-water spring were brown and curled, only the deepest reaches containing greenery, as if hiding from the sun. And worse yet, when they parted the branches (tenderly, like touching a wounded friend) they discovered that the stone walls built around the spring had crumbled and filled the spring box, the drought having sucked the last bit of moisture from the mortar. The spring was just a dry pile of stones on the parched earth.

The old women slowly lowered themselves onto large rocks placed years ago in a semi-circle under the tree, site of many gossip sessions and trysts. Their sadness and fear heightened their exhaustion, and they took out their rosaries slowly.

Because their heads were bent in prayer, eyes closed, and under the shade of the struggling tree, they didn't immediately notice that the sun had broken through the clouds. It rose in height and intensity. Insects sang, then stopped. Canoers with their battered loot paddled home in fear of being trapped in the re-emerging mud. With the last 'amen' Sister Agnes raised her head to see the brutal sunshine just outside the tree's shelter and she blanched: the devastation of the drought was fresh in everyone's minds.

They were right to be afraid: it was as if someone had pulled the plug in a bathtub. The women scurried home faster than they had arrived. What if the walkway planking hit the mud? What if their rain barrels were left out, tops off, in the sun? They knew now for certain that whatever rain they had been able to catch was all the water there was. The water level receded steadily, seeming to not just evaporate, but disappear past opened sluice gates.

The village went from stunned appreciation and relief over the rain to frenzied activity. Women brought their clothing in from the line to protect it from fading. Boys rolled sealed rain barrels under the porch roofs and the potted flowers and vegetables that had gotten a taste of rain were shuttled back into the shade. The plan to reinforce the walkways with more pilings, talked about for too long and not acted upon, was officially abandoned. As the birds flew away, the villagers could see the return of the drought, and knew that soon the sparkling water on the far side of the marsh would drain to flat mud with little puddles big enough for mosquitos but not fish. Already, Esteban's roof creaked, and his porch railings split open. A family who had just last night pulled the prow of their house from the mud packed their things to leave while they wept. Most devastating was the worry that their way of life was over, mixed with sorrow from the sight of limp leaves, shriveling flowers, parched fish, dogs newly suffering under their shaggy coats. It was a primal fear, an emotional thirst, an anxiety that came with the blistering sun.

FOR SISTER AGNES, THE DRY spring and crumbled walls posed an additional problem. Late at night for a full year now she had come to the spring and bottled its water, selling it as holy through an old man who took it to a traveling medicine man, or so said a handsome, smooth-talking thief named Cosimo. The ruse had started out harmlessly: she had not meant to hoodwink people. Attending a mass in a festival town two miles away, Sister Agnes had carried a single vial of spring water as a small talisman for herself because it tasted exceptionally good and was the nectar that kept the village alive. But when a woman saw her touching it fondly, she asked to buy it, as if it was from Jerusalem. When Sister Agnes turned it over to her, the woman was so delighted, seemed so comforted by it (and the coins were so reassuring to Sister Agnes) that the nun bottled up a few more. She had not actually claimed it was from Jerusalem. The woman had assumed its origin, Sister Agnes consoled herself when she was so deep into the fraud than she could not extricate herself.

Rolling those first coins in her pocket she had debated with herself. Why shouldn't she prosper? She was generous to the villagers, though some whispered behind her back that she wasn't. Why couldn't she keep a coat for herself during the coat drive? Or take some of the finer canned foods off the top of the collection that came in from the city each fall, since the villagers probably had never experienced the food and so were not capable of appreciating it.

Sister Agnes was different than they were: she had grown up on the coast 200 miles north in what had felt like a small town to her at the time but in retrospect was an amazing metropolis with cable cars and telegraph, electric lights and restaurants. Being posted in this muddy little backwater village was a test of her faith, she knew it. The archbishop had sent her here for a reason but several times a year she broke down and cried under a pillow over the monotony and simplicity of life with these people. If this location was a test, these little vials of water were its recompense; in the end they were holy in the sense that she took a small basket of them covered with a tea towel from under her bed and prayed over them every night.

She had taken a special trip into the city of Gustavia to buy more bottles and soon she had small clusters of coins in the backs of each of her drawers. She wrote little labels for the bottles at night in her room and hid them if someone knocked on her door. There was no genuine harm in it, was there? It was such a simple way to give someone comfort. An old woman with a bad foot had begged her for one at a harvest festival; a man who had lost his wife and child deserved solace in whatever form it could be given, didn't he? To expand her business, she worked with an old man who made bricks from the dense mud of the swamp and filled his canoe until it rode so low that the gunwale nearly touched the water. When the bricks were laid out to dry, he would paddle her basket to enclaves of migrant workers and farm hands, nearly acting like a holy man himself as he spoke in soothing tones and touched people on their forehead when he bestowed the little bottles.

That's when Sister Agnes had made her mistake: desperate to leave the swamp even if it was just for a weekend, she had hitched a ride with the brickmaker to a Mango Festival twenty miles away, and though she had made no arrangements, was approached by a young mother who asked to buy vials for each of her four children. She met the mother behind the battered carnival wagons but after she held hands in prayer with the woman and watched her trundle back to the festivities, a low, gravely voice called to her.

"I have something here that only you could appreciate Sister," said a man from the depths of a sooty wagon. "And I'll trade you for your... holy water."

He emerged from his wagon belly first. Four plaid shirts and two flowered vests struggled to cover his protruding stomach. With a turquoise skull cap and a belt embossed with dragons, he was a riot of color and patterns, sharp in contrast to the buxom nun in black.

He regarded her with the brooding eye of an opportunist.

"Cosimo," he said, bowing in a false but well-practiced greeting. Then he turned and, with his eyes still surveying Sister Agnes, he reached one hand into the wagon and withdrew a pine box, four feet tall with a leather handle on the top.

The rest of the conversation was a blur to Sister Agnes because he set the box on the top step of his wagon and slid it open to reveal the most exquisite statue of the Virgin Mary she had ever seen. He spoke of Rome, but she saw the flawless blue cape with gold trim, the gentle eyes. She heard 'pilgrimage' and 'blessings of the Pope' but only saw the ruby lips, the perfect hands. What surprised her most was her intense longing to hold it, posses it. Where did she live, he asked her? She haltingly described how beautiful the statue would be in the boat during the floating processions in the swamp, how the light would glint off the water and add to the shimmer of her cape. In the blur of her emotions, she saw her hand giving all the vials in her pockets to this man, Cosimo.

He grabbed her shoulder and she snapped back into reality. "I'll need 400 more, you understand. Or a cash equivalent."

She took her hands from the side of the box and looked into his eyes, dumbfounded.

"You wouldn't want me to discuss... nonpayment... with the Bishop," he said.

He knew where she lived. She thought she had been discrete, but he had seen what she was selling, and was now turning the vials in his hands, inspecting the labels.

"Nicely done, Sister. They look quite...authentic." He smiled slyly, slid the cover back on the box and helped her carry it to the brickmaker's boat.

THE ARRIVAL OF THE BEAUTIFUL Madonna had been celebrated with days of feasting, a stream of pilgrims from other parts of the marsh, heightened attendance at Mass, a happy cadre of women who dusted her and brought her water lilies. The statue was the most unblemished object for miles, its bright blue paint without the chips and dings and splinters that pock-marked the village walls and tables and plates. Sister Agnes was heralded, and the attention and the activity made her nearly chipper. Every morning she had greeted it as companion and proof of good fortune/good taste, talisman, recompense, sublime mirror of her own worth.

Late at night, though, she worried about it being stolen, about being discovered, about thuggish men in colorful vests. She padded barefoot through the church in her tattered nightdress, unable to sleep, checking the locks on the louvered wooden windows; sometimes in a fit returning the Madonna to its crate and lying awake thinking of new ways to hammer it to the altar or strap it to the wall.

She had delivered 200 vials through the brickmaker but had no illusions: once the 400 had been sent, the demand for blackmail payments would begin. Last month the brickmaker had thrown out his back and missed a delivery: she had seen Cosimo flanked by two menacing men on horseback at the edge of the swamp, reminding her of her obligation and its consequences. Over the previous, parched months it had been too dangerous for anyone to navigate the mud to get to the spring, so she had been using rainwater from the church's barrel. If the spring were still dried up and the blistering times returned, she wouldn't have any water to spare.

3

UNDER THE SHRIVELING TREE THAT morning, Orietta
watched Sister Agnes inspect the devastated spring box
and knew that something suspicious was happening
because the nun's voice didn't have the plaintive quality
of a prayer, it sounded like a frightened, guilty whisper,
with ringing hands and a furrowed brow. The nun
scraped her hands desperately pawing through the
rocks. Orietta knew there is no supplicant like the
culpable. She had spent her life hidden but watching.

Orietta heard slow, uneven footfalls on the wooden
planking and Paloma parted the branches of the tree to
join the women. She was still peaked and even the
short walk from the church to the spring, limping to

favor her previously trapped foot, had taken it out of her. She was still speckled with dirt and because of her enormous height, no one had found a blouse big enough to substitute for the tattered rag on her shoulders or her shoes that were mere strips of swamp grass.

The sun had left its zenith and the heat had backed off. Sister Agnes shooed the old women from the sheltering tree. She glared at Orietta and stepped around the muddied, haggard Paloma as she left. "We have to have this water," Sister Agnes said.

When they had gone, Orietta leaned closer to Paloma and gestured back to the nun. "What does she expect us to do about it?" She shook her head. "I'd be careful with that one."

Paloma crouched on the far side of the crumbled box, showing an enormous expanse of leg protruding from pants donated by the tallest man in the village.

"Glad to see you're feeling better," Orietta said. "You slept through a tremendous storm."

Paloma grunted. She regarded the pile of rocks that had been the spring box as if it was a jigsaw puzzle.

Orietta retightened her head scarf. "Can you fix it?"

"The water is probably still there. It just needs a... home."

Paloma stacked the rocks to the side, inspecting the lowest layer for signs of moisture or moss. She got on her knees and put the rocks in a semi-circle on the downhill slant. When she reached the earth, she scooped out handfuls of dry loam. She set stones on the side and bent to smell for water, sniffing in a line closer to the tree. Paloma alternated between sniffing, digging, and stacking, sat back on her haunches in resignation, shook her head and started again.

A puddle of water seeped around her tattered shoe.

"Ah," she said. "There you are."

Paloma used the mud as temporary mortar when the seeping water increased its pace. It began pooling along the edges of the wall and Orietta got on her knees to help.

The two women returned to the church sweaty and tired but hauling a bucket of spring water between them. Villagers on their porches pointed to the women, to the spring, ran for their own buckets and set out over the planks, as a gentle rain started to fall.


THE NEXT MORNING, PALOMA WOKE at the break of dawn, but it wasn't from the soft rain or even the murmured prayers of Sister Agnes who was on her knees in front of the Madonna, spinning a combination of salutations, tearful confessions and desperate entreaties. Paloma limped barefoot, soundlessly, through the church as if tracking an aroma, through the sacristy, stopping outside Sister Agnes' room but not entering, through the kitchen, into the nave and then, with a quickened step, to the altar and the basket of vials at the nun's left side and the bucket of spring water Paloma had carried back, now nearly empty.

Sister Agnes jumped at the sudden appearance of Paloma, who stripped the cloth cover off the basket before the nun could grab more than its edge.

Paloma inspected the labels.

"Holy water?" Paloma challenged, looking from the vial to the bucket.

Orietta, already in her disguise, shuffled barefoot and blinking to her side.

"The sister's a fraud," Paloma said, and handed the basket to Orietta.

"Holy?" Orietta said derisively.

Paloma seized a handful of the glass vials and threw them against the floor where they shattered, soaking the labels until the ink ran, the glass glinting on the scuffed floor. The water trickled through the floorboards back into the marsh.

Sister Agnes leapt to her feet and tried to push Paloma backward, shouting about the audacity of bad girls.

"I worship the Holy Mother's beauty! To honor her. Exalting her." And to finance her own departure, she knew.

The two women were implacable.

"This is none of your business! Get out!" Sister Agnes shouted, and she ran to the kitchen, returned with a fire poker, and chased the two women to the porch of the church, where she swung the poker and snarled at them.

"Vipers! Fallen women have no place here."

She called to Esteban who was readying his boat for the day.

"Get these hellions out of our village! Anywhere, take them anywhere but here!"

Paloma snuck past Sister Agnes to collect Orietta's shoes, and just before the two clambered into the boat, she lunged forward and grabbed the poker from the nun's hands to fling it into the water.

EVERYWHERE PALOMA LOOKED, AS THE dawn broke and Esteban paddled them away from the village, people's faces were tight with anxiety over water. Would it dissipate as it had? Would there be enough for fish? Had they trapped enough in their rain barrels to survive?

Lightening cracked on the horizon and sheets of rain suddenly poured down on them.

"I don't understand this weather," Esteban said, baffled.

Paloma sluiced the rain off the top of her head and tried to rub off the tenacious black mud. "It's just weather," she said absently, as another feather blew from her waistband.

The rain soaked Orietta's scarf until a gust of wind that came from nowhere suddenly pulled it off her head. Orietta twisted and reached for it but could only watch her disguise jig away from her. Esteban stopped paddling at the sight of Orietta's high cheekbones and milky skin, the frame of hair that she gathered in one hand.

Neither woman had any clothing that could cover Orietta, and she nervously turned away from Esteban. Paloma sensed the tension rising in the boat.

There is something about a woman in nature that makes her more beautiful: rain that presses a blouse into clavicle; wind that dances hair around a moon-shaped face; cold that pinks her cheeks; heat that calls up a golden slick across her body; mist that hangs like sugar on her lashes.

"Yes," Paloma said to Orietta as if she had been spoken to. "It's dangerous to be valuable."

Orietta shook her head. "You have no idea," she said with resignation, and Paloma, watching the rain course down Orietta's cheeks to her throat and into her cleavage, vowed to stand between this beauty and danger, to protect her the way one shields a butterfly from wind, to sacrifice one's own gnarled and scarred skin for the pristine flesh of another.


AS ESTEBAN DOCKED THEM, THE downpour stopped, and he arranged with a passing mule driver to take them west across the narrow flatlands to the river. Panicked by Orietta's tremendous beauty, though, Esteban insisted that they take his hunting knife, which he presented to her as compliment and caution.

The mule driver tried to convince Orietta to sit in front of him on the saddle, but she declined.

"She can sit here," Paloma said, steering her to the second mule that had a light load. She helped Orietta up to sit side-saddle and Paloma strapped the knife to her own pants.

"I'll walk," she said pointedly, holding Orietta's knee to steady her, resting her left hand on the pommel of the knife.

"But you're injured," Orietta countered. "You should be the one to ride."

"I said I'll walk," she said sternly, looking at the mule driver.

"Then I won't take you far," the driver said. "A couple of miles."

He grumbled to himself for two hours until they reached a clearing. "Off with you. Araca is just north of here. Little town but...good enough for the likes of you." He gave Paloma a last withering look and turned his mule train southward.

When they turned from the mule driver, Paloma chortled because she recognized where she was: staring out at two river rocks that looked like the breasts of a new mother in the morning.

## Chapter 3

1

aloma stepped into the clearing between the road and the rocks as a woman, not a seventeen-year-old girl, not even a young woman, but as someone who has survived an ordeal, witnessed both treachery and joy and now stood tall.

"As good a spot as any," Paloma said, though without conviction. The clearing was level, with good soil, naturally bordered by jungle. But what she remembered, with a shudder, was that she had chosen to leave this spot before, with near-fatal consequences. She could pretend that it was sensible to stay, or that it was destiny, but she had lost her faith in her ability to choose.

Orietta, for her part, had heard the muleteer say there was a town to the north, but she wasn't going into any town bare-headed, and the protection of this giantess had been surprisingly reassuring on the trip here. She wouldn't go without her. Besides, her new friend was not presentable either: the downpour had drenched her torn blouse, soaked the man's pants that came just below her knees and had run through the shoes she had repaired with marsh grass that now were nothing but sandals.

Orietta, however, knew that shelter from the punishing weather was the first order of business and she took stock of what was in front of her: a strangler fig tree so large that it would have required the linked arms of eighteen women to encircle it. They had had one in the central square of her hometown and the founding fathers had cut a labyrinth in the vines as amusement for the children. She peered between the lattice work of grey vines and the trunk of the host tree, checking for spiders and snakes before the two women dedicated the next three hours to cutting a cave for themselves.

Taking a break, they sat facing each other, Paloma's legs jutting forward, more bright skin against the silver grey of the vines than Orietta remembered ever seeing.

"What did the villagers call you?"

Paloma tossed her head apologetically. "The Jaguar. Jaguar Paloma."

"Jaguar?" Orietta chuckled. "You're more like an emu. Christ girl, how did you grow those legs? Emu Paloma, I say."

They lay down exhausted for a siesta, but after several minutes of wrestling with Paloma's legs, Orietta harrumphed and changed positions to spoon into her new, enormous friend.

"What's an emu?" Paloma whispered.

"Giantess bird of Australia," Orietta chuckled, as she breathed in the clarity of the air after the rainfall and reveled in a survivor's gratitude.


As soon as she came out from the fig tree, after siesta and a lengthy wash, Paloma started trading. She took a stick and dug for wild yuca tubers, used bits of the vegetable to catch two trout and, standing in the river with the water at the cuffs of her too-short man's pants, she traded a fish with a passing angler in a canoe for an extra gourd, which she traded using the other fish for a battered pot. Her height, her piecing eyes that she would not avert, the tremendous presence of her, were so enticing that men paddled hard to get to her and were generous to hide their intimidation.

Paloma was hiding intimidation of her own: rivers frightened her like few other things because a river had taken her other half. Her twin sister Camilla, as a toddler, had stumbled toward the river while their mother hung the wash, and then she disappeared, rolling down the embankment and into the water, never to be found. While Paloma had given up trying to decide whether a river's voice was kinship and kindness, or the siren's call to join her sister in destruction, she had learned to pay attention to the river, to never presume to know the depth of water or the strength of currents, never assume a dam would hold. She swore that holes opened in placid creek beds just as she stepped into the water as if the river was trying to swallow her; she had been the fourth of four to cross a stream and felt the water rise up to claim her while all others were safely on the bank. Twins must be together, the river said to her, join us. We will claim you if you don't. When she dove off the barge three months ago, she had been choosing between forms of death: the men or the river. Today, if she stood between the rocks as she traded, maybe she would be safe.

PALOMA'S TRADING SKILL HAD BEEN honed since she was a young girl in her parents' dry goods shop, displaying an ability to sense the value of objects and trade to her advantage: cookies traded for candy; flowers for dolls. By the time she was eight years old, Paloma was trading in piglets, then lambs. She helped the broken-down old man on the village outskirts get his paltry harvest to market, helped an old woman sell her mother's lace. There was almost nothing she couldn't find a buyer for, so the destitute and orphaned brought tattered cloth or half-burned candles and silently watched as she bundled their things with others considered junk, resold them as precious, and shared the profits. Sometimes she would just pretend there had been a profit and give a tired mother all the proceeds.

By the time Paloma was 12, she was more interested in playing cards and trading than in dating. When she hit a growth spurt and towered over them, young men looked on her as just an oddity. By 17, she had learned the dark side of commerce: the trader who raped her growled about exacting a different price, and then her parents considered him a bargain worth making. The covenant broken with her family, she had fled.

THAT SECOND DAY, ORIETTA CONTINUED to hack away at the strangler vines to expand their shelter; she built a wood pile and smoked the surprising quantity of trout that Paloma threw onto the shore as if the fish had jumped into her hands. Shortly before noon, Paloma walked out of the river, gathered half of their wood pile under one arm and took it back to the water, then returned to stand in front of Orietta in anticipation.

"For you," she said quietly, presenting Orietta with a brightly flowered scarf that had only one small tear.

Orietta took it gently but couldn't meet Paloma's eyes. "Smells like fish," she murmured. But she shook it out with a snap, covered her hair and shielded her face with it, sighing with relief.

Paloma was sorry to see her covered again, like watching the last bit of frosting scraped from a plate.

"What we need is fresh water." Orietta smiled slyly and flung her hand out at Paloma's too-short pants dripping with river water, the rents on her shirt at shoulders and elbows. "Or some proper clothes for you."

Paloma grunted but smiled. "Could be part of my appeal."

"Using pity in negotiations, are you, Emu?"

Paloma opened her arms, palms up, and returned to the river with a smile.

At the river's edge, though, Paloma grew solemn over Orietta's statement: they did need water. The far side of the river was lined with cattle that polluted the river; the nun's spring was too far away and there was nothing in the world that would make her venture into the swamp again. Despite the appeal of the strangler fig tree, they had to settle near a spring or keep moving, perhaps even into Araca, though neither were interested in being around others yet. They could gather rainwater and collect the night's dew, as she had when she was lost, but for real viability she had to find a spring.

Paloma was not going to hack her way through the jungle using a hunting knife, so she stayed on the perimeter of the clearing. She walked a quarter of a mile to the far southern end past their tree, started at the river's edge and walked inland until the thick vegetation stopped her. She looked for animal tracks, peered through the jungle for any clusters of denser vegetation, looked at the destination of birds in flight. Nothing at the south end.

She walked northward toward the tree and spotted a rock with moss on it a few feet into the jungle. They had to have fresh water, and moss was always a good sign. She plunged in toward it, dropped to her knees and dug around the base of the rock but even after an hour, the two-foot trench yielded nothing but loam.

Paloma wrung her tired hands and resumed her march northward. The mossy rock had given her an idea and she noted the position of several rocks, until, at the far northern end of the clearing, a quarter of a mile from the tree, she faced a rock outcropping that rose higher than her head and was fifteen feet wide. She inhaled, trying to smell water. Ferns and grasses fringed the rock.

She smiled and ran her hands across the rock face, trying to sense a change in temperature. She dug at cracks and tried to dislodge pieces of the mound, circling its mass inch by inch. At the far side, near the bottom, moss grew on the rocks and Paloma dropped to her knees in front of it, digging away at the dirt, throwing bits of rock behind her as the water began to pool. She ran her fingers up a seam directly above the pool and dislodged a piece of the rock, then shouted in jubilation as the water spurted out and ran down the rock face.

Paloma put her lips against the rock and sucked in the cool spring water, stepped back to watch it pooling faster. She wanted to run back to the fig tree to get the gourd and the pot, to bring Orietta by the hand, but first things first: she dug at the ground immediately below the fissure to make a pool, running off to fetch more rocks for her makeshift spring box.

Sighing with deep satisfaction, Paloma knew she had discovered more than the spring: she had determined the perimeter of the clearing, a half a mile long and a quarter mile wide. Forget Araca to the north. This spot would do nicely.


ORIETTA JOINED HER AND THE water flowed faster than they could build the walls. The two of them scooped handfuls of it into their mouths and poured it down the front of their shirts while they worked. Clean, clear, chilly, the water tasted like gentle rain on Christmas, or minerals that made something better than diamonds.

Striding into the river between the breast shaped rocks again, Paloma traded a cup of it for a bucket, a bucket of it for a cask, and, ladling it out to boaters on the river, she soon acquired clothing, meat, blankets, fishing lines and household goods. Their cave among the vines became luxurious and soft with linens and a canvas roof.

People boated to the clearing just to buy the water: they claimed it cured their arthritis, cleared up their skin, cleaned their bowels, reminded them of health and hope. Innocence, integrity, of absolution that flowed through their bodies. They said it brought them luck when fishing, protection when traveling; it blessed a baby in the womb; it helped a grandfather make it through the summer. It was the taste that lace might have had, the old women said, like sipping the color of a hummingbird.

PALOMA PUT LIVING FENCES AROUND three sides of the half-mile area that included the spring and the fig tree, with the river as the final boundary and, seemingly overnight, blossoms grew along the top of the fence dripping nectar that brought bats and little dogs. Paloma built a stone fireplace and traded spring water for a swing arm and a set of racks for cooking. She drove pegs into the bankside for the boaters who chose to come ashore and buy Orietta's smoked trout lunch. They set up tables, built benches and one evening after the last boater had pushed off, Orietta wiped her hands on her apron.

"You know, Emu, if we really wanted to put the water to good use, we'd make vodka."

"What's vodka?" Paloma asked, but Orietta gave her a devilish smile.

To Paloma, Orietta was wasting her time on

something inexplicable, but she negotiated for her supplies anyway. As much yuca as anyone could transport, a pipe called a swan neck, and a series of pots way beyond the size for soup. What was the point? Orietta made a porridge from the yuca and tended a fire seemingly forever before a clear liquid dripped out the other side of the twisted pipes. She mixed it with a bit of their spring water. The first sip of it made Orietta twist and dance like she was biting into a lemon.

She gave Paloma a taste that made her eyes water. Orietta mixed it with mango juice and Paloma drank it down, asked for another.

She woke up the next morning on the ground beside the still.

AFTER PALOMA SERVED THE FIRST sips of the spirits to the boaters there was no more wading into the river to beckon customers. The line of them jammed up the docking point between the breast-like rocks. They queued up on the shore even in the noonday sun. Paloma built an enormously long bar for Orietta where she sold the healing water and the jubilant spirits, which Orietta also sold infused with mango, elderflower, or pineapple. She served drinks with fruit whose peals in seven colors grew to be piled high in the corner.

Each night, the women conferred in the strangler fig cave, giddy as little girls. Money. They now had money.

They moved the coins around in Orietta's hand, lifted them and felt them, heard them clink.

"This is working," Paloma said breathlessly. The thought of good fortune had never crossed her mind. Orietta looked over her shoulder suspiciously, then grabbed Paloma's hand and they laughed with abandon.

Paloma expanded the strangler fig cave, circling the tree with hallways that opened into bigger rooms.

FARMERS FROM THE JUNGLE, LONGING for a break from choking chimneys and low roofs, hacked a path north to the compound, bringing the women a plate or cup, a side table they had woven from branches. Tradespeople boated upriver with a coveted rocking chair in exchange for a chance to sit within the sheltering wall of the blooming fence and bask in starlight, sipping, sighing, resting. Women walked all day with offerings of multicolored chicks or newborn goats to trade for the now legendary water and sinful yuca vodka.

Their compound hosted a boater's birthday party, then a Saints day celebration, then evenings of debauchery for no reason at all. Musicians came and went but soon just pitched a tent outside Paloma's walls and stayed. Patrons danced with abandon in the center of the compound where their raucous feet beat the ground smooth, and they ran through the nearby fields kicking up their heels like kid goats. Birds who were mortal enemies clustered in the trees together to watch the festivities. Peacocks sat like kings on the haunches of mules. Spider monkeys, drawn by the fruit peels, played catch with the dogs who created elaborate games and slept together around the strangler fig tree, so many of them in a spiral that it looked like a Christmas tree rug.

Orietta hired cooks and barmaids while Paloma built more tables every week. Cauldrons of soup threw up billows of fragrant steam that mingled with the smell of yeast from enormous wooden casks of beer. A baker who settled just outside Paloma's compound invented little meat pies that could be eaten while dancing and there seemed to be a new aroma in the compound every morning.

The Romani made the saloon a regular stop, and then traders of all kinds converged, so that the untilled area behind the compound wall was rutted by wagons, dotted with fire circles and hitching posts.

Paloma had the far southern wall of the compound completely devoted to transactions: casks and crates were stacked in corners, and she had a special canvas room to keep her dry goods out of the sun. Chickens, ducks and the children of the cook, baker and barmaids cavorted around piles of baskets containing things to trade. Sometimes wanderers brought Paloma herbs that they had gathered on the way and Paloma added them to her thriving garden of the medicinal, nutritious and exotic. She now had standing customers, and her business involved objects that passed through three or four transactions before she was finished and cashed out.

"Don't spend it all in the bar," she would caution some of the men, though too often what she doled out wound up in her own cash drawer again. Some of her poorest regulars, bringing in a useless, broken plate or spoon that had lived in the jungle for decades, would receive a coin anyway, with a signal to Orietta to serve a half-strength drink followed by fruit juice on the house, just to get some vitamins and hydration in the sallow skinned men.

Soon the saloon became a makeshift boarding house. Whether on the road or the river, running away from home even if just for a single night, solo travelers could rent a hammock or a straw mat that had been doused with rosemary water and lie down in the shade. The peripatetic clustered along the outside of the ivy walls of the compound, each with their own fire and their objects in a strict, personal order: fork and knife perpendicular to shoes, or a hat exactly two inches to the right of their pillow. Paloma hired scruffy, wandering children to peel yuca and scoop out mountains of watermelon; women with the desperate, frightened look of a runaway were taken on to make drinks, wait tables, do laundry which they hung to flip in the gentle, dry air, bits of ladies' lace waving at the birds.

2

IN THE EVENING OF THE hottest day of the year, men drank to swallow their anger and Paloma walked slowly through the patrons to break up clusters that seemed fuming at each other, so they cleared out grumbling, shoving each other as they stumbled home.

Despite her efforts to keep the peace, though, in the morning Paloma discovered a thin young woman with a black eye and a split lip cowering in the corner as if she could hide herself in the ivy. Paloma sighed with resignation and disgust, shaking her head.

"What's your name?"

"Marta," the woman said quietly.

"Come on, Marta, let's get you fed."

The woman wouldn't take the hand Paloma offered.

Paloma brought back a bowl of stew, a large piece of bread and a tall glass of mango juice, keeping her distance as she got on one knee and offered it. The girl kept a dusty shawl crumpled in her arms like a shield. Paloma set the food down midway between them, but by noon the bowl was empty, and Marta was gone.

The coffee that Orietta brought to Paloma that evening seemed especially bitter. She didn't know if Marta had been raped but she assumed so, and it made Paloma want to pick up a machete and hack at a man like he was jungle grass. Her own ordeal, heightened by the betrayal by her family, was a rage that visited her without warning, day or night, replete with the sounds of the man's grunting and her door slamming, the jovial face of her father as he laughed at the man's jokes, and was inextricably tied to the devastation of her journey through the swamp.

"We need a gate," she grumbled. "With a lock."

"And a house," Orietta said.


THE GATE PALOMA BUILT WAS large enough for a small truck of vodka casks to get through and strong enough to stop it when closed. All the hammocks were moved outside the compound and the fences at the well were fortified. Paloma hired the traveling Romani to build them a house with doors into the strangler fig cave. With a great commotion, crawling over the structure like the monkeys that watched from the trees, they hammered and sawed and slapped each other on the back. The roof tilted to the east though the doors were slanting toward the river. The windows were a jumble of sizes and shapes. They attached shutters of red and blue in spots without windows and patched their mistakes with boards whose chipped paint revealed the half-a-dozen lives it had lived before. The chimney was bent, and the floorboards gapped but it all locked down tight and when they finished, they celebrated all night as if they had completed the Taj Mahal.

"Never mind, Emu," Orietta said quietly as Paloma inspected the wacky results. "It was built with joy and that's something."

Paloma traded for a machete and a club with spikes, then burnt a sign into wood that she hammered next to the entrance: *Keep Your Hands to Yourself or Go Home Without Hands.*

3

THE SPRING OF PALOMA AND Orietta's second year in business, a traveling rodeo owner chose Araca as his winter headquarters and every year thereafter, at the conclusion of the rodeo season, a string of forlorn young women would appear at the tables of Paloma's bar. In far-flung cities around the region, they had been enchanted by the rugged masculinity of the rodeo men, the way their leather chaps cupped their asses, their smell of horses and courage, their bow-legged walk, muscled arms, and their chapped faces that showed the long hours they had spent walking into the wind toward death. And perhaps just as important as their strength, the men were broken in ways that women find irresistible: plagued by nightmares and loneliness, with sad stories of cruel fathers and bad luck, and sometimes actual injuries.

The women's stories, though their childhoods were varied and frequently happy, had the same cadence after the rodeo: long nights alone convincing themselves that the love had been mutual; surviving vicious denunciations by their family; facing a multitude of dangers on the road, and now, pregnant or with babe at breast, they all wound up at the bar, weeping with surprise that they hadn't been The One for their cowboys, despite having followed them back to headquarters.

After two seasons, Paloma and Orietta could tell who had fathered the woman's child by the look of her: the bull rider preferred the buxom, the dancing pony man liked them thin and small, the rodeo clown pursued an odd assortment of the funny looking.

ORIETTA PUT THEM TO WORK in the bar and Paloma took on the strong ones to load traded goods. Doris, a woman who looked like a Mayan goddess, played the accordion; Gretchen, a black woman with razor-short hair who had become the playmate of the pony man, washed dishes. Paloma had a dormitory built for the women and their babes.

ONE BALMY EVENING, THE INSECT song and the lilting

breeze was interrupted by the sound of Doris crying with her head cradled in her arms on the table. She had never married and now that she had a child she was certain she never would; the women in the saloon gathered around her, cooing their support and stroking her hair but the more she cried, the more they all felt the gaping loss of that singular event: the wedding, the dress, the attendants, the spotlight, the finery and festivities, the marriage license. Soon all the waitresses were sitting with her, lamenting their own lack of a wedding; the barmaid left thirsty patrons with empty glasses and even the women loading the wagons that were to leave for the market at Belmopa within the hour left the crates and joined the glum and despondent group.

PALOMA HAD JUST FINISHED HELPING a drunken monk to a hammock when she saw the women and noted the shut-down of work. She strode to the cluster of them. When they looked at her, the pain in their eyes spoke of hopelessness and self-loathing.

"A wedding?" she asked and shook her head incredulously. "You're crying about a wedding?"

Which child is born to someone married, which to someone who is not – same child, same woman and yet all the difference was a ceremony and a license, a white dress, a white cake, just a party and a piece of paper? How many women have been destroyed, how many children have been made miserable over the absence of paper and cake? It infuriated her.

"You can't force the government to give you paper, but we sure as hell can make a cake. You want a wedding," she said in a voice both flippant and energized, "we'll have a wedding."

Orietta, sorting cases behind the bar, raised her eyebrows but shrugged. "Why not?"

Paloma announced in a voice that was heard to the far walls of the compound. "Weddings for everyone!"

The idea stunned them.

Then one by one they turned to each other. "Why not?"

Orietta considered the logistics. "Tomorrow night."

The waitresses ran to their dormitory and found a white blouse; a lace veil was stitched together from scraps; a white sash was made from a fancy pillow slip that had been traded for vodka. Into the hodge-podge, Orietta donated a white tablecloth that the waitresses spent the morning happily pinning and clipping, chattering about who got to be bridesmaids, and they sent the children out to gather flowers from the riverbank. The mule-driver with the half-loaded wagon offered to be the faux groom.

The party that evening was electric with the glee of broken rules. The dancing and drinking were frenzied. Dogs circled the fig tree like dervish dancers. Monkeys screamed from the branches and the birds hovered above the confab. The modest, one-tiered wedding cake was cheered like a triumph, and the women stuffed each other's mouths with it singing "paper and cake!" Another cask of vodka had to be brought out and the children fell asleep exhausted from peeling fruit. The drunken dance-hall women grabbed at the wedding dress in an effort to be the next bride and tore the lace along the side.

By the end of the evening another six weddings had been planned.

Each wedding was more formal and polished than the last. Paloma asked her contacts on the trade route to find a second-hand wedding dress and by the end of the week the muleteers had brought three from Escoba, two from Hilado and four all the way from Villahermosa on the coast. Five dresses were dyed for bridesmaids; the chairs for the attendees stayed aligned on the edge of the dance floor. Itinerant musicians learned the wedding march; the rum merchant and a couple of gigolos who fit into second-hand tuxedos were hired as grooms or groomsmen, and children gathered flowers every day. When men were in short supply a stable boy stepped in as groom and Paloma set up a tent with a full-length mirror for changing.

All of the waitresses were married once and four of them chose another wedding dress to be married again. After they had acquired a dozen dresses, they had parties where all the women were brides at the same time.

There may not be paper but there was plenty of cake, they proclaimed. In Tartatenango, or Caketown. At the Caketown Bar.

As WORD GOT OUT, SPINSTERS from Hilado in the south came to the Caketown Bar and paid to secretly have the event they had always longed for, that defining event that even widows and nuns were granted. Hardened bachelors from the mule train took a bath and gave their money to Paloma to wear the scavenged tux, be considered a catch, revel in the momentary sense of belonging and the faux love on the faux bride's face. Men and women from nearby Escoba drank, tore the clothing, broke up the furniture and woke up with Paloma standing on the bride's wrist where she had passed out on the floor and would stay until she paid for the damage.

OLD MAN ORJUELA, WHO HAD spent his life weaving mats from swamp grass, was asked to be father of the bride, and with a renewed purpose in life, he bathed each morning, whistling while he hauled water from the river and heated it in a tin bucket over a small fire, scrubbing his crinkly and pock-marked skin. In a fine new suit that Paloma had bought him, with genuine tears in his eyes, he entered the bride's tent and took her hands.

"I'm so proud of you, my beautiful, beautiful girl," he

told the bride melodically. "I always knew you'd do well." With sincerity in his voice, he reminded her of the fun they had during make-believe boat trips, described special faux awards she had won at school, reminding her of how special she was, how precious to him, how lucky the groom. He stroked her face with the back of his hand, inventing a story of the Christmas when she had bought him a perfect gift, spinning out the words that the young women wanted so badly that the ceremonies were frequently delayed by a weeping bride who required time and vodka to compose herself. Some were married repeatedly just for the weightless joy of hearing the old man's praise and the gift of absolution from a father, any father at all.

Tartatenango and the Caketown Bar became a place where everyone was celebrated, everyone had a chance to be the center of attention even if it was just for one night; where women who owned just one dress and had spent their lives on their knees scrubbing floors could revel in the feeling of being beautiful, wearing fabrics they had never seen nor would ever touch again. Their night cost almost nothing but would be remembered forever. Women who had already been married and didn't like their dress or couldn't have afforded a dress at the time plunked down a precious coin to get just one step closer to their dream. The homely and disfigured could spend an evening with a dozen women circling them while they danced, applauding their beauty and encouraging their joy.

Paloma soon had packages to offer: one dress, two bridesmaids, and a bouquet (cheaper if she selected a bouquet already tossed by yesterday's bride.) Even the groom was an extra charge, as women realized that the dress, the attention, the cake, and the party were what really mattered to them. For additional fees, the bride could add music, pay for a buffet, have more bridesmaids and groomsmen. The poor bought churros or rented a wooden cake painted in pastels that would sit on a table filled with faux gifts in festive wrappings.

Women walked out of the jungle in El Dolor with just one coin apiece, then eight arrived on a wagon from Montemadre, each paying to be the bride so that a single wedding party continued for more than a week. Whenever word went out that Paloma had secured a new dress, tradeswomen, teachers, and librarians from nearby Escoba or Belmopa returned to rebook an event. Half a dozen women traveled from Villahermosa to waltz down the isle in each of the 24 dresses on the rack. Six arrived for what they called a bridal tea, with all the women dressed in white and lounging with tall glasses of punch.

A baker set up shop and the wedding cake offerings grew in size and refinement: two tiers, three tiers, filled with mango compote, festooned with fondant ribbons and sugar flowers. A seamstress built a small house near the Caketown Bar and spent all day altering the dresses, adding lace, removing beading.

A hairdresser set up shop and specialized in ornate updos that shocked the peasant girls who had always lived in simple braids. The hairdresser paid several women for their hair, and then fashioned it into the wigs of Marie Antoinette, replete with faux jewels. An old woman with a long silver mane sold her hair to the hairdresser who dyed it red, and the wigs sat on stands, one black with red ribbons and stones, one brown with gold-colored butterflies, and a red one with bits of black lace. Now women could be married one night in black hair with a voluminous dress and the next night as a red head in a sleek gown. The matriarch of the monkey clan, however, loved the red wig and too often snatched it from its stand, and even from the bride's head, to carry it high in the trees above the wedding and preen in it during the ceremony.

A bishop rode out from the capital, Heroica, in his opulent carriage, then changed to a sway-back horse and finally transferred to a mangy donkey, arriving in Tartatenango wearing a moth-eaten cloak as just a sad old man who whispered his request and pressed twice the price into Paloma's hands. A bride, he said, he wanted to be a bride and when no one gasped or flinched or threw him out, he became wildly animated, choosing the dress with the widest skirt, the most petticoats, hung off the shoulder so that his thick chest hair protruded at the cleavage like black lace. To hide his shame, he hired no bridesmaids, but they volunteered for free and held his hands with sadness. Finally, someone whose shame was greater than their own. The Caketown Bar had never seen a more cathartic wedding and celebration, nearly derailed when Old Man Orjuela held the bishop's hands and told him what a great wife he would make, and the bishop fell to his knees in his fancy wedding dress and kissed Orjuela's hands like he was the pope.

SOON, WORD OF THE PARADISE for cast-off mothers that had become Tartatenango and the Caketown Bar, spread along the transport route, driving single women, widows, and the occasional widower, to the gate.

A mother from Santa Anna on the other side of the swamp who had been raped on the solstice expanded Paloma's trade, and with two others from towns they wouldn't reveal, formed a transport business to haul Orietta's vodka to the coast driving a team of strong horses, and their babies strapped to their chest.

Two sisters from the Caribbean who had fled their mother's plan to brand them with a poker as the devil's children opened a restaurant. A quiet woman with the look of an Aztec warrior, with two children from two fathers, became the lace-maker, joined by a silent florist. Toddlers of indeterminable race, abandoned at the doorstep of the bar, were taken in without hesitation. Two women in love with each other opened a cobbler shop; an old woman cast out by her new daughter-in-law took on a young woman and reestablished her butcher shop; a man fond of earrings and feathers was their barber. Gardens flourished on all sides. Seemingly overnight, Tartatenango had a candle-maker and a dry goods store. Saddles and tack were traded and repaired, and a person of undetermined (and unquestioned) gender who carried their carpentry tools in a wooden box helped anyone who hailed them.

A wheelwright, a weaver, men who worked in the fields, who cut the dense river mud into bricks, all built shacks of whatever scraps they could find, settling near the Caketown Bar to cater to the wedding crowd and the mule trains, until the south side was as populated as the official town of Araca.

Their children ran wild through the compound in a jumbled-up pack of all races, genders, and sizes, and soon there were so many that Paloma fenced off an area for the toddlers and three mothers ran them ragged every day. The older children tended the horses, hoed the gardens, picked fruit, fished the river, ran water, and delivered messages all day.

Paloma built a second dormitory for the women and their babes. It was a rough-hewn building with a thatch roof but women first arriving inspected it: the walls were sturdy; the door had a strong latch. And the rows of beds that lined the walls were reassuring. There were others like them, theirs was not a singular horror, they were not alone in their shame.

No one said "you're safe now" because that was too great a promise. They had all come from places where those who promised safety had been cut down by soldiers or brigands: fathers stabbed, brothers captured, mothers vanquished.

"Easy now," the women said, as they dabbed cold water onto swollen cheekbones and pretended that the marks on the newcomer's neck were not in the exact order of fingers. No one turned away from them. That perhaps was the biggest difference: no one pretended it hadn't happened, no one insisted that she hide her belly, pretend to still be a virgin, hide the future behind scripture or sweep it all under the rug.

The first morning after their arrival, a woman would be given a strong cup of coffee and a cheesy *arape* for breakfast, and then a large basket of scrap cloth set in front of her. "Sew yourself a quilt," Orietta would say firmly, and the newcomer would spend the week stitching, crying, sometimes tearing at the cloth in her rage, but within days, she laid squares out on the table, received praise, advice and instructions from other women. After a day or two, she realized there was no shame at all. That was one of the best things about their little gathering: toxic shame was washed away like road dust. A woman arrived in trauma, slept fitfully the first night, woke surprised and suspicious of her surroundings, was greeted with understanding and food, and at some point soon, she held her head higher, walked with more confidence, focused on the task instead of the past. The quilt grew, the rage subsided, and the dormitory became a riot of color and patterns, with white curtains that blew in the breeze while chinks of sunlight streamed through the walls.

"Caketown is where you land when you've fallen!" the mothers toasted gleefully.

4

IN THE SPRING, A CIVIL WAR began and the population of Tartatenango grew with what others considered the spoils of war: a stream of raped and battered women who weren't considered spoiled at all when they reached the little town.

The influx was, in part, because of a prominent but cold-hearted General from Araca who had the strongest lineage, the largest home, and almost enough money to be the president. He marched off. Women returned, among them three women who had wound up in the General's room after a wild night of drinking and in the morning squabbled among themselves as to who was his favorite: the woman who woke up with her head on his shoulder, the woman who was sprawled across his legs or the one who had rolled off the bed and woke up on the floor. The General cinched his pants and walked out without a word and all three of them followed him on his way back to Araca where he was to visit his family and call up recruits. They jostled among themselves for the closest horse, the first fuck, describing loving glances they were sure the General had given to them alone. But when they arrived in Araca and he disappeared back into his family, they reasoned that since they didn't matter to the man there was no sense fighting over him among themselves. They christened him General Heart of Chrome and abandoned him for life in Caketown where the three glided down the aisle, all together as brides. After the first trio, during all the years of the war, it seemed that every woman who walked through the gate after being used by the General was more ebullient and good natured than the last, as if the General had been scouring the countryside to find someone to relieve the gruesome sorrow of his mind and unlock the detached coldness of his heart.

ONE EVENING, A SUDDEN RAINSTORM pummeled Tartatenango, so Orietta thought that a tapping at the gate was just a branch lightly touching the side of the fence. It persisted, though, and when she opened the gate, a tiny woman with black hair slick against her head, had nearly blended into the bushes next to the door. Orietta assumed that she was a buxom little beggar until a baby started crying and the tiny woman pulled an inconceivably small peach-pit of a baby from her dress.

Orietta stopped in her tracks, stunned by the appearance of another child within a child like Russian nesting dolls, as she recalibrated the girl's perceived age, and raised her eyebrows at a nipple the size of a peanut kernel, hungrily sought by the baby.

Orietta quickly ushered her inside the dormitory as if fearing she would be washed away and got down on one knee to towel off the tiny family. But despite the soaking, the newcomer smiled brightly, introduced herself as Jade, and held up her daughter Jewel.

"They say there are no bastards here," Jade said. "All mothers welcome."

"That's right, little one," Orietta said, tearing up.

At first the other mothers were scandalized by the woman's size, thinking a member of the traveling rodeo had taken a child to bed, but when they were told her age, they christened her The Hummingbird, their mascot and talisman who was in motion from before the sun rose until after the last chair was upturned on the final table and the gates shut on the Caketown Bar. The Hummingbird was good for business as well: her child-like size added to the play-time aura of the wedding business, as if tiny teacups and little chairs should be included in the festivities. She seemed to be everywhere, chipper, and bright, assuming the best in everyone and every situation. The children followed her without complaint; the mothers took her solace and advice as if she were a sprite or a cherub who had arrived from some place of greater wisdom and unshakeable privacy.

## Chapter 4

1

I——t is well known that prosperity, like honey, draws flies, and so it was that a wretched woman, regaling against bad fortune that she had called upon herself and that was minor compared to the bad news she ushered in for others, took to the road to Tartatenango.

FADUL, (WHO DIDN'T RECALL SOMEONE loving her enough to use her first name, and so she had forgotten it altogether) was far younger than she looked; a gloomy woman, perpetually squinting above her hooked nose and sunken cheeks, with a distrust that made her twitchy, and she carried herself a little sideways as if expecting a blow. She was pale, nearly gray around the edges from a life of grizzled meat and vague remembrances of unspoken tragedies. Her father had been taken away in the middle of the night when she was so young that she never knew if he had run off with rowdy friends or been violently hustled off to jail.

She had been a precocious child, reading early and when, at four years old, she had displayed a surprising facility to both write and comprehend numbers, her mother apprenticed her to a bookmaker. In a little dress and long braids, though homely, she was assigned to clamber onto a chair at a table with the bookmaker's prospective customers and creditors. They told her she was adorable, asked her name, bought her guava juice, pinched her cheek. But after being amused by her, they disregarded her and freely discussed their top price, the amount owed, their strategy for repayment, or the plan to renege. Fadul climbed off the chair, toddled behind the bar and wrote out the numbers she had heard. She remembered her mother's chortle and the bookie's affectionate head pat that she got just before she was paid enough to make her the family breadwinner.

At six years old she displayed a remarkable talent for drawing, so she was traded to another bookie who put her in a back room to forge raffle tickets. By 10 she was creating bills of lading to launder cartel money, though older women who counted cash in the back room began warning her, in cryptic language with a clear message, that if she got too much older, they would find 'other work' for her to do. Too ugly, the men growled. Even as a virgin, too ugly for that work. Besides, at 12, her skills as a forger were too well-honed to be wasted and she graduated to forging ornate gift certificates to jewelers in the capital, and replicas of ancient stamps.

It had been steady work, but her family's luck ran out during a blistering hot summer when she was 13 and had walked after work through her neighborhood that was putrid with the smell of tropical sun, old fruit, and rotted wood. At home, she discovered the door open to their room, the furniture overturned, no sign of her mother, and just after the emptiness hit Fadul, a woman with heavy shoes and mitt-like hands stepped through the doorway and wrestled her off to an orphanage. She bit the woman's hand until it bled and jumped out of the carriage window twice before two burly guards pinned her arms and wrestled her back inside.

The children's home where she was delivered confused her: she had a bed to herself with clean sheets (though they had to strap her into it for four days before she would stop her escapes.) All the children wore the same, clean clothing that a little nun washed for them every Wednesday. And even though the food was served by broken-toothed women who treated it like slop, it was filling, regular (served at the exact same time!) and no one expected her to earn anything. She thought the sadness of most of the other children to be naïve. Those on their first tragedy were so far behind her. At 14 she had the shell of a woman who had gone through war.

While her precociousness had earned her praise, which might have made another child feel loved and valued, Fadul let it infest her with disdain. The callous way she had been traded from venture to venture and the tricks and subterfuge required to keep herself out of trouble had made her condescending and snide. Her days with the bookies taught her that life held no room for sentiment and that stupidity breeds both addiction and hope. There are few people more dangerous than someone who is both clever and cruel.

AFTER TWO MONTHS WITH NO word from her mother, it was announced at breakfast that she had a visitor, and she grew excited to be reunited with her mother. She washed her hands, straightened her braid and her skirt, but entering the dining room, she didn't see her mother, just the old bookie she had worked for last.

"Where's my mother?" she said, more pointedly than a child should.

The squat old man with a mustache that covered half his face, and rings that covered half of his hands, who never traveled without muscled protection and women who pretended that he wasn't misshapen, motioned for her to sit across from him.

"Where are the stamps? The last batch you finished."

He looked around the room surreptitiously, then lunged across the table and grabbed the collar of her dress. "I find out your mother has taken them, and I'll kill you."

"Take me with you and we'll ask her together," she said with feigned disinterest, unpeeling his hand from her, finger at a time.

He gestured to the floors above them. "I find them without your help, I burn this place to the ground. You know I will. Now, where are they?"

"Where's my mother?"

He pushed his short arms onto the table to raise his egg-shaped girth and kicked the chair out behind him, grimacing close to her face.

She turned away from him. "Panel behind the ice-box."

"Australia," he grumbled. "She's in a trunk to Australia. Or is it *with* a trunk to Australia?" He turned to go, then turned back to her. "Better you don't recognize me if you ever see me. Ever."

THAT NIGHT SHE SNUCK INTO the front office, trembling over the thought of her mother and a trunk. She forged her own release papers and was unchallenged by the night guards at the back gate.

IN THE NEXT TOWN, THE young Fadul set up a discount price tag business, offering facsimiles for the leading businesses, and the women, with shawls obscuring their faces and small children in tow, lined up for a chance to save enough to feed everyone for the month. Could she make enough to get to Australia? She was chased out by the sheriff and the business councilmen.

She stole food from the back corners of fields and orchards, sold stray dogs for meat, lived out of a rucksack in the woods, dressed as a boy, then was taken on for a decade by the Romani. She abandoned her plans to find her mother: too much time had passed, and she tried not to think about where she had gone or how. By the time she was 26, she was jaded and cynical beyond her years and so was perceived as a shriveled, bitter old woman. During a knife fight between two Romani men who would soon discover that she was the swindler behind the issue, she snuck off on her own.

Fadul decided that it wasn't worth her time to forge many small documents like price tags or IOUs for a small return, and she hit upon a plan to forge government bonds of a large enough denomination to make it worth the trouble but small enough to not draw attention.

She used her meager proceeds from transactions through the Romani to buy a dress and a hat one would wear to a funeral or a Calvinist inquisition, and she strode into a bank in a small town to enquire about a bond. She asked the bank manager to explain how they worked, to show her the various denominations, explain the fail safes, while she pretended to be baffled by the idea of currency not based on gold and regarded the whole topic with dubiousness.

"They're government bonds, but can be cashed at a bank?"

"Yes, much easier than riding to the capital, or a regional government office. You can trust us," said the bank manager.

As she stood to leave, dismissing the bonds as beyond her comprehension, she feigned a coughing fit that drove him, flustered, out of the room in search of water. In the interlude, she doubled over the stack coughing, and slid a bond into a wide, flat pocket she had sewn into the inside of her skirt.

On the outskirts of town, she changed out of her severe clothing and walked all day dressed as a boy to put some distance between the bank and herself, then spent a full day and night examining the bond.

Replication was painstaking work, especially as her worktable was the stump of a tree, she was living on low-hanging fruit and sleeping in the bushes. Each of the bonds took three days to make, challenging her eyesight and dexterity for the fine scrolling, and time for the ink to dry. After four failures, she produced one that met with her satisfaction and she woke in the morning, donned her Calvinist clothing, and strode into the next town.

While the village was big enough for a bank, it wasn't big enough for a government office so there was no way to verify the authenticity of the bonds. Besides, Fadul was so sour-looking and prim that tellers were reminded of the beatings they had received from their teacher, or the scolding from their hideous Aunt Gert and they preferred to hand the money over rather than draw her ire.

With proceeds from the first transactions, she bought a horse and small carriage so she could increase the distance between banks.

She rented hotel rooms and stayed just long enough for the ink to dry before putting her pens and paper into the false bottom of a suitcase that she filled with panties she had stained with chicken blood and a corset she had smudged with coal.

The operation had become smooth and lucrative, producing so much cash that she stored it in the lining of the dung bag she hung around her horse's backside. But she knew that she couldn't keep at the same scam, done in the same way. That's how people get caught. And she was getting tired of the road, the requirement to find a different city for each bond, and the labor involved in each one. The conundrum made her particularly receptive when she pulled up beside an old man struggling up the hill.

HE WAS AN ITINERANT VENDOR who had started years ago with the daguerreotype but had been forced to give up his studio when the tintype, with its immediate results and portable camera, swept through the market. Exchanging his equipment for a tintype camera and supplies, he went to fairs and carnivals, festivals, and Saints days, thrilling people with an image of themselves minutes after they stood in front of him. He made decent money until he was edged out by competitors who also boasted a backdrop of the sea or a castle. He lost his horse and wagon to pay a hotel bill, was swindled by carnival managers, and was now reduced to transporting his business by the sweat of his brow. Despite it all, though, he was a chipper man, and considered himself ingenious by attaching wheels to the tripod and saddlebags across the box of the camera, pushing it ahead of himself on all but the steepest hills where he was forced to drag it behind him.

TODAY, THOUGH, HE HAD BEEN bitten by a farmer's dog on a back road and now limped up the hill, grimacing at the same time that he whistled a jaunty tune. His progress was so slow that he would miss the carnival in the next village, and there was no money in the till.

Fadul pulled her horse up short beside him and offered him a ride.

"Oh, bless you, madam! I've always said that people are good and true," he said with a bright smile despite panting as he wedged the camera behind the seats. "Believe in them and every kindness comes your way."

Fadul didn't move to help.

The photographer settled in beside her, rocking on the seat like a child excited over a carnival ride. He was on his way to a place called Tartatenango, he told her, where he had heard there were weddings every day, and he thanked her again for stopping for him.

It hadn't been kindness that had made her stop, more like the allure of the injured to the wolf.

"What's the contraption?" She urged the horse on.

"The very latest," he said cheerfully. "Tintype. Stand for just a minute, wait another three, and you have a lasting image of yourself for posterity. Marvelous improvement."

She concentrated on the road that was now narrowing and rising through steep cliffs, listening to him prattle on: used to be a portrait had to be painted by hand, he said, and Fadul thought of her own operation. Only for the rich. Had to go to their castle or capital city. She wondered if he was trying to expose her. Daguerreotype was better but you still had to deliver the photo after it was done, he said. You go to a fair or carnival, you got all your customers together, so that was better, but no one stuck around. You still had to chase them down to deliver the product. Kept the market small.

His hope was that in Tartatenango his tintypes would fan out across the country in the hands of the satisfied, and he could finally settle down.

Fadul's ability to sense a scam or build a scam was

intrigued. There was something here for her, she could smell it. "How does it work, exactly?" A less trusting person would hear the snake-like tone in her voice: he mistook her self-interest for friendly curiosity.

"Easy as pie," he said, and launched into details of the tintype process, the plates, the emulsions, the revenue. He showed off a few examples that he kept in his coat pocket.

"How big a tintype could you make?" she asked, and she spurred the horse on when he wrestled from behind them a plate just larger than her bonds.

He told her stories of where he had been, but she thought about etching the bonds. Even just printing the black layer and leaving the rest to hand color, she thought, would save her time, increase her production.

Loosening his vest, he described the largest tintypes he had shot, described enormous families from just one woman, and whole congregations in a single frame, then threw his head back and laughed over the lengths people will go to look pretty or strong.

"Took up the entire tintype. I can usually get six from a single sheet. That was pricey, I can tell you!"

"A group portrait," she said, and imagined the bonds smuggled out behind it, hidden within the frame.

"Oh yes, very lucrative!" With a joyful compassion, he wove stories of festivals and their desperate queens, revivals and their preening preachers and carnivals displaying snake women and headless men.

But the more ebullient he became, the darker Fadul's mood. There's nothing adorable about people, and nothing adorable about fools who thought they were. His voice was like a bee in her ear. She wanted what he had: a cover for the delivery of etching plates, a way to smuggle the bonds out in the frames of the tintype. How to get access to this operation, how to take it from him? Driving her with as much force was her need to stop his twitting voice.

Her rancor rose like a fever, infecting her. He took his poverty in stride, he said, and she growled. His tales of exploitation had punchlines of grace and solidarity. Seemingly everyone he met had optimism and forgiveness. She ground her molars; her stomach started eating itself. She needed this set-up, but she'd go mad with him as a partner, and he'd turn them in during a fit of penance, no question. Blackmail wouldn't keep him quiet: he seemed to have no sins, and no family to protect.

"Nature calls, madam," he announced. "Might I trouble you to pause for a moment?"

She pulled the carriage over though the road was perilously narrow. The photographer jumped down, strode to the edge of the cliff and unbuttoned his pants.

"The body's a magnificent thing," he called back to her.

She jumped down in a rage and picked up a large rock.

"I once met a man," he continued, "who lived for six months on just pine needle tea and..."

She smashed him in the head with the rock and he tumbled over the side of the cliff, breaking on an outcropping before falling soundlessly into the gorge. How's that for chipper? She regarded the blood and hair on the rock like vindication and threw it down after him. Silence. Blessed silence.

Tartatenango and wedding photos. As good a scam as any.

She took inventory of herself: taking his life felt no different from taking anything else. It had a false ring to it as soon as she thought it.

Just before sundown, Fadul stopped her carriage in the shade on the southern outskirts of Tartatenango. The music of an accordion and the laughter of children set her teeth on edge. Every tree seemed filled with singing birds. This may not be a place to settle, after all. She sullenly opened the box of photographic equipment and rooted around for an instruction booklet but found none. She pocketed small coins from the bottom of the box, tossed aside pictures of happy little babies on their mother's knee. Without written instructions, she may as well throw all the equipment into the weeds.

The thought of the box tumbling over made her think of the way the vendor had pitched over the cliff, falling as if flying, serene even in death. She hung her head, struggling with a feeling she had never experienced, like a new disease in one's belly. She had never felt this nausea, never thought twice about her crimes except to concentrate on refining the technique or increasing the take.

She forced herself to concentrate. In the very bottom of the box, there it was: a flat plate ready to be cut in smaller pieces, at full size a half inch larger than the bonds she had been making, with a stained, brittle instruction book.

"What's that?" A little boy, standing on tiptoes to see into her rig, startled her with his question.

"Get away from me!"

"But what is it?" He persisted either as a child who has grown up accustomed to hostile adults, or maybe a boy who had never lived with rejection. Either way it was unnerving.

"A tintype. It takes pictures."

The kid ran away but returned with a noisy gang of children asking questions.

She charged at them, snarling nonsense. They screamed and scattered, along with the birds in the trees above her.

She refocused on her tasks: set up the tintype operation that would be her cover. Then, secure supplies and master the etching process for the bonds. Finally, find a broker who would buy the hidden bonds and transport them for resale at a mark-up for themselves. She thought of the dead vendor's description: happy customers fanning out across the countryside with her product. She looked out at the oddity of Tartatenango, the jumble of colors and people, the oddly shaped house, vibrant blossoms and wild assortment of birds. Perhaps a place to find an itinerant partner.

FADUL RENTED THE MOST ISOLATED house she could find and buried her gold under broken boards where a stove should have been. She was rarely seen outside but could be heard swearing and breaking things as she struggled to master the initial tintypes. Two days after her arrival she was seen collecting spring water with a bandage on her hand. The following day the woman who sold her a roast chicken noticed a sprinkle of chemical burns on Fadul's right cheek.

The only other time she was seen was when she threw rocks at the birds. No one had ever seen chirping birds clustered in a dense, multicolored mass as they were in the tree above her house, so many species of birds together, singing at once. Old Man Orjuela took it as a sign of the harmony in their village, but Fadul considered it a torment: they chirped all day and night and just when she dreamt of a little man flying with them, she woke to what she was sure was the shriek of a vulture.

Her snarling at both birds and children established

her reputation as a misanthrope and the interrupted sleep and injuries of her new profession made her look more misshapen and ghoulish than usual. When she invited the tallest of the children in for a test tintype, the entire gang of children ran away.

2

THE CHILDREN'S FEAR WAS A clue to Cosimo, who had
slowly driven his round-topped shepherd's wagon from
the fair where, months ago, he had ensnared Sister
Agnes, through the jungle to this village with a growing
reputation in the underworld. He had spent the
morning skulking around the edges of Caketown
looking for back-door deals, illegal card games, or signs
of a shake-down, his nose to the wind for the scent of
desperation and the opportunity it brings.

He stepped into Fadul's little house as the last of the
children ran by him.

There was nothing unusual about the shabby little
house, and while the equipment was something he'd

never seen before, it was the look on Fadul's face that convinced him that someone was up to no good here. Grizzled woman, perpetually angry judging from the deep furrow between her brow and the snarl that froze one side of her lip. Final tell-tale sign: despite his enormity as he had walked into her house, she had barely flinched, proof of either ice in her veins or a belief that she was the most dangerous person she had ever met.

"What's going on here, madam?"

She sized him up. "Tintype. Would you like a portrait of yourself? It's the latest thing. Sit for one minute, wait another three, and you have an image for posterity." The words of the dead vendor chilled her, but she continued. "As my first customer, it's on the house. Sit, please."

Cosimo sat on a small chair like an elephant on a stool and watched her fiddle with the plates, the camera, open the lens, cap it, and disappear into a cordoned off part of the little house. Out of habit, he surveyed her house for something worth stealing, someplace she might be using as a money cache. She had a single coat hanging on a hook, a box lid for the camera with the initials "RJ" engraved in it, and it looked like the bed in the other room had warm blankets but no frills.

"What's your name?" he called to her.

"Madame Fadul," she said flatly as she handed the tintype to him inside its little paper booklet.

His eyebrows shot up at the sight of himself. He quickly closed the cover, looked at her, slowly opened it again. He had never seen himself except in the occasional mirror or a reflection in a pond: this was too revealing. He dipped his head in silent appreciation when he left: thank you was too strong an expression for exposing him.

He walked slowly to the Caketown Bar for a drink that he needed more than usual, and by the afternoon, there was a queue outside Fadul's door of bridesmaids in costume and muleteers in newly shined belt buckles. They were flanked by trees hosting a cacophony of squawking birds.

COSIMO TOUCHED THE TINTYPE INSIDE his pocket as he drove his horse and wagon toward a fair a day's ride away. He had animal traps arranged in size on the outside of his wagon, from one that could sever the leg of a man down to the smallest mousetrap and, in addition to trapping rabbits, or if he was very lucky, a wild boar, he would rent out his services to villages and farms, trapping rodents. The fairs brought trapping business, card games that he could win even without cheating, and commerce like the swap of a Madonna for vials of fake holy water.

He was not a bad man: he had off-loaded the water business to a snake-oil man because he couldn't take the desperation on people's faces as they turned over their last dirty coin. He didn't hurt people with glee, or victimize anyone except for money or food, and during times that were that lean, it was just everyone for themselves. He tried to avoid stealing from mothers or farmers, though that cut out many of his potential victims, whom he didn't really consider victims except when he stole out of their purse out right. In all other cases, the person who was swindled had bought into the drama of the story and what might be their own share of what was being offered, trying to make a quick profit themselves, and so had gotten basically what they deserved. If they lost at that game, it was similar to playing cards: their permission had been given at the first shuffle. All of life was like that, as far as Cosimo was concerned, chasing the chimera of a good deal but getting caught in unseen details.

He was a big man, despite not knowing where his next meal was coming from. He was a great lover of buns and rolls and huge loaves of bread, ripe fruit, anything he could put into his mouth from bitter tobacco to the breasts of women. His father named him Cosimo because de Medici was the greatest trader in history, his father said, spooning out a meager soup in front of the fire at night. He built empires with daring, courage and skill, just like you will, son, he had said. His father had been a tinker who had built their wagon with its rounded green top, shelves and secret compartments on all sides that his father would open with a flourish to present his wares. Though Cosimo's current business was unscrupulous, and on a scale the very opposite of de Medici, he was very scrupulous in his business, knowing exactly how much profit he had gathered from any theft or transaction, and he never swindled the same person twice, which he thought would have been cruel. Cosimo considered his thieving an act of revenge, as he had spent his life thin and hungry, riding in this wagon next to his father who struggled to sell pins for pesos and convince people that pots could be re-hammered and reused. His father would repair shoes or harnesses in front of the fire, while Cosimo read aloud to him from the single book they owned, beginning again the evening after they had concluded.

At the card game that evening at the fair, Cosimo propped the tintype of himself upright on the table. "You seen anything like this?" he asked the players. Good strategy to divert their attention.

They laid their cards face down, but he noted the way they had sorted them in twos and threes. They passed the tintype around, making jokes at his expense.

An old bald man recognized it. "I've seen these. Little guy. Chatterbox named Johnson, drags his camera to all the fairs. Didn't see him at the last one. Where'd you get this done?"

BACK IN TARTATENANGO, COSIMO WALKED into Fadul's

house without knocking. "Tell me what you're really doing, Madam Not-R-Johnson."

Fadul pivoted away from him, panicked in a way that she had never experienced. Cool under pressure: that had always been her saving grace, but now it had deserted her. Acrid sweat broke out on her forehead. Could he know that she had killed the little man? She fiddled with equipment to buy her time. How had this latest sin become so visible? She was a murderer now and her dreams knew it. She was convinced that the clustering birds knew it. Now this monstrously large man knew it.

"What do you want?" She kept her back to him. A good con man might see it in her eyes.

"I want in."

"Into a little tintype operation? There's hardly profit for one." Fadul knew a trickster when she saw one, but partnership was always a risk: work with someone who was a con artist you eventually become the victim but work with someone honest and you go to jail when their conscience flared. Loyalty was just another scam. She had always worked alone and though she had experience with the long con, she had only ever seen temporary alliances that shifted as soon as the risk and reward changed. Fadul had always worked with people who had a lot to lose or a lot to fear. In this case, though, she was the one who had a lot to lose and for the first time in her life, she was roiling inside with fear.

Cosimo stepped a bit closer.

"Where is Mr. Johnson?" he asked quietly. Her refusal to turn around told Cosimo a lot. A con artist who has just bilked someone isn't this nervous since a simple theft can be explained in a thousand ways.

"Retired." She still kept her back to him and had run out of things to fiddle with.

"Voluntarily?"

"Again, what do you want?" She shuddered to think that he possessed a secret that could have her hung. What if she brought him into the operation? Spread the guilt. Ensnare the blackmailer. This man had mobility, an obvious delight in theft, and the heft to take care of himself. She supposed that expansion required partners, no matter how unwilling she was to trust. And right now, she needed someone else to buy a large etching plate, while she was distanced from the transaction.

He stood closer behind her, almost enveloping her with his girth, but said nothing.

"I do have a task I will pay handsomely for," she said, pushing him aside and reassuming her cool, detached tone.

Cosimo immediately noticed the resumption of her shell. The game was afoot, again.

"I need supplies," she said. "Tintype plates. Other... supplies. But all I have by way of money is a government bond. Take it to a bank... near the coast...

not here... where you can buy the supplies, you see." He had unnerved her. She was usually smoother than this. "Return and.... I will make it worth your while."

He nodded, as he had when given the tintype of himself. He wasn't an errand boy, but the secret of her scheme was here. She gave him a list and the fake bond, and despite his misgivings, he mounted his horse and rode for the coast.

COSIMO TOOK THE BOND TO an older man who was in his network of thieves but who kept a decent wardrobe when someone genteel was needed for a con. Surprisingly, the sale of the bond to the bank was completed so quickly that the man calmly sipped coffee at their rendezvous cafe before Cosimo returned. Cosimo looked around carefully, as he was convinced that an easy con had a trick inside, but he took the money and strode to the store for the supplies Fadul had requested.

The vendor took the list and laid out a stack of plates, two bottles of liquid silver, one of fixative. When he got to the etching plate that was last on the list he paused.

"This one is not for tintype, you understand," he said, stroking a mustache that covered his mouth. "It's for printing."

The wheels turned in Cosimo's mind. Printing. Bonds. Tintype. Ingenious. "You can't make advertising flyers with tintypes, my friend," he said, smiling broadly, his arms out in an expansive gesture that had always beguiled.

Before sunset the following day, Cosimo returned and waved his arms to shoo away a carpet of birds that now covered Fadul's walkway.

"You're a smart one," he said with his hands on his hips. He thought he saw the tiniest smile tug at her crooked mouth.

## 3

PALOMA INSISTED THAT FADUL BRING the camera to the weddings and distribute the tintypes at the receptions. Luckily for Fadul, the arrival of the tintype in Caketown was so novel and added so much to the wedding business that the homely woman behind the camera was largely ignored.

Orietta, however, was suspicious. "Buy a more festive dress," she told Fadul. "You're not photographing funerals."

Fadul looked at her askance, sneering at Orietta's sack-cloth dress and the headscarf and sun hat that hid her face. Fadul was unmoved by the frivolity of the mock weddings and the hopeful faces of her subjects.

She didn't join in the dancing or salute the bride: the cavorting was as irritating as had been the incessant chatter of the tintype vendor who was now rotting in the ravine. At night, she was unable to sleep from the sound of music and laughter, which added to her torment by the birds, and as she was busy half the day and all evening with the wedding photos, and etching, printing and coloring the bonds took up most of her nights, she became even more haggard and thin.

Soon, though, the birds followed her as she walked to the weddings and screamed from the surrounding trees. The colorful collection of birds was gone, with only crows black as coal and dull brown weaverbirds remained.

COSIMO BOUGHT A HANDSOME SET of clothes so he could sell the bonds in banks himself and then started borrowing pieces from the costume wardrobe. An elegant man in a three-piece suit and a walking stick cashed in bonds in Escoba; a man with a goatee and a leather vest cashed in one in Santa Anna. He changed his country of origin and his accent, wove elaborate stories of himself, doffed a half a dozen different hats on his way out of a half a dozen different banks. When he returned from selling three bonds, he rode a new black horse, gleaming and healthy with its mane plaited and tack covered with silver studs.

He reluctantly put Jade in charge when he rode out

for transactions and supplies, with strict instructions that she should put Fadul's dinner plate at the doorstep but never go inside. Cosimo was uneasy over implicating the tiny mother in their scheme and resolved to find another worker.

He sent word out through his thieving network and his compatriots arrived to pose for a photo and take the bonds directly.

"Relax," Cosimo said to them, shaking their tight shoulders. "Have a drink. Have a dance. Get married," he said, and the men shook the dust off their hats and looked around suspiciously. The wedding business worked its charm, though, and soon they were freshly bathed and costumed, sobbing over the hands of Old Man Orjuela about where they had gone wrong. In the morning as they set out with a tintype of their bride and a series of bonds, they were changed men: though it was faux, the look of love on a woman's face, and the pride of their faux father showed them a life that could be, and they plodded out of town distracted, weighing the what-ifs and the what-could-have been-dones.

When Cosimo was on the road, the tintype operation ceased to be involved with the weddings: Fadul was now completely hemmed in by birds who were perched on her roof and on the grass outside, so thick on the windowsills that almost no light entered the house. Cosimo found her cowering inside, unwilling to leave the building. The birds had descended on her the last time she ventured out, cutting her face with their claws and her dreams were nightmares of attacking birds, women in trunks, men flying from cliffs.

"Not to worry," he said to her, with tenderness he didn't know he had for his grizzled partner. "I'll bring the tintypes here. You can do your part without leaving."

The arrangement suited him well: he was expansive and joyful, fawning over the brides, as he slid in the plate, opened the cap, slid out the plate. Sometimes he served as the groom with such solicitude that he was requested by name. He started the dancing, encouraged the drinking, and sang love songs at the top of his lungs. Little Jade the Hummingbird brought him extra rum, and pastries in the morning.

The next month Cosimo showed up with a Romani clan for a group photo and when they all sobered up and dragged themselves out of Tartatenango, Cosimo rode out and bought the portrait back from them with so much skill that they were convinced that they had swindled him.

SIX MONTHS INTO THE LUCRATIVE arrangement, Cosimo was carrying a particularly large cache of bonds in the frame of a portrait when four Rebel soldiers rode out of the forest and surrounded him. He didn't have time to haul his rifle from his saddle before he was in their cross hairs. The liberal Rebels were a raggle-taggle group, dusty, thin and poor, only distinguished from farmers by the black triangle they wore on their shoulders. They demanded a redistribution of land to the poor, free education for all, seizure of the church's property, the equality of women, and the abolition of bastard status. The demands made the Conservative government forces and their priestly mouth-pieces apoplectic, and they waged war as if routing out the devil. Battles raged in the south, with brutal skirmishes being reported in the jungle and on major trade routes. But Araca was the home of the Conservative General, so no one suspected that Rebels would frequent the area.

The Rebels surrounded Cosimo, taunted him as a rich man and delighted in stripping him of his fancy clothing and hitting him with the butts of their rifles. The oldest resolved to string him up as an enemy of the revolution.

"I'm a thief," Cosimo protested. "Just a simple thief. But I can make you rich. See that package?" He pointed to the portrait they had thrown into the mud looking for a money bag. "It's a tintype. Look behind the frame. They're yours. The bonds are yours. Like cash. Or better yet," he said, as they tore open the brown paper wrapper, then the backing and looked at the bonds, "let's fund the revolution!"

With the muzzles of four rifles pressing against his skull, he had divulged the arrangement with Fadul. Live to negotiate another day, he had reasoned.

He arrived at Fadul's little house with bruised knuckles, a cut lip, a gash on his cheek, very little of his clothing, and an escort of the four Rebel soldiers. The hungry warriors breathed in the smell of grilling pork and mango juice, confused by the wedding arbor, while Cosimo gathered supplies for a drunken, angry celebration around a cooking fire that night.

Cosimo gathered supplies and set up the large camera near the fire.

"First, a group shot."

The rebels, mostly from the jungle, had never seen a tintype before. They drunkenly shuffled themselves together.

"No record of us," the captain slurred and waved the others away.

Cosimo put his hands on his hips. "Why else would you be here? You will have the tintype. Nothing is left behind for anyone to find."

They cautiously clustered again, draping their arms around each other's shoulders in brotherhood. The captain reluctantly joined them, but when the tintype was presented to them five minutes later, they hooted and pointed at themselves, mocked each other with joviality. They jockeyed to be first for an individual portrait, which they studied with sadness and awe before they tucked them into their pockets and secretly planned to send them home to their mothers.

The thought of the bonds, however, made them

giddy as they stumbled around with mugs of beer and turkey legs in their hands: Tartatenango had solved their problems. Their insurrection would be funded with the government's own money.

# Chapter 5

1

The Caketown compound was a common stop for small merchant boats and anglers, but it became a waystation for the mule trains, with its pastures on the southern border, a willing and able trader in Paloma, a bathhouse, a dancefloor, and plenty of yuca vodka. The mule trains came from the coast in the north, headed south to circle the bay and the marsh, set out north again toward Le Ceiba Grande on the coast, east over the spit of land that crossed the bay to Villahermosa, and headed south again.

Whenever the trains arrived or departed, the air was brown with dust. The smell of healthy mules and dusty men nearly overpowered the fragrance of fruit peels and flowers. Their arrival made the earth pound, from the tromping animals beyond the horizon announcing their advance, the quickened footsteps of everyone from bridesmaids to bakers, the earth-shaking arrival, the foot-stomping dancing, and plodding departure.

Shortly after the appearance of the rebel soldiers, a mule train arrived that was so long that the rider in front had unloaded and climbed into a bath before the last man had passed the gate and dismounted. Gonzago, a commanding man in a fringed leather jacket, with thick black hair that hung below his shoulders and eyes the color of beef broth, was the head of the operation and last man in. He turned over the reigns of his horse to a young boy before slapping the dust off his pants with his enormous hands.

As he stepped through the gate of the Caketown Bar, a swarm of children who were chasing a monkey with the red Antoinette wig ran into his legs but flowed on like water except the last one, a toddler who fell over Gonzago's boots.

The driver picked him up by the back of the shirt and, raising the little child high in the air, smiled up into his face, then set him down gently.

Paloma was wiping down tables when she caught sight of his kindness, and as he moved into the bar and ordered a drink, she was intrigued by the way he swung his hair back when he chuckled. He looked sad, which meant he had a heart that could be broken, and she thought his kindness made him seem more wise than cunning, though she knew to doubt that.

She watched him courteously accept a shot of vodka from Orietta and drain it without hunger. He crossed the bar and requested a bath, and when he returned an hour later with a shining face and slick wet hair Paloma wanted to be close to an inexplicable aroma coming off him, a scent she believed was from all the places he had been and all the women who had bedded him.

When the musicians began unpacking their instruments, he strode across the dance floor and asked her to join him.

"Not often a man can dance with a jaguar," he said quietly.

She chuckled a bit chagrined. "You've heard that story, then."

"The jaguar who turned into a woman?" He pulled her close and whispered in her ear. "Legendary."

That first night, they danced so long that others had to take over Paloma's chores. Gonzago was a full head shorter than she was, and he reached up to run his thumb from the side of her nose to her cheeks with appreciation. Her parents' choice of men had grabbed her by the arms with a violence that had turned sex into punishment but every time the memory made her stiffen with anger Gonzago spun her on the dance floor so she could look him in the face. He told her of his childhood on his family's meager plot of land, of his beloved and long-passed mother who had grown herbs in window boxes circling their tiny house so that it smelled differently depending on the position of the sun and the direction of the breeze. Rosemary in the morning from the eastern window, he whispered to her, cilantro as the sun went down.

"Where are you from?" he asked her quietly.

She looked at her shoes. "The marsh." She said it tersely and started to pull away, but he spun himself around in circles, his hair fanning out.

"And your family?" he asked, as he pulled her into him.

"Dead."

He looked deep into her eyes and saw the lie.

"To me," she said quietly.

He protectively pulled her hand into his chest and kissed her knuckles.

"Lovely family you have here, though."

It was true, and she hadn't realized it. Jade the Hummingbird, Doris, Old Man Orjuela, and most of all, Orietta. They were family. And what of this wise man?

She invited him into her room, and they made love as if it were the first time Paloma had ever walked into a lake. The next night they made love as if they were shipwrecked. They lost themselves in the river of their black hair. Every night when they were spent and the saloon deserted, they danced through an inexplicable blue and translucent mist, like swamp gas, that now hovered over her compound at night. In the morning, purple flowers with obscene stamens that gave off an aroma no one could identify had erupted around the perimeter of her house.

Gonzago was a genie who put the tragedy of her past back into the bottle. As her first lover, he introduced her to the scratchy hairy handsomeness of men, the glory of pillow talk, the sanctuary of his arms. She traced the outline of his muscular chest, rubbed her face across his stubbled cheek, slept with her lips behind his ear.

While he was there, Paloma was magnificent: the clarity of her gaze, the new depth of experience it telegraphed, the mirth in her smile; she was older and wiser, luscious, and firm. Towering over others she was like a great tree; when she was in new bright dresses, she became a holiday for all, cheering people by just walking by with her fragrant reminder that beauty is a form of hope.

The weddings that took place while Gonzago was there were more highly charged and passionate, while some mothers, pained by the sight of real love, took to their beds with their babies and their grief. Older women clustered at the compound's edge, pretending to want Paloma's medicinal plants but curious about the sound of a rapture that had been banished from their homes years ago.

Orietta, however, worked long, joyless hours.

Gonzago strode loose-limbed and barefoot through

her compound, his shirt, shoes and musty leather jacket consigned to a corner of her bedroom. In his absence the mule train had three insurrections, the last ending in a knife fight that had no conclusion other than a reshuffling of bedrolls and campfire placements. Paloma spent languid days bathing and sleeping in a hammock on her porch, waking to give instructions and only once shuffling over to the south wall to make a trade.

On the sixth Thursday of their time together, though, Paloma woke to the sound of the mule train wagons being loaded and she ran through the village looking for Gonzago. He was fully dressed, his boots polished, the fringes of his leather jacket jumping as he orchestrated the assemblage. Come with me, he pleaded. He would build her a beautiful wagon with every comfort, he said.

She refused. "When will you be back?" She thought she sounded a bit like a child when she asked.

He tied his hair back with a leather strap and resettled his hat. "The route depends on the deliveries," he said, and she thought it had the ring of a well-used excuse.

She had had more than enough wandering and the open road held no appeal, she explained. Besides, she had a business to run, so like many other women before her, she let him go, overly confident that he would return.

She stayed in bed the rest of the day, trying to put

her mind and heart back together as if collecting scattered belongings after a storm.

That night the mist failed to appear and the following morning the purple flowers fell to carpet the edges of her house.

Without Gonzago, Paloma felt as if she had nothing. Despite the bar and her trading business, she had no love, no child. Jade ran the wedding business with seemingly no assistance while also doting on her daughter, and Orietta was heads-down at the distillery with apparently no need for anyone or anything else. That day, Paloma went about her tasks surly and withdrawn. She walked away from transactions because she didn't care about the outcome, having lost the thrill of the chase. Her enthusiasm drained and took her compassion with it.

2

THAT EVENING, MARTA, THE WOMAN who had been assaulted and disappeared, returned, hugely pregnant and just as skittish, but she received few indulgences from a grieving Paloma.

Marta cried when she arrived, which was expected when a nightmare seems like it's over. But Marta lay on her bunk with her face covered and when women started to worry about her, they brought her bowls of stew and bread, coming in with tenderness but leaving with suspicions when the woman gave them no thanks, just gobbled the food and hid again. She was sullen and wordless, lying in bed until Paloma arrived on the third day, holding a broom.

"Are you injured?"

Marta shook her head no but turned toward the wall.

"This isn't a flop house," Paloma said sternly. "You're here, you work. Sweep the dance floor." She pulled her up by her elbow. "Then Doris could use help with the laundry, or Gretchen with the dishes." She pushed her forward and put the broom in her hand. "And say thank you once in a while."

Marta slowly swept the floor, but late that night, went into labor, waking up the entire compound with her screaming.

The mothers crowded into the bunkhouse, barking suggestions, describing remedies; they ran for hot water, for drinking water, towels, talismans, they rubbed her back and patted her hand and shortly before two in the morning, Marta gave birth to a boy. While the crowd around her cheered, Marta started crying again.

She pushed the baby away, refused to put it to her breast. When he cried, she put a pillow over her ears.

The plaintive sorrow of the baby's cry tore at them. Doris rocked him but the hungry baby continued to cry. Mothers gathered in clusters to discuss what to do, who had had trouble before, what it foretold of the child's life, what kind of mother would allow it. They cajoled Marta, tried to soothe her into nursing, tried guilt as a last resort but she was implacable. After hours of crying, Gretchen, newly delivered and still nursing her own daughter, marched into the bunkhouse, and put the little boy to her own breast.

It quieted the baby but didn't relieve the women's worry or cause a change in Marta. She wouldn't hold him or change him, and though Gretchen nursed him, his crying could be heard throughout the compound whenever he wasn't at the breast or asleep. Everyone grew restless and on edge: they had all been abandoned at one time or another and the sight of a woman doing that in their midst brought up too many memories, too much buried rage.

On the fourth day, Paloma couldn't take it anymore.

"It just takes some women a while," Gretchen said weakly, knowing it wasn't true in this case.

"We can't torture him while we wait," Paloma said, and had Gretchen strap him to her back while she sat on a bench. When she stood, he was far above everyone's head, and quiet.

"He's got a bird's eye view," Gretchen said.

"An emu view," Orietta called out in jest from behind the bar.

Paloma wore him all day for three days, present at inspections of cargo, at negotiations, weddings, and the baby slept soundly through the hubbub and hilarity of the bar, changed and fed by Gretchen. Paloma didn't dare kick Marta out: she was afraid the baby would wind up abandoned by the side of the road if she did. A dozen children had been abandoned at the doorstep, but they had the mother in hand here and would keep them together if they could. On the other hand, since when did they have a right to judge a woman's mothering?

The following morning, though, as Gretchen brought him to Paloma after nursing, Paloma marched into the bunkhouse with the baby in her arms.

"You don't care about your own son?" she sputtered in a biting tone.

"He's a rapist," Marta said, gritting her teeth. "He doesn't deserve to live. Every time I look at him, I see..."

"You stop right there," Paloma said sternly. "You raise him right he won't be. Besides, he's half you. Are you going to let half of you die?"

Marta said nothing and turned toward the wall.

Paloma grabbed Marta by the elbow and hauled her out of bed, dragging her to the door. She flung it open to the compound where women hurried across the dancefloor with baked goods and arms full of folded laundry.

"How many of them have been raped, would you say? Touched in some way they didn't want. Used for their bodies and discarded. Punished for love that was lost. How many?"

Marta sighed deeply but couldn't look up at the woman towering over her. Her milk had come in that morning even without the baby at her breast and it soaked the front of her dress.

Paloma gripped her shoulder. "Hate the act, love the

child. I don't want to hear a word about neglect again, you understand me?" She pushed the baby into Marta's arms. "Feed him."

PALOMA STORMED FROM THE BUNKHOUSE across the dancefloor, followed by the surprised looks of the working women. She flung open the door to a storage room and closed it behind her. Orietta was sorting crates of fruit and was surprised but stayed quiet when she saw her friend's face.

"When are you going to take that off?" Paloma challenged Orietta, who worked with a broad-brimmed sunhat over the scarf that hid her hair. Paloma gestured to the compound. "Anyone here threatening you?"

Orietta was surprised by the fury on Paloma's face.

"Is it any of your business?"

"Yes, it is."

"It changes people, Emu. They look at you differently, like you're scenery. They want something from you. Or they resent you. Plot against you."

"Yeah, it's tough," Paloma said, though it sounded like sarcasm. "But all of these women have stared into the face of people like that. People who think they're easy, who think they're property or bound for hell. Or that they're a giant. Or a jaguar," she said, her voice rising in intensity. "But they stand tall. The only one in hiding is you."

Orietta snarled a warning.

It was the first time that Paloma had thought poorly of Orietta, had questioned her integrity and, almost as important for Paloma, her courage.

Deceit was not tolerated in Tartatenango; not between each other, anyway. The government, the church, the gentry, they could all choke on it and it was assumed that anything you received from them had a dark side, an insult, or an injury. But among themselves, when so many around were bearing their souls, licking their wounds and trying to get back on their feet, it was an act of distrust to refuse to throw your lot in with the rest of them.

Paloma would not back down. "You're the only coward here. And worse yet, you're not afraid of them, you're afraid of you."

Orietta looked Paloma up and down with disdain, though it masked her discomfort. "I'm no coward!"

Paloma challenged her with a wordless look. Then instantly regretted her challenge.

PALOMA HAD BEEN THE ONLY one in Tartatenango allowed to see Orietta's beauty and even then it was a brief pleasure: she had been able to catch a glimpse of her sleeping, when she carried her chamber pot through the house, lounged on the sofa, or walked from the kitchen to the parlor with breakfast, her scarf off, her neck exposed and smooth, a sudden glint of sun from the window on her hair.

Orietta had said that she stayed hidden because the reaction of people made her feel separate and lonely, so Paloma tried to make it clear that she was not awestruck. The truth was, though, that Orietta was so beautiful that Paloma felt that a glimpse of Orietta was a nectar that could feed her for days. Orietta was beautiful in a way that made Paloma suddenly aware of her guts, and just as quickly, made her feel naked. Orietta took up all the space of beauty, making flowers look pale, and the fine fabrics of the bridesmaids like rags. And every morning, just before Orietta donned her scarf and hat, Paloma took one enormous inhale, as if she could hold her breath until her friend took off her disguise again.

"Since you're here," Orietta floundered, tossing mangos back into their crate. "I've been meaning to tell you... It's too crowded here to... expand my still. I need to find another place to..."

"To hide?" Paloma asked, though more gently now.

"To grow."


PUSHING PAST PALOMA IN THE storage room, Orietta whistled to her foreman, Juan, and walked north just a few hundred yards from Paloma's fence. Her business was doing well, her bottles of vodka, unmarked but well-received, were being carried in small quantities to other cities. She wondered if growth was possible. She and Juan spent the rest of the day pacing off an area, debating, then changing the outline of her parcel. She would have to go into Araca to see if it were available for sale. High time she deposited her money in the bank, anyway, she reasoned, and she should ask for a loan.

She was a hard-working woman, sunup to way past sundown and her clothing, a simple shift dress with a bib apron beneath the hat and scarf, wouldn't do for a trip to the bank in Araca. Orietta bathed, changed into her other coarse shift dress, retied her scarf and reluctantly strode down the dirt lane to a seamstress.

A second seamstress had set up shop on a tiny patch of land that seemed to totter on the exposed roots of old trees. It was the northern-most establishment of Tartatenango, as if she were the gate keeper between Araca and its ribald neighbor to the south.

"Where are you going in this dress you'd like?" the seamstress asked.

"To the bank." Orietta said it with finality, aggression, almost a resentful tone.

"Very well. Strip to your slip and remove everything else, if you would," she said, gesturing to the scarf.

When Orietta emerged from behind the accordion screen divider, the seamstress thought it was a magician's trick: the dowdy but respected Orietta walked behind the screen and an exquisite beauty walked out.

"Oh, my Lord, girl." She was stunned, mouth open. "You are... blessed. You are..."

"In a hurry, madam, if you don't mind."

Orietta wanted to just turn one of the bridesmaid's gowns into daywear: that would be good enough, but the seamstress wouldn't have it. She had just received a bolt of a robin's egg blue silk but Orietta insisted upon Navy with long sleeves and the two women went around in circles for quite a while regarding the neckline.

"How about this? I'll put small buttons all the way up to the top and you can button it up when the occasion calls for it." But she arranged the fabric to show off the smooth, firm cleavage of the newly unveiled Orietta.

"Not a word about this," Orietta commanded. "Not about the dress, not about me, do you understand?"

"Most women would want news of their beauty shouted from the rooftops," the seamstress said.

"Not a word!"

The seamstress bowed with deference.

3

A WEEK LATER, ORIETTA EMERGED from the accordion divider in a Navy dress with a tucked waist, the tiniest pleats accenting the bodice, a flounce skimming the floor, mirrored by another at her sleeves. The seamstress tied a bow in the back and one on each arm.

"This will not do!" Orietta grabbed at flounces that covered half of her hands.

"Stop, stop! I will remove them but don't..." she slapped at Orietta's hands. "...tear it." She quickly cut off the flounce and stitched the sleeves while still on her customer, barely finishing the last knot before Orietta shook her away.

Orietta twisted her thick hair into a simple knot on the top of her head and paced out the door.

She had ordered the tallest teenager to find a horse and carriage and dust it off. She requested a tuxedo jacket and top hat from the costume rack be given to him and assigned him to drive her into town.

"A lady does not walk."

WHEN ORIETTA STEPPED FROM THE carriage, she pretended she didn't notice that her driver had no shoes, but she walked imperiously toward the bank with a small purse and a briefcase. She was dressed for battle, her clothing both armor and weapon.

Women pushing strollers brought their hands to their clavicles in surprise, holding their breath. Gardeners digging in the park stood and removed their hats; those unloading wagons set the crates on the ground as they paced toward her for a closer look. They rubbed their hands through their hair, pulled on their beards. Women shifted a child to the other hip and patted their own hair.

Her beauty was a marvel, the downy skin, the long neck, delicate wrists, shining hair. Her features were mysteries that reaffirmed beliefs: symmetry existed as evidenced by her perfect eyebrows; balance was true in the world because of the way she walked. Her beauty lit up everything, seeming to clean even the most decrepit corner of Araca; dust was soft, water was clear, clothing on the line was now honorable. When seen near her beauty, colors became sharper, saturated like new paint, and rust became patina.

At the bank, the long-suffering line of patrons parted, agog, and she strode up to the grill work of the teller.

"Orietta Becerra to see the manager, please."

Orietta had arrived in a state of irritation. Fussing with her hair and her dress had annoyed her and despite her insistence, there were bows on the back of the skirt. But decorum counted for a lot and there was no time to make another dress. She was here. Time to proceed.

Men came into the bank and leaned on counters, looking her up and down. Older men tipped their hats, bowed at the waist but kept a respectful distance. The loan officer came out from the back of the bank and asked if he should open a window, offered her a chair, another pillow. A customer volunteered to run to the bakery for pastries. The room became electric with the mounting intentions of men. The teller and secretary were instantly convinced that they had developed a special relationship with her: the loan officer with the pillow knew the secret of what must be a bad back. The secretary who brought her an *aromatica* knew that Orietta preferred her unique recipe. Every little touch of her hand became a secret bond.

And at the same time, the opposite was true: even

the most beautiful woman there suddenly felt like a caterpillar in comparison.

When the bank manager, Rodrigo Cardoso, came out of his office, it was the very plainness of him that fooled Orietta. He was not scrawny nor obese, medium height, unremarkable eyes, standard haircut for a man of his station. His clothes were not flashy and yet his attire was not severe like an undertaker. As he had been just alerted to the arrival of an astounding beauty, he chose to not get excited or hop around like his employees who had brought the news.

His nonchalance was reassuring to her. To Orietta, the banality with which he greeted her made her think it was out of respect, that he would conduct business with her in a business-like manner, or that perhaps he was accustomed to the finer things.

But the truth was that a steady state was the one he preferred. Solid. Not excited nor glum; unaffected by the flim-flam and silliness of life. That was for children, not for a man with a keen eye and superior negotiating skills. And since this woman was in his bank, this was a transaction, and all transactions involve negotiations.

"How may I be of assistance, Senorita Becerra?" He said it with feigned detachment, as he fought the impulse to plop in his chair and drink in the look of her.

Orietta and Cardoso went into the fortified safe and she was assigned a safe deposit box. Cardoso returned to his desk and busied himself with the paperwork, while she counted out the small quantity of gold coins and bills.

When she returned to the office, he motioned for her to sit across from him. "Senorita Becerra. Your address?"

Orietta considered her options: Paloma's accusations had cut her to the quick and she was in no hurry to deal with her further. Why not cut all ties? Nothing would ever be the same, anyway.

On the other hand, she also knew enough about the right and wrong side of town to know that alerting people in Araca to the wild bunch on the southside would not be to anyone's benefit, including hers. Identifying with the home of ruffians would not help her.

"I'm new in town. Do you have a recommendation of rooms available to a respectable lady?"

"I would be happy to inquire."

"Thank you kindly. Next order of business: I'd like to discuss a small loan. I'm here on behalf of Magdalena Elixirs. The business needs to expand."

Cardoso just heard snatches of what she said, as it was interwoven with thoughts of her with her hair loosened in his bed; her interest payments; her with his children in hand; her on his arm; the incessant chink of yet more gold coins being counted behind him. She was bewitching. Her beauty in this place was a water lily in the mud. He was the most powerful man in Araca. Only appropriate that he have the most beautiful woman.

4

ORIETTA PACED THE SECOND-FLOOR furnished rooms she had rented, checking that she could not be seen from the street with her drapes slightly open, appreciating the balcony out the back shaded by a tree that was far enough away to repel intruders.

"And your trunk?" A young man who had escorted her seemed desperate to help while nervously shuffling his feet.

"It will be sent along directly," she said in what she hoped was a confident tone. She blushed over the rashness of her move, her impetuous refusal to return to Caketown.

"Is there anything else I can...?"

"No, no. That's quite enough...Thank you."

As he closed the door, Orietta spun toward him. "Actually, could you please have this seamstress," she said as she scribbled the seamstress's name on a nearby scrap of paper, "come to me here."

The boy bowed, blushing over inclusion in what could be lace and lingerie, even if it were just fetching the seamstress.

Orietta was jittery as she assessed her situation. She hadn't thought past the march to the bank, and now that she had exposed herself, was there a way back? If her Tartatenango workers saw her like this she would have no one who treated her like a genuine person. The only way to preserve the precious life she had in her business with her Caketowners was to wear her simple clothing. She couldn't work in this frou-frou dress, anyway. But if the banker or the Araca folks saw her as she preferred to dress, she would be mistaken for a scullery maid, not seen as a respectable and successful businesswoman. The thought surprised her: she was successful. The distillery needed her to be able to negotiate with these people.

She missed her mother as she paced the floor, stumbling over the voluminous hem. Her mother had been right all along about staying hidden, and now Orietta had been banished from another home.

And Paloma! She was enraged that Paloma had

pushed her into this revelation against her will. Untrue, a voice in her head said. Her own ambition had driven her to take the loan, which meant going into Araca. And the distillery meant too much to her to abandon.

But even Paloma, after all this time and all they had been through, was more interested in how Orietta looked than who she was and that cut her to the quick. There was no coming back from that abandonment. That betrayal. No returning to Caketown. Or their little house in the tree. Or Emu with her legs splayed under a table, indulgently watching the bridesmaids dance.

She choked back tears but realized that she could cry, or she could fight. The north and south sides of town never met: the north out of privileged ignorance and the south out of fear. The maids who walked north from Tartatenango into Araca saw the back door, the kitchens, the chamber pots. They didn't see the town folk in Araca and wouldn't cross her path. They didn't saunter through the square with nothing to do but take tea. The town folk in Araca sent their footman to the tinsmith or the second chambermaid to the seamstress in Tartatenango and none of them would go directly to the distillery. Ever.

A dress and a hat. Ridiculous that her life had become defined by these. Like paper and cake for the others. But if she had both kinds of dresses and hats, could she have both lives? She needed both lives.

Sadly, she would have to live in two worlds now.

So, two worlds it was.

The seamstress arrived later that afternoon and found Orietta stripped to her slip with her hair plaited into two simple braids. The plans for the new distillery were strewn across the desk.

"I need something to wear that is..." Orietta struggled.

"Like what you wear in Tartatenango."

"Exactly."

"Something that guards your...privacy."

Orietta took the woman's hands in hers. "Thank you, my friend."

The seamstress mocked-up a cover-all that was similar to a monk's cassock, with a huge hood that shielded her face and they planned that she would wrap her head scarf and don her sun hat at the factory.

"And for this world," the seamstress said, "you'll need at least one more dress."

"Yes, yes. Whatever you think, but simple."

"Tailored jacket. Straight skirt."

"Exactly!"

The seamstress remeasured her arms, then her bust. "Of course, if you want to be invisible around these people," she gestured out the window at Araca, "just carry a bucket. No one sees a woman with a bucket."

## Chapter 6

1

Paloma had watched the carriage set out for Araca with a sinking feeling. The previous evening, she had watched Orietta pull gold coins from the myriad of hiding places they had created in their house, calculate their worth and divide them in half. Paloma had said nothing, made no objection to what was left for her share.

She was glad for Orietta's new venture with the distillery and for several weeks had talked excitedly with her late into the night about the specifics of it, its expansion, the growing number of people she would be able to employ. They sketched out labels together, devised a route where Paloma's shipping business would take the crates of vodka to the coast and inland. But her departure from the compound had not been part of the plan – or had not been recognized by Paloma as part of the plan.

At the bar, in her concealing headscarf, Orietta had worked all day almost unnoticed by anyone except her workers. But Paloma noticed her industry, her efficiency, her shrewd presence, and she noted small happenings in Orietta's business so they could talk about it over an *aromatica* late at night.

It wasn't that she couldn't live without her. It wasn't that Orietta would be that far away, if the markers she had seen in the field on the other side of the spring were any indication, but she felt her belly shriveling with a parched loneliness, nonetheless.

She had pushed Orietta too hard. Why had she even mentioned the scarf?

As Paloma turned back to her work in the bar, a warm breeze blew away the morning river-mist. By mid-morning, the wind had become oven-hot, followed by a befuddling dust storm like no one had ever seen, coating the dancefloor and the backs of the mules, pooling at the base of the bar.

Jade hurried around the dormitory, Jewel strapped to her chest, ordering the mothers to close the windows and cover the cribs with sheets. The bridesmaids and groomsmen ran inside to stuff rags and straw into the cracks in their bedroom walls and the seamstress closed for the day to prevent the dust from ruining the lace and embedding itself in the felt of the top hats. The monkeys stole all the wigs and huddled in a protective circle around them as if they were babies.

"Jungles don't have dust storms and they don't blow from a river," Old Man Orjuela said under his breath as he stood on the dancefloor with the dust collecting in the creases of his elbows and neck. He licked it from his lips and spat. "Tastes rotted like the marsh," he said, watching the muleteers cover their beasts and the dogs huddle under the dancefloor. "I don't understand this weather."

Paloma looked around and shrugged. "It's just weather."

Late that afternoon, Paloma was heartened by the sight of the carriage returning to Caketown, though it struggled through the dust storm, and then she became especially unhappy when the boy in his bare feet, using his top hat as a shield, informed her that Orietta had given him specific instructions to return without her, as she had taken rooms in town.

"In Araca?" Paloma pulled the boy behind the bar out of the wind. No one went into Araca. Araca was sleepy and old, a few larger homes owned by mining moguls and a logging baron, now old men with their wives in rockers on the porch. Cities like Araca were filled with people who had...opinions. A working woman with a child on her hip would be sneered at and if she were black, she would be turned away. Everyone in Caketown knew how the exclusion worked and just steered clear. She didn't know anyone who had ever been to Araca except for a couple of women who were domestics, and the produce merchant who drove his wagon up to back doors. Why bother going there? Just this week in Tartatenango a tanner had set up shop and his wife made the most amazing etched leather. A smokehouse was being built and the gardens nearest the jungle were wild with blooms and vines.

Several times during the evening, Paloma carried her dish rag into the dust storm and the lane, looking for Orietta, but she snapped her towel in frustration and returned to tend to the few patrons who huddled in a corner out of the wind, covering their glasses with their hands between sips.

Paloma decided to enforce closing time and she shut but did not lock the gate. Closing the bar was a rare occurrence, since the incessant arrival of new travelers made the Caketown Bar a place that only seemed completely still when there was a midnight rain pelting the dance floor, or in this case, an inexplicable dust storm. Paloma walked into the lane one last time, peering through the swirling dust for any sign of Orietta, then guided the last drinkers on their way.

"Get along," she said. "Get home safe."

As she watched the last patrons totter down the

road, leaning on each other's arms, their shirts up over their heads as protection from the dust storm, Paloma was drawn by a sharp ping to the south. Metal on metal.

The wind settled and the sand puddled where it fell.

It was a clear and bright ring, not a machine, and it was either a new sound or one she hadn't heard over the nearly uninterrupted dancing and general high life of the bar. It drew her down the lane. Four hundred yards south of the bar, Paloma saw the circle of light made by a furnace and the whooshing bellows like the wings of an enormous bird. It was the new blacksmith shop, opened just a week ago. The muleteers had been happy about it, and overhearing them, she knew it would be good for the transport business as well. She hadn't seen it, being too busy with the bar, and she had assumed that the smith would wind up on one of her barstools one of these evenings.

This evening, though, she was drawn forward by something other than practicality. She walked south, enchanted by the flame, and as she drew near, the violence of the blacksmith plunging red-hot metal into cold water mesmerized her. She lost herself in his serene motions, the insistence of his hammer, the satisfaction of watching iron bend to his will.

And she was drawn to him as a man when the blacksmith set down his huge hammer and hung his leather apron on a peg, wiped his hands carefully and rolled down the sleeves of his surprisingly white shirt, walking toward her as if she had been expected.

He was enormously tall, wider than her everywhere except her hips, and they stood closer than one would on first meeting because it was so rare for either of them to stand face to face. The blacksmith had just one eye, the other socket healthy and smooth, neatly stitched closed. Sparks had etched a scar like a flowering tree into his dark, close-cropped hair.

"Gabriel Herrera, senorita," he said with a surprisingly formal bow. "I hope I haven't disturbed your sleep. It's cooler at night. And the horses are calmer."

She was tongue-tied. Without stepping away or dropping her gaze, she invited him for breakfast in the deserted bar.

As she swung open the gate, the moonlight hit the flowers, the multi-colored fruit peels in their now-dusty pile, the sleeping dogs who had emerged when the dust storm subsided to shake themselves clean and resume their positions around the strangler fig tree. The red and blue birds flapped themselves clean and watched Paloma before tucking their beaks and going back to sleep.

It may have been because they were alone, because the hour was without expectations; because they were the same size; perhaps because with none of her employees or hangers-on around, she could talk about her business as she couldn't with anyone else. But Paloma revealed more than her business: she laid out her life to Gabriel, being raped and running, her ordeal in the swamp, her current prosperity. Her worry over Orietta. Her confusion about Marta who had rejected her child. He listened intently, not hungry for gossip, but absorbing details and murmuring kindly, looking down at the table when she struggled with painful memories. She made him trout smoked in banana leaves that night, made fresh fruit juice, brewed dark coffee. Boldly, Paloma ran her finger up the trunk of his scar, as he described the death of his parents, the smithing accident when he had lost his eye, and he spoke softly without meeting her eyes as he described the lonely wandering of recent years.

After that evening, she closed the bar every night, and the ping of his hammer became a much-anticipated sound, while the late nights with him in her empty bar now meant the world to her. When Orietta's foreman pulled up all the stakes and announced that the spirit business would be built in the jungle to the northeast, halfway between Tartatenango and Araca, the time with Gabriel was the best solace Paloma had ever known.

Over the following weeks, Gabriel courted her in an old-fashioned way, showing up in the early afternoon in a long black topcoat with a small bouquet of flowers that he carried far in front of him as if it was an overfilled mug. He would stand under the flower-laden archway at the eastern edge of her compound and wait until she joined him. He never came into the Caketown Bar in the evenings to join the raucous, foulmouthed, hedonistic bunch, though he never denigrated it or her involvement. And though she bathed, wore her best dress, and started putting flowers in her hair (piquing the curiosity of the bridesmaids), they ended their evenings with him bowing over her hand like a courtier. He just preferred a quiet walk to the bakery, the gathering of families under trees in the forest, a buggy ride, and on weekend nights when he didn't work, a quiet evening with a book. He lived in a small house on the far southern edges of Tartatenango that he had built himself in the weeks before opening the smithy, and he decorated it with small white linen curtains trimmed with embroidery, and chairs that looked like they would buckle under the size and weight of him. Every day, with sand and a stiff brush, the blacksmith scrubbed himself on his back porch as if doing penance. He cut his food with precise motions, chewed slowly, drank with deliberation, and was refined though not snobbish, as if refinement were simply a gentler way to be.

He taught her to read. He asked her to marry him.

JADE WAS SO THRILLED WITH the prospect of their Jaguar marrying that she climbed on a table and danced. A real wedding. Real love. She had watched their courtship like the dance of exotic birds, and sometimes wept at night remembering how once she had had someone who had looked at her adoringly.

On hearing that they were going to host a genuine wedding -- with a license but the formerly mendicant and now eternally Drunken Monk officiating – the Caketown Bar erupted with cheers. The cadre of seamstresses and tailors – usually in fierce competition with each other – joined forces for the task of modifying a tuxedo for the broad-shouldered blacksmith and they fell into a fit of laughing when they saw Paloma's gangly legs and heavy men's boots sticking out under the longest wedding gown. They all dug in their storerooms for enough fabric to make a dress and when she tried it on, she preened and glided around the saloon like a queen, then burst into unbridled laughter.

As the day grew closer, Cosimo lead a cadre to bring the best flowers from deep jungle clearings and dangerous cliff sides. The baker, usually content with lard frosting and old flour, sent off for exotic chocolates and imported vanilla beans. The floor was polished, the chairs dusted, cobwebs removed, and dried puddles of vodka and fruit juice were scrubbed off the walls.

Paloma thought of her parents for one fleeting moment but the rage that surfaced was so fierce that she banished them from her mind. She was jubilant again and would whistle as she soft shoed her way between the tables of the cantina with its busy kitchen and dining room, dance floor and bar. With Gabriel, love was quiet and kind, and Paloma settled into a serene warmth that made her think she was floating in a warm pond.

Though they had planned to have just a small wedding, every trader, dancer, and mule driver who had raised a pint or downed a shot there arrived and cleaned themselves up. The women who ran her transport business returned from the coast. Half of the customers from the wedding business arrived to watch a real wedding. The old women who had listened at her bedroom, the children who had been brought in from the cold, Doris and Gretchen, Jade and Cosimo, scrubbed the bar and made the food. All the bridesmaids insisted on being included and though they didn't know him well, all the groomsmen tended Gabriel and stood at his side. People emerged from the jungle in their best clothing carrying small gifts. The entire town, who owed their well-being, the health of their children, their livelihood, their sense of belonging and pride to this woman, carved and stitched and polished little gifts and set aside the day to attend. Twice as many chairs as usual were set up and yet, when the event came, people crowded into every passageway, nook and cranny of the bar, peering around posts and sitting on the fence tops to bear witness. The monkeys wearing wigs sat in the treetops, awestruck and quiet, and even the crows that blanketed Fadul's house seemed to turn to watch the festivities.

The only dampener on the day was the lack of Orietta. Paloma had sent an invitation that Gabriel wrote out for her by hand. When there was no response, she sent the teenage boy with the top hat to bring another invitation. There was no response. While dressing for the event, amid a bevy of excited bridesmaids, Paloma asked if Orietta had arrived, insisted that a chair be saved in the front for her and glanced at the empty space before saying her vows.

AT THE RECEPTION, GABRIEL WALTZED with Paloma all evening, oblivious to the outrageous celebration that surrounded them and spilled into the streets. Every band that had played there, returned, and with so many instruments playing in different parts of the compound it was musical bedlam. Fadul watched the dancing from a space between the birds' wings, sometimes convinced that the animals moved in time to the music of Doris' accordion and the wash-pan drum played by Old Man Orjuela.

Jade had had Cosimo build her a bench to stand on so she could see above the bar, and she monitored the rush of people to the vats of vodka and mango. Two hours into the celebration she had to use a spatula to slap the hands of the heavy drinkers away. A Romani clan mistook the party for the arrival of a competing family, and they stormed into the Caketown Bar with pitchforks and cudgels, then pulled up short when they realized that the legendary Jaguar Paloma was a bride, and they exchanged their weapons for jugs of rum and found handkerchiefs for their tears.

The morning after the wedding, with Paloma and Gabriel blissfully asleep, the river overflowed its banks at the breast-shaped rocks and coursed into the Caketown Bar, turning the dancefloor into a waterslide. The children spent the day hurling themselves across the floor and into a pool at the edge of the property. The bridesmaids changed into diaphanous slips that they pretended were swim costumes, frolicking and falling with the children. Grandmas put chairs into the water to watch that the joyful children didn't wash away.

By noon, the river had broken the banks of the pool it had cut into the compound and the river raced through the streets of Tartatenango. It filled Fadul's little house with an inch of water, but the birds wouldn't budge from the outside. Chickens were lifted to rooftops and dogs climbed haystacks to stay out of the water, while the monkeys carried the Antoinette wigs high into the treetops. Old Man Orjuela brought stones in the hopes of helping the farmers channel the river to the fields but as the water rose, the farmers gave up and bartered for ducks instead.

The water receded that evening as Paloma walked from Gabriel's house to the bar and she was shocked at the children caked with brown mud, the dancefloor in need of shoveling, and the fields ripe for planting in rich, black, river loam. She looked back toward the Magdalena.

"Sister, sister," she smiled, and said under her breath. "Glad you made it to the party."

## 2

THOUGH ORIETTA WASN'T SEEN IN Tartatenango, her name was on everyone's lips, as she hired most of the able-bodied men and women to build her new distillery three miles to the east between Caketown and Araca.

Jade, with Cosimo's help, set up a nursery for the babies so the women could work, and the walls of the distillery went up quickly, the brewing kettles arrived on wagons, the bottles were delivered by the caseload.

Orietta went back to the bank for another loan and met with the balding, portly loan officer. He was the least busy man at the bank, but he was kept on because Rodrigo thought a two-man operation, a teller and a president, with a secretary, seemed paltry and weak. It was worth a salary to keep up appearances. The loan officer sat behind a large desk in a room no more than five by ten, with a dark wainscoting to the waist and frosted glass to the ceiling. As Orietta stepped into his tiny office, he was startled speechless, then fumbled around behind the desk that pinned him in the room while offering her a chair.

Unbeknownst to Orietta, the loan officer was so smitten with her after her first arrival in the bank, that he had thought of nothing else. He had spent his evenings studying Latin: it was the mark of a gentleman (he had heard) and there was something about it being a lost cause that appealed to him. But since meeting Orietta, he spent his evenings over a cooling bowl of soup imagining her in a cherry forest in a pink dress, in a pine forest in fur, floating above his bed at night.

When she came in for another small loan it was approved immediately, no questions asked.

And when she sent in a request for a doubling of that loan, he agreed but insisted that she come in to sign more papers.

Another trip in what she called her town dresses, she thought unhappily, as she surveyed the development of the distillery. She supposed it couldn't be helped.

The look on the loan officer's face when she arrived, though, told her that her presence had more to do her looks than her loan. She scowled and twisted her gloves in her hand as he sweated and stammered through the paperwork.

Just before signing, she leaned over his desk.

"Oh dear, it's missing a zero. I asked for 200,000," she said, pressing her breasts into the desk, her skirts rustling, and she pointed at the number so her perfume would waft in front of him.

Hunched over the papers, his head popped up and he looked like a frightened chipmunk. "200,000?"

"I can wait while you change the papers... if you don't mind my being in your office." It was an enormous amount of money, far more than she needed. A test of her power. Akin to revenge money.

"Stay," the loan officer stammered. "I can change these now."

With the loan, Orietta added a loading dock to the back of the distillery, bought a larger pot, more yuca, her own horse-drawn wagon, and hired another half-dozen villagers. Those who weren't constructing were growing, harvesting, peeling, or mashing the yuca for Orietta. They built shelving and tables, worked together to devise a layout for the production, a circular flow for the wagons' arrival, layout for the packing line, racks and hooks for the workers' coats, found holes to plug against the rats. She had a market stand built in the coatroom and the employees brought in extra potatoes, ears of corn to trade, chard and spinach, mangoes, herbs from their kitchen garden. They did it together,

Orietta and Juan, the women on the bottling line, the men who dug the driveway. Everyone voted on the label design, and when the first bottles of Magdalena Elixirs were taken by the workers to the Caketown Bar, they toasted it with pride.

Paloma hosted the party with a bittersweet indulgence, wishing she could toast her friend's success, with her friend.

EVERY MORNING, A DOZEN WOMEN and men headed three miles northeast to work but every morning, Orietta was already there in her cassock, scarf and sunhat, having slipped out the back door of her apartment building with a bucket, unnoticed. Her employees thought she lived at the distillery, sleeping on a little bed in a room off her office.

The distillery meant everything to Orietta. The noise, the smell, the industry, the respect she was given for what she knew and the authority she had built. She had won prizes for her looks, but never for anything she had done. Making vodka had started as a whim, using a process she had seen in a book, but the satisfied looks on the customers' faces, and the repeat orders filled her with a pride she had never known. Each step in the growth of her business was a surprise to her. She hadn't known that she knew anything about efficiency or production lines, or even managing people. Little by little, bottle by bottle, the business had made her more direct, and she felt it had taught her a skill few women knew: to ask for what she wanted, calmly, succinctly, without flirtation or guilt. Magdalena Elixirs had made her, as much as she had built Magdalena Elixirs. But she doubted herself the minute she thought it. That may have been her goal, but in the bank, she had used old tactics, enchanting the loan officer, purposely distracting him. Maybe Paloma was right: she was afraid of herself; of the things she would do if allowed to trade on her looks.

Still, she loved her business, and the Tartatenangans. The best part of each expansion was the chance to see a mother's face light up: food for her child, maybe enough to move out of the dormitory into her own place. Shining faces rejuvenated by a little hope.

THE MOVE TO ARACA, HOWEVER, continued to prove challenging, as Orietta began receiving invitations to social events that required her to leave her apartment in town dresses. Women invited her to join their garden club, to stroll with them on Sundays either to press her for details of her previous life (looking for scandal), to bask in her reflected glow or to claim membership in the beautiful-women club.

Too frequently, her progress down the street was impeded by men with invitations or inappropriate questions, who bowed in front of her or blocked her way. They begged her for a moment, for a glass of port, a cup of coffee, for an introduction.

Worse, clusters of men gathered in the evenings under her balcony, serenading her with guitars and violins, sometimes at cross purposes, or reciting hyperbolic poetry, and most of the evenings devolved into fist fights and drunken, morose weeping.

The only invitation she accepted was that of Rodrigo Cardoso, still under the illusion that his flat demeanor spoke to his acceptance of her as a businesswoman in her own right. The very ordinariness of Cardoso made him attractive to her. He was predictable, quiet.

They met for tea, but she sat at the spot furthest away from him as was proper. Gossips were hungry for any sign of attachment. She met him at church and sat with him in the first pew but would not let him walk her home across the square. They had dinner in the best restaurant in Araca, at a table Rodrigo had ordered placed in the absolute center of the room so they could be seen. She did, however, ask him for a favor: she mentioned the singers and poets under her window and that night a policeman dispersed the crowd and took up a permanent post there.

After three months of meetings, Rodrigo tried to take her hand across a carriage when she wouldn't sit by his side. "I think you understand what is to be done here," he said to her, as they rode out into the country.

"I beg your pardon?"

"You deserve a man of means, my dear. I am the most prosperous in the region." Seeing that she was unmoved, he became flustered but continued. "I am... enchanted with you, of course. And I would like to think that... you may grow to be fond of me. It is my belief that we should marry."

"Is it now?" She looked at the forest to her left. "I am an... unusual woman," she said with embarrassment, "...in that my work is very important to me."

"Yes."

What she heard was an affirmation of her business acumen. What he heard was himself one step closer to her bed.

She married the bank manager without much resistance because she decided that it was safer to be attached to one man than pursued by many, especially as he had stopped the brawling musicians under her window from ruining her sleep. He insisted she wear his mother's wedding gown and his grandmother's ring, and she was glad to be without the burden of yet another gown choice. The seamstress fitted it while Orietta poured over her ledgers. His hunger for her accelerated the wedding plans, and his stature in the community filled the pews of the church with his business associates. She didn't invite her parents. She had only one regret, but it was so debilitating that it filled her mind throughout the service, the dinner, the dancing.

She had not invited Paloma or her beloved Tartatenangans.

# Chapter 7

1

The sun was glinting off the water of the *Cienaga Grande* marsh as three nuns from the coast disembarked from Esteban's boat to the deck of Sister Agnes' floating church. They were a delegation on important business, Sister Agnes knew, here to solicit her involvement though she wasn't sure in what, but at the very least, to rest here for the final leg of their journey, compliment enough.

The first greeted Sister Agnes as the two behind her saw the beautiful statue of the Madonna and, with barely suppressed glee, hurried over to it and fell to their knees. This was the moment Sister Agnes had been waiting for: others who discovered the genuine quality of her acquisition could revel in the Madonna's beauty, the aquamarine of her eyes, the lapis lazuli of her cape, the rosy pinkness of the baby Jesus. The statue was a worthy prize, now admired by important people, and the feeling of vindication and camaraderie made Sister Agnes very receptive to their request to join them on the journey. She barely heard the details of their destination, blinded by the relief of being with other nuns, of the prospect of rowing away from this detested village. It didn't matter where they were going, or that they prayed in the evening for so long that Sister Agnes' knees hurt, or that they had insisted on a Spartan dinner of broth and bread despite her offer of trout with mango salad. Here was her longed-for escape, perhaps the first leg of a journey that would take her to a real town, with real streets and shops. She packed everything she owned, though they had promised to return her by the end of the week.

Sister Agnes sat in the very back of Esteban's boat watching the village shrink, clutching her rosary and, while the other nuns thought she was praying for the well-being of the village, she was begging to never return, until she realized that she had left her blessed Madonna behind and she jolted with so much force that she made the boat sway. She wept with her face in her hands until the boat docked on the far side of the marsh.

A PORTLY WAGON DRIVER HELPED the nuns clamber from the boat into a wagon and they bounced over the rutted roads. "What's your business?" he asked cheerfully.

"A blasphemous tavern at the river's edge, desecrating the holy sacrament of marriage." The oldest nun, who had declined the trout and insisted on broth, had heard about it from a shopkeeper who had purchased goods from a muleteer who made it a regular stop.

"Ah, Caketown! Jolly place!" He smiled broadly and chuckled. He knew it well, stopping in whenever he could. "Good people. Good times." During his first stop, drunk on vodka, he had stripped off his clothes and danced wildly in his long john's. During his ensuing visits, he had woken up in a hammock, once flat on his face on the dancefloor, and once curled up in a bush with a stray dog. The withering look of the nun at his side made him clear his throat, straighten his shoulders, and keep his stories to himself.

The local priest in Araca had no idea what the nuns were talking about when they knocked on the rectory door and insisted on shelter. Caketown? Ridiculous name, and he did not frequent bars. But he would not deny the nuns shelter.

In the morning, the nuns marched south, the severe oldest nun and Sister Agnes driven by righteous anger, the younger nuns admiring the river, the flowers, the fragrance of mango. Without missing a beat, the nuns arrayed themselves across the road in front of the Caketown Bar, on their knees with rosaries flipping through their fingers as they prayed.

They were a formidable blockade when seen either from the front or the back. Jade watched with frustration as customers looking for some daytime drinking kept paddling downstream, as wagon drivers made the sign of the cross and turned around, as shipments were returned, undelivered. Even travelers just passing by pulled on the reins and redirected their horses and mules.

That afternoon, when the sun had baked them until one of the young nuns swooned, the gate opened, and Paloma strode forward with a large platter.

"Mango juice?" she asked, bending low so they could select a cup. All but the leader eagerly gulped the refreshment and thanked her.

The head nun rose and commanded the others to stand, though they came up just to Paloma's chest.

"Marriage is a holy sacrament! You blaspheme with your false vows."

Paloma smiled indulgently, unmoved by the nun's protest. "What part is sacred, exactly? The dress?"

"Of course not!"

"The party? The cake?"

"The vow one takes before God!"

"I can assure you, sister, no one here is taking any vows, and most certainly not before God." Paloma smiled broadly, then was startled by the nun on the end of the line.

"Sister Agnes!" She scoffed: the fraudulent nun here to protest fraudulent weddings.

"Jaguar Paloma!" Sister Agnes blanched.

"Nice to see you again," Paloma said knowingly, as she held the tray on the tips of her fingers and ran her other hand down the thick rope of her hair.

AT SUNDOWN, THE NUNS RETREATED to a makeshift nunnery the priest had arranged but Sister Agnes was not among them. Nor was she there the next day.

By the third day, the vendors and craftspeople of Tartatenango had rerouted their deliveries to the back entrance and built a flowered arbor at a side gate. The wedding parties were rescheduled for night-time revelry, after the nuns disappeared at sundown.

What the nuns hadn't expected, though, was the generosity of the Caketown citizens who brought them little pies and hot coffee, chairs with pillows to sit on, and their kindness coupled with the seductive smell of barbeque and mango juice, had made the nuns festive and they showed up in the mornings with a spring in their step. They moved their chairs into the shade at the side of the road and one by one, prayed with more thanksgiving and less approbation. After a week, they greeted the children on their way to fish in the river, though the oldest, angry nun admonished the children to behave and grumbled life lessons to their backs as they skipped down the road. The nuns greeted the rum runner with cheer after she had brought them small medallions of the Virgin Mary. They blessed the dogs, the horses, said prayers for the muleteers who asked for safe passage, and were frequently joined by the bridesmaids who knelt in the dust and held their hands to pray. Even the oldest nun while walking to Tartatenango wondered aloud how the *arapes* they were served could be so buttery and light.

BUT THE DAMAGE HAD BEEN done and its impact was greater than its effect on the wedding business: suddenly Araca became aware that Caketown existed, that the citizens of Araca did not live in a world where nameless, faceless servants and delivery people brought them what they wanted from the far corners of the world and then disappeared into the ether. There was a thriving but separate city, with streets and wells and homes, some mere shacks but others with tidy kitchen gardens and pathways lined with stones. Here were people who ordinarily would live cowering in the shadows but in Tartatenango, they walked the lanes in broad daylight, greeted by those who chose to be oblivious to their deformity or their sin. The raggle-taggle citizens of Tartatenango had reveled in their mutual acceptance and the joy of living with their own special brand of beauty, had thrived within their flexible generosity, and had not been shunned, sneered at, considered unworthy, dirty, or flawed since the day they arrived.

Now, for the first time, the lanes that radiated out from the Caketown Bar were not safe spaces, no longer hidden from the disapproving stares of the moneyed class, the religious clan, and the authorities.

They were visited for the first time by police who rode their horses down the narrow lanes, stopping to peer into the little houses, to study the faces of the muleteers and clusters of men, to slowly ride with their stirrups close to the shoulders of Doris as she carried laundry and water. They leered at the women, made loud jokes among themselves about the 'bastard' children.

When a zealous officer pulled his horse up in front of Cosimo's wagon, Cosimo slowly took his feet down from the railing.

"What's your business here?" the officer demanded.

Cosimo gestured to the traps on his wagon roof. "Exterminator. You have rats somewhere?"

The officer looked at him askance. He gestured to Fadul's house covered with birds. "What's going on there?"

"Abattoir," Cosimo said, grimacing with feigned disgust.

The policeman slowly turned his horse away.

The police assumed all the horses had been stolen

and the chicken feed was tainted, that the women were whores and the rum sub-standard. They walked through the bakeries as if they were inspectors and tracked mud across the dancefloor on their way to peer into the hammocks. Pointed questions were asked about the movements of the Romani. The loading mule train was watched over with suspicion.

That afternoon, Jade curtained off a portion of the women's dormitory as a changing room, though it hid cupboards where the women with especially suspect pasts or brutal men in pursuit could hide.

The nights at the bar started out with a gloomy resentment and fueled with liquor, a recounting of insults. When Doris brought out her accordion, the dancing was angry and wild.

THE ONLY NUN WHO REGRETTED arriving in Tartatenango was Sister Agnes, whose blood was so chilled that first day by the sight of the enormous Jaguar Paloma that she never returned to the church or the blockade. She slept in an empty hammock and stayed on the back streets. To Sister Agnes, Paloma had been formidable as a young woman, even though she had just survived an ordeal. Now she seemed even taller, was certainly more regal, her astoundingly long black braids glistening like the fur collar on a queen's mantle. The twinkle in Jaguar Paloma's eye disarmed her and the recognition frightened her.

In fact, the joyfulness of Tartatenango shook her. She had been sent to the convent when she was just eight years old, without a visitor since and the drone of prayer, the silent meals, the abnegation, was all she had ever known. Her service in the floating village had been limited as well: one school, two boats delivering supplies, and fish, endlessly fish. There was one bar and she had thought of protesting about it when she first arrived, but the wives and mothers reminded her, not lifting their heads from their sewing but bobbing their heads in unison, that it was a relief to be occasionally freed from their husband's demands, it was better that they let off steam outside the house. A single priest attended to three churches, two on dry land accessible by a good road, so he rarely visited the floating church, and when he did, he mistook his scarcity for rarity and treated Sister Agnes as if she was lucky to have him stop by, as if he was saving Sister Agnes first and foremost.

But this place, this noisy, dirty village had a pulse, a vibrancy, an unpredictable nature, a special hue to it as if something had brightened the colors. The second morning there, she shuffled down the dirt lane that ran from the flowered wall of the Caketown Bar, past the bakery, the leather shop, the tinsmith. She stopped at the edge of a communal garden and breathed in the rich smell of the black earth so recently enriched by the flood of Paloma's wedding night, inhaled the fragrance of the rosemary, basil, and the tomatoes growing bright red and inviting. Where was she, and how could she possibly go back to that wretched floating church?

"A good day to you, sister!"

The salutation shocked her out of her confusion. The Drunken Monk sat with his back against a thin tree, his legs spread stiffly out in front of him and his cassock up around his knees. He waved her over with drunken enthusiasm and patted the ground beside him.

She thought of scolding him and marching on, but she had fled from the other nuns in front of the bar, who, as far as she knew, were kneeling in the dirt all day reciting prayers. Given the choice, she sat on the ground with the monk.

He patted the ceramic jug of rum in his lap, uncorked it, passed it to her.

In the months to come she would tell herself that she had thought the jug was full of water, that the monk had tipped the jug back and all but forced the rum down her throat, but what she could not deny was the glory of that first sip. She had never tasted rum; nothing but the smallest sip of consecrated wine had ever passed her lips and so she was completely unprepared. No doubt she sputtered over the burn but all she remembered was the way it had softened her, how the second swig, enormous compared to the first, took away all urgency, in an instant polishing off the edge of her anger. She stopped counting the swigs, laughed at one of the monk's jokes that was irreverent if not downright blasphemous. No matter. There was time enough to repair the damage with prayer. She was wrapped in a warm blanket, drifting on the cloud of rum in her mind, so comforted by the way the liquor shrunk the world, relegating to the mists everything outside the small circle of her, the Drunken Monk, and the jug.

As she passed out, her head and wimple hitting the loam with a thud, the Drunken Monk seized the jug from her lap and chuckled to himself.

COSIMO FOUND THEM IN THE morning, snoring side-by-side, the jug safely propped against the tree. From his vantage point they looked like a fallen cow: the enormous breasts of Sr. Agnes in black, the enormous belly of the Drunken Monk in brown. Cosimo knew an easy mark or a willing accomplice when he saw one and these two were the best kind: like any mark, wracked with shame but driven by addiction. Better yet, they possessed the authority of the cloth, above suspicion, entre to special rooms, so-called private meetings at all times of night for topics that could not be revealed. Almost as good as a police officer on the make. He stored this revelation in his mind for future use.

2

ARACA'S AWARENESS OF THEIR SOUTHERN neighbor
changed Caketown. The young men who ventured south
chuckled over the roughhewn horse troughs and the
makeshift planks across rivulets, the crude street signs
burned into bits of wood. When they brought
adventurous ladies from so-called good families to the
Caketown Bar, Paloma overheard the lists of the urban
improvements they wanted, and she saw their little self-
important smiles. The dresses, hats and shoes, the
parasols the women carried to stay out of the sun were
viewed with suspicion and resentment by the
bridesmaids. Never mind that these new arrivals filled
the Caketown Bar and Paloma's coffers every night.

They demanded matching glasses, chairs instead of benches, and somehow thought that dogs were more vermin than companion. The conciliatory birds took to fighting again and flew away. Paloma had the local carpenter scrape and re-paint the wooden dance floor just to quiet their complaints about dirty hems and muddy boots.

Wealthy women began arriving from glittering La Ceiba Grande for wedding parties and they stepped out of their carriages in dainty shoes: a matron and her four daughters had four parties and one screaming fight that the towering Paloma had to break up. A monied widow surreptitiously arrived, wept through her ceremony, and left immediately afterward. Jade, who ran the wedding business now, knew that the rich were more interested in being able to select a deluxe package than in what the package actually included, so she now offered Platinum and Gold offerings that were little different than the usual but priced high enough to have élan. She filled a calendar with fake events to create the perception of shortage and shook her head when they pleaded, then she retired to her rooms and emerged again, having "worked magic" for them, she said.

BUT NOT EVERYONE WAS HAPPY about inclusion of wealthy clientele: the dancing girls now had to waltz serenely and soberly. The monied brides treated the fay and loose-jointed grooms-for-hire like undesirables, and the wealthy bridesmaids snickered at the wildflowers in their bouquets and the crude tent that was the changing room. Old Man Orjuela was at a loss for compliments that would appeal to women who had everything.

"Just tell them their babies will be beautiful," Jade said glumly.

Worse, word of a village of un-moneyed men was reported to the Government.

Late at night a month after the nun's protest, a squadron of Government soldiers swooped down on Tartatenango to conscript every man they could find. Pounding on doors with the butts of rifles, pulling at the flaps of make-shift tents and flipping over hammocks, they rousted young men from their beds, pushing them into the center of the dancefloor, while others chased down those who tried to slip down the labyrinthian alleys and into the jungle.

The middle-aged men protested that they were needed on the mule train or the army would have no food. Mothers of toddlers held them in their arms or pushed the very young ones into their skirts. Women who had already been raped by soldiers either cowered or glowered. Women with teenage sons shrieked and pulled at their arms, at the sleeves of the soldiers, but when they saw that all was lost, ran for boots, jackets and pants so the boys didn't have to march away in long-johns and nightshirts. Old men wept over the heads of their canes remembering their younger selves, their sons already perished, and the nightmares ahead for the taken.

The tanner was conscripted. The tinsmith and his son were both taken. The mule train's numbers were cut in half. Cosimo was on the coast delivering portraits with their hidden bonds, for which Jade gave thanks.

Fadul was awakened by the sudden flight of all the birds that blanketed her house and at first it felt like absolution, until the horse hooves shook the ground, and the air rang with the distinctive shouts of authority. Convinced they were here to lynch her, Fadul hid under her bed, shaking, but in a corner of her mind willing to end the torment of the birds and her own conscience. Her choices were eliminated when the birds resettled on the house.

Gabriel, bruised and disheveled from struggling, was marched from the blacksmith shop to the bar with a rifle pointed at his back.

"This one's a blacksmith," a soldier shouted, and Gabriel was motioned to a horse that he refused to mount.

"Ride or walk, smithy, I didn't care," the commander said, "but you're now the one-eyed blacksmith for the third Battalion of the Republic's cavalry."

Gabriel glowered at him but already had a black eye and cut lip from the struggle and the soldier behind him pressed the muzzle between his shoulder blades.

They road out of town, the conscripts who had been unable to retrieve their clothing jogging between the horses, in their broken-down slippers, while the rest buttoned their pants and their mothers pressed packets of chorizo and rosaries into their hands.

Paloma, who had first run to the blacksmith shop to hide Gabriel, now ran after them. With her enormous strides, she chased down four of the last riders, who pivoted their horses and brandished their weapons.

Paloma charged at them, challenging them to get off their horses for a fight.

"Go home, my love," Gabriel called to her as the soldier with the reins of Gabriel's horse continued down the road. "They don't fight fair, these ones."

The soldiers squirmed in their saddles and would have laughed outright but for her size and savage intent. The youngest of them flung his long leg over the neck of his horse and, landing with a jaunty disregard, he raised his rifle to his shoulder and paced towards her.

"Go home, woman."

"Or what? You'll slink back and kill us in our sleep?" She spit in the dust.

Jade had followed her, and panting, adjusted little Jewel in her arms. "Paloma, come away."

"So pretty, skinny giantess," the soldier said, looking over the women being left behind. "We may come back for the rest of you anyway."

There was pandemonium in the bar. Paloma stomped empty fruit crates into kindling, shouting obscenities as she threw anything within arm's length.

Other than the steady stream of women used by the General and the soldiers, the civil war had not touched Caketown, but now they were sharply reminded that Tartatenango, while a home more welcoming than any they had known, was no longer beyond the reach of the law or the government.

Few young men were left: two fay boys had ducked under a bed and covered themselves with crinolines, and a man whose left leg was so much shorter than his right that his gait pitched him from side to side like a boat in a gale. Old Man Orjuela sat with his head bent as he pondered the relief of being too old to be taken and the fear of being so old.

A HALF-DOZEN REBEL SOLDIERS ARRIVED late in the afternoon of the following day, thinking they were there to collect from Cosimo their cut of the latest bond sales. Only Cosimo and Fadul knew of the arrangement, and they stood outside Fadul's house, screwing up their courage to confront the crows and enter. But they had been seen, and soon, an angry mob of women demanded to know why the Rebels hadn't been there to protect them from the government conscription. The soldiers were taken aback by the reception but so frightened by the news that the enemy was close that they rode out of town without even watering their horses.

The bridesmaids let Paloma plan a rescue because it focused her rage as she paced the dancefloor, though none would join her plan, and when she fell to inconsolable weeping, the citizens of Caketown left her bent double in a chair with her head in her hands. She felt Gabriel's loss more acutely as the hour for their breakfast drew near, and she couldn't bear to go to their little house alone, so she spent the night at the bar, finally silent but with a heart injured in a way that even the swamp had not been able to do.

Her family had all but thrown her to the wolves; she had foolishly let Gonzago go; and every morning, despite waking in Gabriel's arms, she ached over the schism with Orietta. With Gabriel, she had walked so close to the edge of respectability: the official wedding, the little house, the promenades, the reading lessons. She had been seen, understood, loved. For the first time, she had felt she was part of a couple, no longer alone.

While Paloma's grief vacillated between fatigue and frenzy, the Caketown Bar seemed to run itself: patrons stuffed bills into an old crock and sympathy kept them accurate. Jade had the wedding business well in hand. The muleteers and traders continued their commerce, quietly, outside the walls, without her. She slept in the house that she and Orietta had built adjoining the strangler fig tree, moving aside the inventory she had stored in it since marrying Gabriel and moving in with him. Sometimes she didn't sleep at all, nor did many in Caketown, as they lay listening for sounds of a war too far away to be heard but close enough to have destroyed their families.

A month after her husband's conscription, Paloma half-heartedly mopped the dew off the dance floor and when she looked up toward the road that was shrouded in fog though it was noon, she saw the blacksmith, tall and proud, sitting on a large horse. She dropped the broom and hurried forward, but the horse and rider evaporated into the fog before she reached them.

"Gabriel," she called, and started down the street but there was no sign of him. "Gabriel!"

She looked up the road as another horse, with a smaller rider, stopped in a cluster of trees at her property's edge. He didn't move, and except for the occasional, soft snorting of his horse, Paloma would have believed that he was as much a specter as the blacksmith. She stood in the archway entrance to her property, clutching the sides of the arbor to steady herself. An owl landed in the tree above the rider. Paloma waited. A fox came out of the bush and looking side to side at each of them, retreated.

When Jade shook her shoulders, Paloma was sitting under the arbor, her hands still clutching the frame. In her lap, disintegrating from the dew, was a letter from the Government informing her of the blacksmith's death. The rider and horse were gone.

Paloma sat immovable, unresponsive for several more hours as the girls who worked for her fell to their knees around her, touching her hair, her shoulders, wailing in commiseration.

"I saw Gabriel in the fog," Paloma said weakly.

Jade did her best to hold her, though the tiny woman's arms barely reached the giantess's shoulders.

THAT NIGHT IT WAS NOON-time hot, and the tears of the bridesmaids mingled with their dripping sweat to soak the beds. Snakes and iguanas wandered the dancefloor befuddled by heat with moonlight. In the morning, a dense cloud of fog descended on Tartatenango like mattress stuffing and so many people walked into fence posts and tripped over their own dogs that children and chickens were sequestered inside for fear of being trampled. Old Man Orjuela was paid a coin to use his cane and lantern to escort women to their work. The muleteers became so disoriented that they refused to travel and even the call of alcohol could not get people to stumble toward the bar for fear of breaking their ankles or getting lost. Smoke up a chimney could not penetrate the fog so the generally raucous Caketowners huddled without food or fire listening to the only sound in the village: sturdy palm fronds crashing from forty feet up and leaves of other trees unseasonably cascading to the ground.

Jade, crouched in the dormitory with other mothers, organized a memorial for Gabriel in the hopes it would give Paloma comfort, but scheduled it for midnight when there was no fog. Traders from all corners arrived with flowers but hovered on the outskirts of the blanketed town until the inverted night burned the fog away. Several clans of Romani nearly drove into one another in the white-out, so they declared a temporary truce for fear of bludgeoning their own children and they roasted a pig in the dark. The bridesmaids scrounged for black dresses and cried in each others' arms as Doris played a dirge so melancholy that the bellows of her accordion, already soaked with fog, dripped with her tears. The nuns who had come to protest but learned to love the Caketowners, got on their knees again to pray.

Cosimo improvised a speech littered with fractured references to his father and good men, the honor of hard work, and he broke down, along with the rest of the assembled crowd, when he stammered about the power of love. The Drunken Monk and Sister Agnes hid behind trees, listening, where they were found blacked out and blanketed by fog in the morning.

3

ORIETTA HAD SLIPPED OUT OF her house in a simple black dress with a heavy black veil and took a circuitous route to the memorial in the hopes that her dual identity would not be discovered. She tied her buggy up and walked the last quarter mile, unrecognized by the steady stream of muleteers and farmers who paced toward the bar, slump shouldered and silent. The unreasonable heat surprised her: she hadn't thought that there were cooler breezes on what was now her side of town, and she unbuttoned the collar of her dress but wouldn't remove the suffocating veil.

Orietta could see the enormously tall Paloma from the back of the crowd, even though there were more than a hundred people in the courtyard and Paloma was bent over with grief. Women grabbed at her hands, knelt at her knees and cried, men doffed their hats and were immobilized as they tried to fight back tears, but Paloma was speechless, looked without seeing, and let her lifeless hand fall back into her lap.

Orietta spun around and leaned against a tree, covering her mouth with her gloved hand. Paloma enraged, Paloma exhausted, these were all things she could tolerate but Paloma rendered lifeless. That cut Orietta to the core.

As her tears soaked her glove, though, a tiny voice inside her started to chirp of jealousy. Paloma had had the love every woman wanted. True love, reciprocated love, authorized, condoned. If Paloma's life was a mess it wasn't her own fault (as Orietta's was). But to see Paloma in this much pain also proved that they were not friends at all. A friend would have been the first to know; a friend's solace would have been sought. For Orietta to stand here at the back of the crowd like a farmer who brought her bananas was a refusal of intimacy as severe as any other. Orietta had been deemed not worthy or trusted enough to give Paloma assistance. Orietta pushed herself off the tree, indignant, just as the little voice switched to recrimination: she had caused the first schism; she had refused Paloma's wedding invitation though it had been sent twice; and had married without even requesting

Paloma's presence. The depth of her anger showed her, again, the intensity of the feelings she had for Paloma. She hurried to her buggy, silencing jealousy and guilt, but relieved to not witness more of Paloma's pain.

As THE MEMORIAL LIMPED ON in the night, Paloma looked over the crowd. No Orietta, again.

4

LIKE ORIETTA, ALL OF TARTATENANGO found Paloma's grief difficult to watch, to see their hero struck so low. The city had been founded by her resolve and made famous by the embellished stories of her jaguar strength. Her months in the swamp were spun into stories of years, and even children knew the tale of how she had sprung from the mud of the Cienaga del Tigre, half-woman half-cat, a ferocious force of nature. To see her now, day after day, staring into middle space, listless and defeated, made them all feel more vulnerable, and the demise of one of the only marriages in the village made the faux weddings seem cruel. The ripple of her misery made the men who had been left behind or who had arrived after the conscription drink more, and the muleteers to revive old grudges. Children woke up crying for no reason and mothers buckled under the pressure of their burdens and curled up in their beds with their babies, shirking work.

PALOMA SAT ALL DAY BETWEEN the bar and the fig tree house in an old nightgown while the plates of food she wouldn't eat filled a table beside her. At best, dressed and working, she was despondent and irascible, holding a bottle of fiery *aguardienta* and a bottle of rum tucked under each arm as she swiped at tables with a cold rag. After her customers had ordered, she did a tight turn on her heel and withdrew with a harrumph. She kicked dogs out of her way and had nothing at all to say to the children who clustered by the kitchen, accustomed to the odd chicken wing or mango slice. Without having been in it since the night of his conscription, she gave the little house to Old Man Orjuela, who agreed to care for it only until she changed her mind. The blacksmith shop was now so crucial for the mule trains that riders sent word out everywhere they traveled and a man who called himself Whippet, so scrawny that all doubted he could even lift the smith hammer, arrived from the coast to offer his services. Paloma hired him but insisted that he never work at night.

She became an undependable employer, even at the

bar: she spent some days silently in bed; sometimes she could be heard screaming and throwing things against the wall.

During one of her frenzies, Paloma emerged from the fig tree house holding a hatchet and dragging a spare door, ready to wreak havoc, when she caught sight of four rifle-totting riders who dismounted and swatted at the crows as they entered Fadul's house. They were Rebel soldiers, but Paloma couldn't see their insignias, nor did she register the lack of caps worn by the Army. As far as Paloma was concerned, they were the murderers of her husband, the thieves of Tartatenango's youth, destroyers of her heart and life. Growling, holding the hatchet, she stormed to Fadul's house, causing the birds to lift en masse and circle the roof. She threw open the door.

The Rebels' rifles were leaned in the corner out of reach, and they were so startled by the enormity of the woman that they froze.

Fadul threw a cloth over the etching they had been inspecting.

"Gentlemen," Fadul said tensely, "Senora Paloma Marti Herrera."

"Paloma?" The soldiers looked at each other, then back at her. "You mean *Jaguar* Paloma?"

Paloma continued to glare, twirling the hatchet in her hand.

"We thank you for your efforts on behalf of the

people, Senora Jaguar," the captain said. "When we overthrow this corrupt government, we will take down the church with it. Expand inheritance to bastards. Give equality to women. Your cause is also the cause of the rebellion."

Paloma stepped around them and threw the cloth off the secreted object.

Half of the rebels eyed their weapons, uncertain if the legendary woman was an ally, while others crowded toward her with bright eyes, excited to tell their hero of their ingenious idea. They pushed against each other to describe the bonds and the tintypes, the frames and the smuggling. Our allies sell them to a bank, the bank collects the money from the government.

"They will fund their own demise," the captain hissed darkly.

Paloma tilted her head as if snapped into action. This plate was the sharpest weapon she could imagine. Bitterly, Paloma turned to Fadul.

"How fast can we make them?"


WITH PALOMA ON BOARD, THE operation accelerated rapidly. Paper arrived in the core of cloth bolts; ink pots were hidden in rum casks; fake bonds went out in false-bottom boxes with the mule trains. Anglers boated them to the coast with their catch. Advertisements for corsets and bloomers were decoupaged to boards, with the bonds hidden inside and carried out of town like the evening paper. Bags of flour, sacks of seed, laundry, anything that could hide the bonds was pressed into service. Paloma shifted the contact point for the bonds away from Fadul's house, moving it to storage sheds, then to corn cribs and back. They varied the shipments that carried them, the route, the destination, the pattern of boxes with and without until the system was so complicated that only Fadul knew the quantity produced and Paloma knew the whereabouts of the bonds.

More wedding participants were part of the smuggling operation. The freedom fighters, themselves, succumbed to the allure of the weddings and the kindness of Tartatenango. When they returned between battles, they gathered wood for the smokehouse, helped in the gardens, and strolled hand in hand late at night with the bridesmaids and the laundress. Their mothers were these people. Their sisters lived with scandal, and after six months the families of Rebels began walking out of the jungle, arriving in wagons and on horseback. More than one soldier wept with the kind hand of Old Man Orjuela on his shoulder as he whispered to the faux groom about bravery and his credit to the family. And as they marched off to battle, many looked back at the village built of scraps and tenacity and thought 'I fight for Tartatenango.'

# Chapter 8

1

Cosimo went through a sea-change as his residence in Tartatenango continued. Though the Rebels had taken the new black horse, he rode his old horse out to conduct business instead of taking his wagon and whistled as he returned. He staked his wagon down, pretending it was to protect it from the wind, and he let his horse graze with others after years of keeping her tethered close to his wagon for a quick get-away. He donated to the bar's kitchen a basket of wild mushrooms that he had dismounted and picked himself. There was a new lightness to him, a joviality that had shed its dark, predatory undertones.

Cosimo felt that Tartatenango was more like home

than his usual route to fairs or with the circus since carnies always had their eye on the angle and the con. Most of these residents were like his father, rest his soul: a simple man trying his best to provide a service, hone a craft, but still shunned for his feeble results. Cosimo was among his people here: he could see their scars peaking from the sleeves of their shirts, the faint remnant of childhood trauma in their eyes, the unshakeable skittishness of victims in their responses.

Cosimo had soaked in the baths, washed his clothes and hair, trimmed his beard, as if for a holiday or homecoming. It was in this relaxed state, sitting on the porch of his wagon with his face up to the sun, that he caught sight of a bundle leaned up against a tree. It was too upright for a rag or a pile of trash, but he stuffed a pipe with tobacco, watching it with mild curiosity. A goat with two kids grazed nearby and sauntered over, sniffing it. The kids jumped with excitement and the goat dragged what was a blanket, spilling the contents onto the grass.

It was a baby.

Cosimo threw aside his pipe and launched himself off his porch. If he shouted at the goats they might double-back and trample the little child, who might already be dead, considering how passive and quiet it was.

He circled behind the goats and shooed them away, then scooped the baby up, and the look in the infant's eyes cut Cosimo to the core. Unflinchingly, his little eyes spoke of resignation, of misery beyond protest. Of abandonment and hope abandoned with it. Cosimo held the baby against his chest, then hurried to his wagon.

The little boy was covered with flea bites and rashes, patches of caked-on dirt. He was small and his ribs showed. Cosimo was tempted to rush into the bar and demand to know who its mother was, how it could have been left there, but he realized that returning the child would not improve the baby's plight.

Cosimo filled his palm with clean water and let the baby suck it from his little finger, talking to the child quietly. He threw the filthy diaper out of the wagon and carefully washed him, dabbed him with salve he used on his own hands, wrapped the child in his softest shirt. The ministrations didn't change the look in the baby's eyes, though his breathing seemed to Cosimo to be deeper and more regular. Cosimo held him to his shoulder, little head cupped in his large hand, and Cosimo wept. Wept for the boy, for the pain that could push an infant to silence, for Cosimo's own loss, his mother having died or deserted him so long ago that a mother wasn't a person, it was the hollow feeling of cold wind swirling in his ribcage.

For the rest of the afternoon, he kept the shutters on his windows closed and the door just slightly ajar so no one would witness the tears rolling down his face as he mashed plantain into porridge or see him when he broke down weeping for himself, his father, sometimes for his mother. He changed the baby the minute he was wet, though he was running out of dish towels and shirts used for swaddling. He held the baby against his chest while the child slept, the little ear against Cosimo's heart. And while Cosimo listened for the sound of a woman returning to the tree and discovering her baby missing, he was unwilling to actively look for her for fear he would hit her while enraged, or break down in front of everyone, or worst, he realized, that she would take the baby away.

He fell asleep with the baby in his arms, jolted awake to make sure the infant hadn't rolled off his chest; slept again, reassured on a deep level; woke once with the baby silently staring at him. Cosimo lit candles and fed him, changed him, gave him water. The most important thing, he reasoned, was to reassure the baby that he wasn't alone in the world, and the tears rolled down his face again, reassuring himself.

The baby hungrily ate breakfast, which seemed a good sign, but Cosimo had to admit to himself that he needed things from the community of mothers: a bottle with a nipple, diapers, properly sized clothing.

Though he had only had the baby for a day and a half, Cosimo had already grown protective. He had taken off his bangles and chains as too noisy and harsh, had removed all of his colorful vests to keep them clean and to keep the buttons away from the baby's face. As he had slept in his clothing, his pants bagged without a belt and his tall, laced-up boots were far under the bed. But what was utterly buttoned-up was his conviction that no one would take the child away.

Cosimo saw Jade at the edge of the dancefloor close to his wagon, as she wiped the morning dew off the tables and barstools. He looked around to be sure they were alone and, silently, pulled the top colorful shirt away from the baby's face and showed her.

Jade sighed and shook her head. "That's Marta's son."

"I found him yesterday propped against a tree. The goats nearly got him!"

"We were afraid she would do something like that."

Cosimo blustered and gestured incredulously. "I won't give him back to her. I won't!"

Jade had never seen him looking so unkempt or in such a state of undress. There was nothing hard about him now; while he had never seemed all that sinister to her, he had had the edge of a hustler. Now he looked like a little boy and a rumpled dad at the same time. Jade pulled out a chair tucked in between them and climbed on it so that her head was at Cosimo's level. She stroked his cheek with her tiny hand and hugged him closely.

As the sun was setting, Cosimo watched Marta come back to the spot where she had left her baby and fall to her knees in the grass. She clutched her head as if she wanted to crush it.

Cosimo shifted the baby to his left arm that was hidden by the door. The kind thing would be to comfort her, make his proposition to adopt the child. But she didn't deserve the reprieve, as far as Cosimo was concerned. He couldn't bring himself to reveal the whereabouts of her baby, and he closed the door quietly, trying to convince himself that his secrecy was for the baby: if she knew, she would demand the baby's return and that just endangered him further. But it wasn't for the child: the pain of losing his mother had surged from a place he didn't know existed, causing anger he hadn't known he had. He, for one, would never abandon or surrender this child.

JADE SLIPPED INTO THE WAGON the following morning, seeing Cosimo nearly doubled over, weeping.

"Alright now," she said firmly. "This child has had nothing but weeping since before it was born." She set down a small bowl of *changua* egg soup that she had under a checkered cloth. She put her tiny hands on each side of his face and looked into his eyes. "Show him that there's joy to be had, no matter where, or with whom." She dug her fingers into his beard and shook his face. "Build him a happy life." She gestured expansively to all of Tartatenango. "Remind him that we're all happy he's here."

Cosimo wiped his tears. Jade pulled her little infant out of its riding sling and laid her on the bed. Cosimo followed suit, lying the infant down and then standing tall.

Jade pulled on his shirt. "He's too young to see that far. Get right up to his face. And smile, for goodness sake!"

Jade taught Cosimo things to feed him when the baby had gas, was constipated, how to heal a rash, to use the diapers she loaned him. Hold the baby's hands and slap them together. Move his legs, hold him close and sing him songs.

"Sing? I only know dirty sailor songs," Cosimo said.

Jade laughed. "For now, that will do nicely."

Word got out that Marta's son was with Cosimo, and mothers knocked on his wagon door at all times of day and night to whisper advice. They brought him little hats for the baby, an extra shirt, a soft spoon. And at every visit, they reminded him that Marta had left Caketown without a word to anyone, unlikely to return; and they asked him what he was going to name the little boy, since Marta hadn't given him one.

"Bart?" Cosimo said. "How about Alejandro?"

He walked through Tartatenango wearing the baby like Jade did, chattering away to him, which made the mothers smile. "How about Caesar," Doris shouted to him with her arms deep in a wash tub.

"Emmanuel!" called a bridesmaid.

"Matias," said Jade, as she stacked fruit for pulping. "Matias, son of Cosimo."

Cosimo teared up over the suggestion, and Jade averted her eyes to afford him privacy, but spoke firmly. "Happy Matias, son of joyful Cosimo."

Cosimo held the baby close to his face and whispered to him, not with the nonchalance of a father, but of an adoring mother, and kissed him before settling him again.

"This town isn't just *for* mothers, it *makes* you a mother," the bridesmaid chuckled.

"Time for a christening party?" a fey groom asked with a flourish of silk scarves.


LIKE SO MANY EVENTS IN Tartatenango, the christening was a combination of mayhem and jubilation.

The children needed frilly white clothing and Paloma, only slightly less weighted down with sorrow, donated one wedding dress to be cut up for the occasion. The women traded and lent their most respectable clothing to one another, as the costume closet held only outrageous wedding attire. The restaurant added baby food to its menu. The bathhouse ran day and night. The seamstress and all her assistants were exhausted. The band practiced subdued, religious music that not one of them knew. Word went out via the mule trains welcoming anyone, and three black sisters with one white newborn each walked out of the jungle to join in and never left. The forgery business was suspended for the day so all could take part in the festivities, though Fadul, who tried to duck out of her house, was chased back inside by the birds. Old Man Orjuela was assigned to keep an eye on the Drunken Monk to keep him sober enough to say prayers over the make-shift font of water. Cosimo was the only man presenting a child, and his shoulders rose above the women's heads, though he was hunched over on a small stool like a horse in a classroom.

The event exposed old wounds, of course. The bridesmaids without children felt barren; the faux grooms and muleteers were lonely. The mothers participating lamented the absence of their own families; mourned the children they had miscarried or abandoned to the church. And Cosimo worried that the child never seemed to see anything, express any emotion, or move with curiosity, just laid with dead eyes. He even ate with no reaction, as if moving his mouth and swallowing were the only things he knew.

After the christening, Caketown threw a party of course, and though there was plenty of rum and vodka, fresh guava juice and cake, chicken that had been on the spit all day, attendance was sparse, as the mothers returned to their beds with their babies, tearful over the absence of the baby's father and their own parents, some reliving the moment they had been cast away.

The christening was the first official recognition of Cosimo's new family, but the child became his son several days later. Matias slept across Cosimo's chest, his little ear on the big man's heart, kept from rolling by the log-like arms of his father. That morning, Cosimo woke himself with a raggedy snore and opened his eyes. Matias was looking directly at him, seeing him, as if finally arriving. Cosimo smiled broadly, then laughed from his belly when Matias flung his little arm over and grabbed the big man's beard.

"Welcome to the party, little man."

2

JADE WAS HAPPY FOR COSIMO but understood the sadness of the other mothers. The Hummingbird's baby, Jewel, had been conceived in love with a sharecropper who lived in a thatched house one hill over from Jade's family, in coffee country. They had grown up together but, as teenagers, when her mother and his father saw them holding hands after Mass, they had been forbidden to see one another and Jade was subjected to screaming denunciations and warnings. His father threatened to cast his son out, though who would work the four acres of coffee fields they had was not mentioned. He and Jade met in secret, pledging undying love, agreeing on patience while reveling in the delicious forbidden fruit. But when Jade discovered that she was pregnant, her lover blanched. His father was not to be crossed, he said, and the boy had no idea what he would do other than tend coffee.

The delicate white blossoms of the coffee plants that bloomed for just three days every year were usually cause for celebration and prayers of thanksgiving, but the morning her lover turned from her, they were a ghostly portent for Jade. Soon the coffee beans would glitter like beads in the morning mist, pearls in the spring, rubies in the fall. But whatever the shape or color, they meant her mother would begin walking up and down the terraced slope, bent over, pulling weeds, spreading manure, picking the coffee cherries as she had done since before she was Jade's age until now, when she struggled to stand straight, and her hands were gnarled and chapped.

For Jade, pick or stay home, it was all the same without her lover: a broom, a rake, a rosary, on your knees, on your back, offering the breast. If she stayed off the steep coffee terraces, she still faced a life sweeping a dirt floor as if there was a destination, one unending stroke at a time. Everyone said that girls who left home were raped or ruined or both. But if she stayed home, already pregnant, she could only imagine the violence ahead from her mother. The shroud-colored hills drove her to snatch the best embroidered shawl off her mother's bedstead, tie her second pair of panties and only other dress into it and burst out onto the road leading down the hill.

With every mile she walked it was the same: children staring off into space, women with their heads in their hands, young men leaning in doorways marking time. And with every new ride, weighing danger vs. distance, her sense of trust and wonder dissipated like effluvium behind her, replaced by wariness, then cynicism. She stole a knife from the first man who demanded sex for transport; she feigned a medical emergency to hitch a ride on a wagon; she insisted that she was a pilgrim to sleep in a church.

Her independence, and her perceived age, though, made her look suspicious, and she was pushed further away from the righteous side of towns. After the first night sleeping in the rough, nuns barred her entrance to churches and refused her assistance.

By the time she reached El Cuadrillo far to the south of Caketown, she had been taken on as the barker with a troupe of female contortionists who drove men to drunken hysteria by the flexibility of their legs and the positions of their vulvas, and when the men passed out on the floor dreaming of upside down and sideways sex, the women picked their pockets, then burgled shops by dropping through impossibly high windows. They cast her out when Jade's pregnancy kept her from twisting through the bars on doors.

After another week of wandering, exhausted, afraid

the baby would arrive while she was roadside, completely ignorant of childbirth, Jade fearfully presented herself at a Catholic hospital. Her arrival and her surreptitious departure were the only clear memories she had of the birth. The confusion, the searing pain, the mortifying nudity and bizarre-seeming fluids that came out of her, coupled with the angry, judgmental nuns, turned it into a dark kaleidoscope of grotesquery. Screaming, confused, alone, the sudden arrival of her daughter shocked her, amazed her, and she was startled by the voice close to her.

"Don't let the nuns take it anywhere," whispered a young woman mopping the blood from the floor. "Not even out of the room. They ship off the bastards and you'll never see it again."

"Help me. Please."

"As long as you have the baby at the breast, you're safe until the morning."

The young woman brought Jade another diaper, a bag, a chunk of bread and a small piece of sausage that they secreted under the mattress. "Take the blanket when you go."

"Go where?" Jade whispered.

The young woman considered the question sadly. "On the outskirts of Araca. There's a place. I hear all are welcome."

Jade slipped out well before dawn and took to the road with her beloved Jewel.

Like all the women of Tartatenango, there were foods that reminded Jade of the privations of the road. The small sausage lasted her three days and was the last sausage she would eat. Some women wouldn't drink rum, some wouldn't eat yuca, others couldn't stand the smell of pork. In Caketown, one didn't ask for a recounting or explanation.

Tartatenango was her home, she reassured herself, where she and her baby were safe, and that's all that mattered to her, as she lay down in the dormitory, hearing the soft weeping of other women.

## Chapter 9

1

As a maid brought her fresh lemonade without being asked, Orietta put her feet up on a tufted stool and regarded the flounce at her hem as part of a private joke.

Most women took off their finery when reaching their home, out of the proper dresses for the shop girl or the teacher. Orietta, on the other hand, did it the other way around: upon arrival at work, she jettisoned her feathered hat and silly crinolines for the rough hewn, shapeless cassock the seamstress had made her, a heavy apron that she cinched tightly, and she tied her concealing scarf and wide-brimmed sun hat over her hair. She pushed up her sleeves, going from lady to yeoman but smiling more broadly than she ever did at home.

At the end of the workday, when all her employees had gone home and the stable boy had outfitted her horse and carriage before he left, she hung her basic dress on a peg in her distillery office and resumed the costume of the decorative wife. She had eight dresses and she wore them in the same order every week, beginning with the navy blue, then the brown, the camel, purple, black with white trim, black with red trim, on and on without fail; she had a sky-blue gown for summer parties and burgundy for winter gatherings.

HER HUSBAND NEVER ASKED HER what she did or how she spent her time. Their routine was simple and clear. He had coffee and eggs in the morning before he went off to the bank while she had a 'lying in as was fitting for a lady,' Rodrigo said. In fact, she was already at work at the distillery, having gone off in the carriage and changed in the office. As long as she was back home when he came in for a late dinner, he asked nothing of her, and made no inquiries. He assumed that she spent her day reading: one of the maids had left a dime novel on the sideboard and he had absently inspected it, looked at his wife with an indulgent smile. She was offended but just before protesting, she reconsidered. Hiding what was valuable was the way she had always protected herself.

Rodrigo and the staff thought she was easy-going, but it was just that she didn't care how the house looked, even for parties. It had been built by his father and was outfitted with his family's furniture. Drapes, china, throw pillows: they meant nothing to her. The house staff followed a very strict regimen, so the house seemed to run itself, and the maids administered to her as if paying homage to a queen.

The only demand she had made of her husband and the house was being able to take over the back parlor to use as a sitting room and she preferred work so much that, at parties her husband gave, she would slip away and continue business correspondence or settle the books. Without children, all she ever thought about was her business.

Every morning, in the carriage on the way to work, she grew chipper. Changing into her cassock, scarf and hat, she relaxed. She joked with the women on the bottling line, conferred with the men finishing an expansion to the warehouse. At breaktime, she cut into a guava with her foreman and staff, her elbows on the table, laughing. She knew whose child had hurt his ankle; she knew whose little girl needed more protein in her diet, she knew their birthdays and how they had earned their nicknames.

Coming home, she retreated behind a cold facade.

Her husband wasn't sexually demanding, which he considered unseemly, and the associates he brought to the house (more now that he had such a beautiful wife) did not expect a woman to contribute to the conversation. No one could imagine that she was really running a distillery, so she was able to live deep within the shell of her beauty, seen but unknown.

Sometimes late at night, though, as she lay under perfectly starched sheets in her own bedroom, she thought she could hear laughter and snatches of music from the Caketown Bar, though it was too far away, and she would fall asleep with images of women in matching dresses twirling on the dance floor.

THE LOCATION OF THE SEAMSTRESS'S business had kept Orietta's secrets safe: Caketown residents had never seen her beauty and so word of an exquisite being who had bewitched all of Araca brought no one to mind. Her workers who came northeast every morning from Tartatenango never saw her arriving or departing in high-class attire. To Araca, it was incomprehensible that the wealthy and astounding beauty who was wreaking havoc on their men was really just a shrouded, dowdy worker at a distillery. Women who asked about her family or birthplace were silenced by their men who wouldn't hear of derision aimed at their private goddess. Men who were curious became frightened by the power of her husband: one did not cross the man to whom everyone owed money by asking questions about the integrity of his wife. After Rodrigo heard that there had been snide comments at the local tavern, the barkeep was visited several times by the chief of police (indebted to Rodrigo for some substantial gambling losses) and just for good measure two casks of ale were split open and spilled. Her beauty was like a vapor that mesmerized those around her, stupefied them so they wouldn't dare ask a pointed question about her people or hometown. And even if they had asked, seeing her, they floated on memories of what they cherished most, awash in desires for what they wanted. To some her eyes were those of a puppy; to some her beauty was like sunlight on flowers; to others she was rich honey cake. Looking at her, they harkened back to the day they were happiest, lounging on the branches of a fruit tree, or the time when they were a child with a hand on the breast of their mother.

SIX MONTHS INTO THEIR MARRIAGE, however, things took a very different turn.

At lunchtime in the middle of the week, Orietta walked into the dining room while pinning on what she considered a ridiculous hat, and saw Rodrigo sitting glumly at the head of the table, steam from hot coffee snaking across his face. A large canvas sack of money that she was taking to the bank was splayed across the table in front of him, its cord loosened a bit and a dozen gold coins bright against the dark wood. She had left it to fetch the damn hat.

"Testimony to some success, my dear," he said darkly.

Orietta positioned the hat pin and pulled her gloves further up. "Yes. It was good month."

"Month? This is from one month?"

She scooped the coins back into the bag, twisted up the cords. She usually kept her money in the safe at the distillery, then reinvesting every scrap of it into more yuca or better bottles, expanded production. Anything left over, she deposited in her safe deposit box at the bank while Rodrigo was conducting a businessman's luncheon across town. The bank teller lit up when he saw her step through the door and didn't mention her visit to the boss because of the sexual fantasies he cherished after her visit.

"I need to get this to the bank," she said curtly.

Rodrigo stood up suddenly and trapped the bag in his hands. "I'll take it for you, dear. No need to make a special trip. The little elixir operation has an account, of course?" His voice had a hollow ring.

She averted her eyes, twisted her hands in their gloves.

"Of course. That's kind of you," she said. "You'll bring me a receipt."

"Not to worry, sweet wife," he said as he picked up the heavy bag and kissed her on the cheek before he left.

WHEN SHE GOT TO THE distillery, Orietta paced her office without even removing the loathsome hat. She knew that tone of voice, that hollow ring. It meant 'you don't deserve this,' 'you can't have this, you're a woman.' It was 'trust me, I'm not stealing from you, I'm protecting you.' It was the sound of her lover's voice when he assured her that he would divorce his wife. Or when he said that it wasn't deflowering, it was being ushered into womanhood. And when the town got up in arms about it all, the tone said that he wasn't betraying her and leaving her to defend herself alone, it was that he was sure his absence would help things blow over.

2

THE WEIGHT OF THE BAG of gold hanging at the end of Rodrigo's fist motivated him in a way he hadn't experienced before. It was a significant amount of money, made greater by his surprise and its possession by a woman. And at the same moment that he had seized it from the table, he felt a stinging rebuke. More money than he made, clearly.

IT HAD BEEN A MERE six months since they had married and so he had assumed that her little elixir business was just a shed with a couple of women following an old-time perfume recipe. A hobby, like making jam. Old biddies canning beans. His business associates never mentioned it, and they all assumed Orietta read little books all day like their wives did. But the sack he carried wasn't a month's proceeds from a tiny operation. This was far too much money to have been produced by a woman's capabilities.

He carried the bag directly into the safe and counted it himself, slipped a half dozen gold coins into his pocket. He wasn't subverting her, or under-cutting her, he reasoned, he was just righting the natural order, restoring cosmic balance because a woman out in front of herself can tip the entire ship. He was rescuing her, in a way, keeping her from doing something silly. He handed a deposit slip to the teller while lost in his thoughts.

That night he slept poorly, vexed by the idea of his wife moving more money than he made in a month. How was this possible? The next morning, he asked the maids for the location of Magdalena Elixirs, which made them stammer and turn to one another.

"It's southeast of here, sir," the cook said. "I'm told you can't miss it."

He set out anxiously, alternatingly spurring his horse on in fear then sitting passively in the saddle in contemplation of the beauty of his wife and how adorable her little endeavors must be. Perfumes. Little sachet pillows, maybe.

The Magdalena Elixirs distillery, however, loomed in front of him when he emerged from a stand of trees, and he pulled his horse up sharply. Not a little shed, it was arguably the biggest operation in town. Far larger than he had expected. Proper roof. Solid walls. A steady spiral of steam from the boilers. He could hear yuca being chopped and thrown into vats, the clink of bottles, the call of workers from one end to the other. He had only issued a single small loan, nine months ago. A paltry sum. He assumed it was for a little shipment of flowers or something. He had paid more attention to the woman than the transaction, so he didn't really know. How could it have been built so quickly, and so large?

This couldn't be hers. This must be a mistake. Run by her uncle, perhaps, or brother, though she had never spoken of either. It had to only nominally be hers.

He felt foolish staring at the building that was at least twenty feet wide and deeper than any barn in the area. Holding his horse by the reins, he paced around the outside of the building to the loading dock. Men hauled wooden cases with burned-black logos. Twenty solid cases were stacked to the side of the wide loading dock.

She employed men. Couldn't be. And there were more men here than the two men who worked for him at the bank. Not possible. No man would work for a woman.

Which meant that a man, a very prosperous and capable man, owned the distillery. There was no other explanation.

And yet she had boasted of ownership, hadn't she? No. Most likely, her pronouncement in the bank the first day they met was just an expression of loyalty. But to whom? She had said that she 'represented' Magdalena Elixirs. Perhaps she was the bookkeeper. Not running it. Just recording it.

He startled a stable boy at a side door.

"What are you making here?"

"Vodka," the boy said proudly.

"Vodka? Who is the boss here?"

The boy caught a glimpse of Orietta walking back from the dock, hidden within her rough-hewn clothing. The boy pointed and Rodrigo whirled around just as she moved out of sight.

"And where does the boss live?"

"Tartatenango," the boy said. He had never seen the face of the heavily veiled woman whose carriage was kept there, but he was friendly with the simple, hardworking woman who owned the place.

"Tarta...what?"

"We call it Tartatenango, Caketown. South of here. Jaguar Paloma's got a tavern. Good fun."

The south side. The policeman who had been there several weeks ago said it was nothing but shanties and mud roads.

Riding back to the bank, Rodrigo ground his teeth. A prosperous man he did not know. One capable of generating a sizable amount of money. But Rodrigo hadn't checked the books in months: very little happened in this town. He didn't generally look at the books except just before the quarter end, and they always looked exactly like the books of the quarter before it. A teacher's paycheck, the meager contents of the collection plate at church, the same dividends deposited by the patriarch of a mining family, the steady salary of the timber company's lawyer. The whole town came alive on the same day that the checks arrived: the coal was delivered to the houses and the maids did the extra shopping, the vintner delivered from the horse-drawn wagon, and gardeners knew they would be paid, so Araca buzzed and clomped and shoveled and shopped, and then, on the second day, settled back into the near-silent satisfaction of the do-nothing life in Araca.

RODRIGO HAD ALWAYS SPENT HIS time reading the business section of newspapers, including ones he had imported from the capital and from nearby Colombia. Sitting behind his desk at the bank, he read books on the exploits of the American Robber Barons or the Hanseatic League in Germany long ago. He spent many hours over lunch with the town lawyer and the dry goods owner who fancied himself a real estate man and were frequently joined by the head of the police department, Chief Sanz, a good man who loved his wife so much that they were overrun with children, and who had a gambling problem on top of it. Off the book loans, losses written off in other ways: it was a kindness Rodrigo was extending to him.

But what of his own wife? He pulled his horse up short: how could she have been entrusted with that much money? One doesn't simply put a bag of gold into the hands of a little lass.

And then the idea struck him like a branch overhanging the road. She would have to be the owner's mistress. No other logical explanation. She must be having an affair. Or at the very least, this usurper must be in the love with her: men fell hard after just a sideways glance. He saw it every day, just walking down the street with her. Perhaps this man had involved her in the business as an endearment. To be around her daily. There was no question but that someone was in love with her.

His stomach turned when he realized that he was a cuckold as well as being unseated as the most important man in town. Untenable. He spun his horse around and considered storming into the place.

No, he thought. Keep the element of surprise. Destroy the man first.

The thought of being deposed like this gave him a splitting headache as he rode back toward Araca. Leadership was in his blood, he knew it, or he clung to it: the only memory he had of his father was of a great man on a horse, his boots black and unmarred, his jacket with shiny buttons and epaulets with fringe. As a young boy, Rodrigo had pressed himself into his mother's leg, her hand smelling of the chicken she was roasting for dinner, her plain cotton skirt stained from cooking. He imagined that his father had been called away for some important battle, and that made his absence understandable, patriotic, heroic, which made his own little boy sacrifice of life without a man in the house heroic as well. And yet he knew that these days, unlike the man he considered his father to be, he wouldn't put his life on the line for anything or anyone. Not his country, not his wife; he wouldn't even take a bullet for the Pope.

Upon returning to the bank, Rodrigo Cardoso slapped his hat on his desk and demanded the ledgers on the bank's deposits and financial health. What he discovered made his situation worse. He had given Magdalena Elixirs a small loan, but what about all these subsequent loans? Especially this last one of such an enormous size. There were no assets held as collateral. There wasn't a payment schedule or proof of income! How could that be?

Rodrigo called the loan officer into his office and two men wrangled about it for more than an hour, Rodrigo shouting and pointing at the loan papers, the loan officer shifting on his feet while looking at the floor, then throwing up his hands. Her beauty, he stammered, bewitching. But Rodrigo glared at him, daring him to saying something lascivious about Orietta. The loan officer slunk away.

It enraged Rodrigo: the bank was highly leveraged to this mystery man. Worse, to be forced to share his wife if not physically than at least to allow this man to bask in her glow, was to be usurped at every turn. Untenable.

Rodrigo returned home without a receipt for his wife. He poured himself a tall glass of rum and called for her.

"You lied to me."

Orietta stiffened, assuming a regal stature. "I beg your pardon?"

"At the bank you presented yourself as the owner..." He chuckled to himself, laughing at his foolishness. "But now that I see the extent of the operation...A bit of a grandiose claim, don't you think dear? Owner!"

Orietta dragged her index finger along the top of the table and poured herself a rum, buying time.

"The extent of it?" Orietta asked.

"Yes, I rode out there today. It's an impressive operation. Foolish of me to misinterpret you. You... handle the money. You're the bookkeeper most probably."

Orietta's breathing was shallow while she pondered her options. She was brutally insulted that he thought that she was just the bookkeeper, but if she insisted that she was the owner, it meant that he actually owned half of the business. He would take it over instantly, all the revenues if not the actual running of it. Hiding her ownership would be worth it, though. Exposing herself physically in all these stupid hats was not going that well, but one thing was certain: she had to hide her ownership of the business. Apparently, some situations require more subterfuge than a headscarf and a hat.

Rodrigo took a gulp of rum and decided against challenging her directly. He had planned on pointedly asking her for the name of her boss. For proof that the man wasn't her lover. He wanted the satisfaction of forbidding her to continue there. But if she was as loyal as her possession of the gold attested, she would warn this businessman of the banker's interest. And Rodrigo had a perfect entre to the business: his wife was the bookkeeper, which essentially meant that Rodrigo himself was both the accountant and the bank. He was an honorable man, trustworthy, he reassured himself, but all he could think of was how to chip away at this man's resources.

"Bring me the coins as you did yesterday, little one," he said, "and I will deposit them for you. No need to trouble yourself."

Orietta stood very still. Little one! Even her father hadn't called her that. She needed to buy time to think up a plan. She nodded slightly and swept out of the room.

Orietta plopped down into a chair in her sitting room. She was accustomed to men being unreasonably jealous, misinterpreting the hungry looks she never requested but still received. Or threatened by the extent of her success (which surprised her as well, frankly). But it hadn't occurred to her that Rodrigo would discount her altogether, attributing her efforts to a man just because she was successful. And while she had learned how to turn men's greed against themselves when it came to her looks, converting it into titles and prize money, this was about business, so it required more stealth and sophistication. She had a safe in which to hide her money at the distillery, and a safe deposit box for which she held the only key. The nearest bank was two hours away by carriage which would make her gold the target of highwaymen so working with another bank was out of the question. His bank had visibility into only a portion of the company profits through the account she held there, though no access to its books. Her Achilles heel, though, was that the bank held her loans, including the large one that she had taken out on a whim, as revenge, and that had financed their massive expansion.

At dinner that night, Orietta ate little and said less.

"It's been requested," she said as she fingered her wine glass, "that an accounting of deposits for Magdalena Elixirs be provided." She wasn't lying. She was the one who requested it but that still meant that it had been requested. In her office at the distillery, she had retrieved her ledgers from the locked drawer of her desk and drawn a line just above the last deposit, the one she had been forced to entrust to her husband.

"Has it?" Rodrigo asked as he cut his meat into equal sized pieces. "And when shall I carry another bag of coins to the bank for you?"

"I have been relieved of that task...for some reason," she said as she set her glass down.

What he delivered from the bank the next evening was audacious: funds received but then depleted with fines and fees, special assessments with obscure names, all levied since his visit to the distillery but backdated. Quarterly payments that were just now due. Annual assessments that started next month in a pay-ahead cadence.

The letter accompanying the accounting made it clear: these fines and fees would have to be paid.

That would smoke him out, Rodrigo thought. He looked forward to the mystery man storming into his office, enraged, maybe disheveled and frightened. It would be good to make it clear who held the reins in this town.

They were in the front parlor and he plopped down on the settee as she studied the bank papers. He picked up a needlepoint pillow with lace trim. "Did you make this?"

"No, of course I didn't make that," she said with disgust. What she had made, though, was the one hundredth bottle of vodka, a real accomplishment. She and the crew had cheered and raised a glass to it. "I have a headache. I'll take my dinner in my room."

WHEN RODRIGO ARRIVED HOME THE following evening, Orietta had opened a bottle of tequila that had been kept in a sideboard since Rodrigo's father was alive, and she looked forward to the look on her husband's face. She lounged on the sofa, her shoes on the cushion, her arm splayed across the back. On the low table in front of her was an envelope with the bank's threatening letter in front of it.

Rodrigo looked at her, gave his coat and hat to the maid.

"What's this?"

"From Magdalena Elixirs."

He seized the envelope and rifled the bills inside.

"If you could just sign the receipt," Orietta said sweetly.

Rodrigo was infuriated to see that this man had been able to collect cash so quickly. And still he was a mystery.

They sat down to dinner, but Rodrigo continued to seethe over the mystery man at the distillery.

"Who is this man?" He growled at her. He tore at a piece of bread as if attacking his own mouth.

"What man?"

"The man who owns Magdalena Elixirs, of course!"

She sighed deeply. "I've never seen this man."

"You're telling me you've never met the man who runs the company?"

Orietta held her wine glass and looked him in the eye. "Do you think I'm part of an inner circle? A board of directors? Privy to an executive suite?"

He backed down. "No. Of course not, my dear." He ripped at the loaf of bread. "Can't shoot the messenger, after all."

The irritation over this upstart would not leave Rodrigo: he was an outstanding member of the community. How could he be usurped by a low life from the south side? He needed a promotion, but he was head of the bank. Who was more important than a businessman, he wondered, as he downed his rum?

A politician. He poured another rum.

The mayor.

The next evening, he had his teller from the bank over for dinner and floated his idea of running for office, as he stormed up and down the parlor floor with a tamale in one hand and a beaker of port in the other.

"Well," his guest said lazily, one leg over the armchair while he twirled a crystal glass of rum. "That would let you squeeze him from both sides: trouble with the bank. Trouble with the law." He said it half-heartedly, but Rodrigo seized on it as a solution to his problems.

How better to manipulate the law, he thought, than actually *be* the law? It was an excellent time to fulfill a life-long dream: he would run for Mayor. Araca had never had a mayor. The moral guidance of one priest, three policemen including the chief, and himself at the bank – that's all Araca had needed. All that Rodrigo needed as well, since most of them were in his pocket: the chief of police had taken out a side loan from Rodrigo, and Rodrigo's father had given the church money for the spire. But money is power and if the mystery man had money then power would have to be wielded against him in another way.

He paced up and down, flinging his arm out while muttering to himself, the rum sloshing onto the rug.

When his guest, the teller, had staggered home, Rodrigo called to Orietta with drunken hostility and announced his intentions to run for mayor. "And you," he pointed at her with anger, "will be by my side."

She stood rigid and silent, then nodded her head like a butler taking an order.


THE FOLLOWING WEEKS, THE PARLOR was filled with men pacing with Rodrigo as he pontificated. They strategized, double-checking that the young boy taking notes wasn't floundering. One recalled his glory days advising men in the capital. One walked through the house whenever he could, hoping to catch a glimpse of Orietta in her dressing gown or with her hair loosened.

And with the politicos came two ruffians who worked at the behest of a burly man named Pablo with an oft-broken nose and a cauliflower ear who smelled heavily of lamb. Pablo kept his henchmen at the side of Rodrigo's house where they absently kicked at the flower bed. Pablo paced in front of the building, lifting and re-setting his bowler hat, ordering the coachmen around and scanning the area. He kept a knife in his boot, one in his vest, and a rifle in his wagon. No one would admit to having invited him and his minions, but no one sent them away.

Rodrigo's campaign was formulated, and a general election was announced from the pulpit and the steps of the police station.

During her husband's campaign, the persnickety dresses and silly hats that she now had to wear all evening were burdensome to Orietta, and she found it distasteful to be brought out on stage like a show pony. But she had become too cautious to protest, even more withdrawn since witnessing the fury that drove him to be mayor, and the way he looked at her like she was the source of his rage. The skulking men who wandered the house, and Pablo's patrol outside, made her lock the doors to any room she was in.

3

RODRIGO PAID TO HAVE A pavilion with wooden Victorian flourishes and sculpted cherubs built in the middle of town, and he delivered bellicose speeches every Sunday on the need for Araca to be a modern town which required a modern mayor. A voice for this splendid town in the provincial capital, Rodrigo shouted. Araca needed someone who understood how to bring justice and safety to the city, though no one had previously thought their safety was in jeopardy and justice was something that had always been on their side.

The candidate Cardoso didn't campaign on the unincorporated south side so the night before the election, Paloma slipped behind a tree in the Araca square to listen to his final speech, with Orietta sitting impassively on the dais. Paloma peeled a jicama with a small pen knife, scowling as if she wanted to flay someone. Cosimo had accompanied her, and the fine people of Araca walked by them without seeing them, assuming they were wait staff or wagon drivers.

"That's the most beautiful woman I've ever seen," Cosimo said with a dreamy tone to his voice, unable to take his eyes of Orietta.

Paloma grunted. They listened to half an hour on the dangers of modern life, Cardoso's overblown abilities, and Paloma scoffed as he ended with a rousing call for his victory.

"In all my years..." Cosimo said, "she's exquisite."

Paloma didn't correct him or reveal Orietta's identity. She was insulted by the indecent exposure to any passerby of Orietta in all her beauty, knowing that they queued up to hear Cardoso because it included a chance to see her, as if she was a circus dog. Orietta had run away from Tartatenango because of an argument in which Paloma had shamed her for hiding behind her veil, and now that Paloma saw the way the world was reacting to her beauty, she understood. She had been wrong. And now she had ruined the best friendship of her life.

The night of the election, Rodrigo and his campaign underlings paced the floor of the bank, which they had convinced Chief Sanz to use as a counting house, and since Rodrigo had run unopposed, they returned to his home, triumphant, jubilant, drinking his best brandy and congratulating each other as if they had overcome the insurmountable.

After the election, the new mayor ordered the police into Tartatenango. The officers were silent, standing still at an intersection with their arms crossed, scrutinizing those who walked by, recording the names of the businesses on each corner and whether there were fenced-in backyards. Inventory. The new mayor demanded a census of the south-side.

Rebel soldiers had a close call, arriving to collect bonds, but spotting the police, rode quickly into the jungle and moved the collection point to a clearing two miles away and it took all day to get word to Cosimo that he should ride out at sundown.

The following week, Araca police officers dismounted and demanded identification papers of those driving wagons, informed them that business licenses must now be bought at the mayor's office. Men claiming to be health inspectors stormed into the bakery and confiscated the day's wares.

Caketowners looked at the ground, pulled down their hats, held a basket in front of their swelling bellies. They ducked into buildings and alleys, and at every visit, the police siphoned off another drop of freedom and joviality.

## Chapter 10

1

Amid the fanfare and pontificating of the mayor's campaign, and the mesmerizing quality of a sighting of Orietta, a dwarf who had studied medicine at the Sorbonne, Oxford and the University of Bogota, walked into Tartatenango carrying a carpetbag almost as wide as he was tall. He lifted his bag onto a tree stump, his walking stick beside it, and climbed up, his feet in ornately etched shoes dangling just inches below his knees. He opened his case and its shelves step-laddered down to the wood. Unlike most hucksters and purveyors of tinctures, the man quietly surveyed the village, occasionally grunting and humming in bemusement, but not calling out or making grandiose claims.

The suspicious women arrived at the tree stump first, demanding to know who he was and what he was doing there. Jade peered at the diplomas that, while proudly displayed across the inside lid of his traveling case, bore marks of grubby, skeptical hands and acts of rough treatment. The women inspected him like he was sculpture, or an interpretation of a man rather than someone who had feelings about the mismatched lengths of his legs. His sharply pointed beard and pencil thin mustache could barely draw attention away from his piercing green eyes that regarded the women from behind round tortoiseshell glasses enormous on his small, flat face. Like the diplomas, they gave him an intelligent look, like spectacles on an owl.

The women peered at the tools, vials, and powdered packets inside his case but just crossed their arms in front of their chests and looked at him askance.

"A doctor," they muttered among themselves. "Wouldn't let him touch me, that's for sure!"

He ignored the comments, clambered to stand on the stump beside his case. Two months ago, over dinner with a lady friend, he had heard about a town where all were welcome, and he had perked up, but when he was told that it was a town filled with pregnant women and new mothers, he set off on a stagecoach the next morning. With them clustered around him today, he bowed.

"Dr. Simon Bolivar Valdez," he said, then shoved his hands deep into the pockets of his waistcoat. "I set bones and break the worst of fevers. I have stitched up entire battalions, pulling men from the piles of the dead and patching them together to lead happy lives. I have administered to schools of children with the pox and delivered the Duchess of Valois of her 13 children."

The women regarded each other: every pregnancy reminded them that they were without professional care.

"I am misshapen everywhere except my mind, and my hands. And I carry pain-killers that will soothe even the worst of labors."

At this, the women crowded closer.

Doris the accordion player pushed to the front of the crowd, favoring her hand that was wrapped in makeshift bandages, now stained and crusted with green and yellow pus. She had caught the fat of her thumb on the sharp end of a wooden crate but had turned down all offers of assistance: it was her hand, after all, precious the way a dancer protects her feet.

"Oh, my dear, that's infected." He reached out and cradled her hand before she could withdraw it and, at his touch, she let out a little gasp, but an ease flooded her body. Her shoulders dropped and her face relaxed. She and her skeptical companions leaned in.

His hands were even more unusual than his stature. Ivory white, smaller than any woman's they knew, let alone any man's, they were only slightly larger than a toddler's, silky smooth without callus or scar, nails clean and trimmed. But oddly, they glowed from inside, a bioluminescence that he said had come from doing the breaststroke in an Amazon tributary filled with glowing plankton. They illuminated his medical bag as he dug for an ointment; shone through his jacket pockets when he fiddled with change; made his whereabouts visible to dog and man. In the darkest night they helped him fit key to lock without a candle.

With Doris, he carefully unrolled the crusty bandage, cleaned the wound with a blue liquid and the crowd of women flinched: Doris had recoiled any time someone reached for the injured hand but today with her hand in the palm of his, she stood mesmerized, breathing deeply with a sudden serenity.

Jade smiled to herself: finally, someone smaller than she was, and someone to help.

His touch did more than heal. More than calm. Incandescent, with less pressure than the kindest mother, more spark than the finest storyteller, Simon Bolivar, like his namesake the great savior, possessed the ability to restore trust, to relax a woman into safety. As the skeptical watched him over the next few days sitting in front of a small fire, tending to a growing number who stopped by for assistance, they dismissed his works any way they could ('just a scratch, anyone could heal that', 'she's always been quick to complain, there's probably nothing wrong with her anyway') while the previously infirm extolled his abilities and the old women tied his gifts to meteors and goddesses of old. The children at first made fun of his feet and then seeing his work, claimed he could jump over trees ten times his height and rivers wider than oceans. He had pitched a large tent and his small chair in front of the fire was soon joined by a circle of chairs, boxes of gifts and foodstuffs, offerings woven from river grass and cut from rare wood that mothers had insisted their sons drag out from the deep jungle.

Soon the traffic to his campsite was steady, tapering off in the late night but never idle, when women with no discernible ailment would emerge from his tent with a beatific smile muttering about the magic of his tiny hands. What assistance was he giving now, the old women wondered?

The last to join his circle of influence were the pregnant women, especially first-time mothers, despite it being his specialty. Terrified of being without medical help when their time came but fearful of jeopardizing their children or exposing their bodies to such an odd little man, they approached him warily. But after the first delivery, when no one believed that a narrow-hipped woman had given birth without screaming in agony, it was proven that under his alabaster fingers, small enough to enter the birth canal, mother and child were ushered into their new lives with gentle coaxing, tender leadership, a compassion that they increasingly believed was not of the human realm. Flooded with a white light from his hands, the baby settled into a heavenly float, mother into a levitation-quality bliss. He welcomed an entire generation of Caketown babies who glided into the world on the cloud of his hands believing that the world was far better than it was.

The promise of childbirth without pain brought mothers in droves: those just showing arriving on horseback, those about to deliver waddling, fearful, gripping the flowering ivy fence of Paloma's place to make it one more step toward him.

Tartatenango now had a new reputation: Old Man Orjuela soothed the ego and Simon Bolivar Valdez healed the body.

When he wasn't tending to childbirths and ailments, he could be seen on the dancefloor with his tiny hands glowing as if lit from inside, a candle inside a white paper luminaria. He assisted at the next christening since the Drunken Monk could not be counted on to be sober. He touched wedding bouquets as if anointing them. On festival days, he walked through the crowd as a knee-high glow. His hallelujah hands were raised like torches on a Saturday night and though no one could see his body in a throng of dancers, his progress forward was a beacon, women growing giddy as the light neared them.

His late-night visitors continued, women entering

his tent with lace slips and ribbons showing, leaving with rumpled hair and a delicious sweat on their cleavage. The old accused him of being trained more in bacchanalia than medicine but the women smiled when they heard it. "Same thing, my friend! Same thing!"

He gave the nuns (now on fine cushions on chairs in the shade) another reason to disapprove of Tartatenango: God said women were made to pay for Eve's sin with their agony. How dare they shirk their misery, especially at the hands of such an abomination. God wills women's suffering, they muttered, and wondered when the bridesmaids would bring their morning *arepa* and a cup of Paloma's excellent coffee.

2

THE WAR SNAKED ITS WAY through the mountains, swamps and jungles of the country, leaving in its wake indeterminate victories and the wailing of mothers. The Conservative army split the trees with artillery, and butchered anyone in their way, including the parents of twin girls, Magdela and Maria, whose father managed to tie the 12-year-olds into large burlap sacks and hoist them onto a fleeing wagon of turnips before being cut down and left for the crows.

The girls bounced over the rutted roads, trembling, snuggled together in the subdued light of the sacks and, even when they were old women holding hands in rocking chairs, they couldn't determine why they suddenly rolled off the back of the wagon to fall in the doorway of the Caketown Bar. Was it kismet? Had the driver jettisoned them to avoid trouble ahead, or, seeing the nuns by the road, decided it was as good a spot as any to off-load troublesome cargo?

The girls had been weeping quietly for their parents since the sacks were cinched but what mattered most was that they were together when they landed.

The girls were identical, inseparable even during their difficult birth, as if neither had been willing to emerge first. They nursed at the same time in the same way, learned to walk on the same day, spoke each other's names as their first words, and not only wouldn't sleep without each other in the same bed, they exhausted each other with their pledge to fall asleep at the same time.

The girls had grown to be tall and thin, with dark hair and large eyes, both with tiny noses and full lips and they could be found from crib to classroom with their hands entwined, frequently kissing, so close that teachers in their original village simply called them both Magaria.

Upon their arrival in Tartatenango, the bridesmaids ushered them into the bar to keep them out of the hands of the nuns. Jade and the seamstress brought them cast-off clothing and the girls worked late into the night to make identical outfits, even if it meant they each had half a lace collar and a jumbled but equal number of buttons.

When the girls were presented to Paloma, she could see the mosquito of grief buzzing around their heads. They were the oldest motherless children there, and Paloma was one of the only childless women, all three of them preternaturally tall, as if they were born from her.

Some hoped their arrival would give Paloma someone to care for now that Gabriel had died, but the twins just made Paloma's grief more labyrinthine. Instead of the straight-forward mourning for her husband, she now struggled with the joyful opportunity to parent, which came with a reminder of the daughters she might have had if the war hadn't taken her beloved, and even more acutely, of her own twin Camilla who she had lost when they were toddlers. It hurt to look at these young twins, and she waved them into the ramshackle house in the strangler fig tree and ordered that they peel mangos for the bar. Paloma was stern with them and rarely looked them in the eye, announcing that they would join the first group of Caketown children old enough to go to school in Araca, without asking if either knew how to read or write. Every tender look between the twins heightened Paloma's sadness until it could be smelled in the air and felt on the cheek.

THE SUNDAY AFTER THE TWINS arrived, the loam oozed a black tea; the buildings sweated, and the mules were up to the tops of their hooves in mud. The ground squished under the feet of even the smallest child and clothing on the lines dripped more after hanging than before. Good for the gardens, the villagers said, until the following day when they saw the seeds and shoots floating downhill to bob in the puddles at fenceposts that by the end of the week had grown waterlogged, then were unearthed and floated downhill. Chickens' feathers became matted, and they shivered in their nests, unable to lay eggs. Dogs developed mange and cats refused to budge from the thrones they had built of bed pillows. By the weekend, flying bugs fell to the ground after take-off, their wings useless against the humidity while unseen insects could be heard chewing in the night and in the morning, they brazenly walked single file across the dancefloor to devour another load-bearing wall. Mango peels were black and stinking within an hour of removal; the floor sprouted a green moss that made dancing treacherous and stained the hems of the bridesmaids. Worse yet, the weddings gowns and top hats became dotted with a green mold that made them smell and only grew worse when they were aired in the scant minutes of sunshine. The monkey queen picked at the green mold clumping on the Antoinette wig and cried. The seamstress closed up shop and carefully folded all her bolts of cloth, ribbons and lace into sacks of rice that she hung from the rafters. Jade put the wedding business on hold. Dr. Valdez washed his instruments and vials twice a day and scurried from house to house scrubbing mold off wound dressings and dabbing newborns' eyes.

Paloma's moods vacillated so quickly she appeared to be flinching from bug bites: anger that her sister had foolishly walked into the water; tender love while remembering the feel of her little hand; rage at her parents for not protecting them; gratitude for the chance to see sisterly love again in the eyes of Magaria; crippling abandonment; guilt to be alive that gave way to a righteous belief that she was allowed to live her own life, differentiated from her sister.

Paloma concluded that the world ran on luck, driving both the evil of the world and the good intentions of the best person, using a helter-skelter refusal to be ordered and comprehensible. Accidents were just lack of luck; it had been unlucky that her sister had tottered into the water.

With the clawing stench of rotted moss clinging to everything, especially her own skin, Paloma decided that if luck were that powerful, she would build a temple to Lady Luck.

With a renewed vigor that her staff hoped was a good sign, Paloma had Cosimo help her build a craps table from an old granary door, and a six-foot Wheel of Chance using bike spokes and barrel heads. After Paloma had hammered and painted, she unveiled a new wing of the Caketown Bar, a casino.

People thought she had done it as celebration, but

that first Friday night, she raised her arms and turned to all four corners of the compound.

"Life is random, my friends. You try your luck the minute you open your eyes."

Mothers, wives, and the nuns on the roadside were not happy that she had added gambling to the temptations that haunted men and made the jobs of women at home so much harder. Jade was saddened to see Paloma so bitter. Disregarding them, Paloma hawked the games aggressively, almost demanding people play. She prowled the streets of Tartatenango late at night, hawking her new wares.

The first taker, and most frequent customer, was Sister Agnes.

The nun, who had aged during her months of debauchery, had lost her wimple in the mud and her hair was growing in as if she had been struck by lightening. She smelled of rum and though she passed out most nights with the monk under a bush or tree, no one threatened her in case she still held some sway with the afterlife. The morning she discovered the Wheel of Chance she paced toward it as if on procession toward the holy statue that had driven her down the wrong path in the first place. Her eyes lit up, she held her breath as it click-clicked from good outcome to better, though as to all addicts, the win was better than the prize.

3

FADUL WATCHED THE WHEEL SPIN from behind the tiny triangle of glass not covered by crow feathers and scoffed at the nun's gullibility. She could pretend that she was above it all, but Tartatenango made her heartsick, the glimpses of the baker walking by when the smell never penetrated the wall of birds to reach her nose. The children running around like bees, inexplicably happy, jumping and laughing, more like oblivious animals than little people, with food on their faces and happy dogs to lick it off, a mother swooping in with the front of her blouse wet with breast milk.

Mostly, Fadul worked like a washerwoman as she pressed the ink into the plate, pulling a wide squeegee through the thick wave of color, back and forth like a shirt on a rock, a dress on a washing board. Others danced and drank, while Fadul inhaled ink fumes and became more bitter and blank. The weddings, ribald and overly emotional, people with arms around each other in kindness: it made her queasy.

Fadul was sitting in front of her triangle of window, watching the Wheel of Chance in the puddle of light from the bar when she saw two small white pods, like glowing stones, move toward her house. The crows watched, shrugging their wings and resettling. Dr. Valdez knocked at her door.

"Madame Fadul," he called through the door, though it made the birds squawk. "I am Dr. Simon Bolivar Valdez, the doctor of Tartatenango. I'm just checking to see if you're alright."

Fadul had pressed against the wall as if she could be seen.

"May I come in?"

"Don't let any of the birds in," she said, and unlatched the door.

The engraving plates were hidden under heavy canvas cloth, but the smell of ink permeated the house as the dwarf doctor and the bitter woman introduced themselves. Fadul was shocked over the tiny bespectacled man with the enormous case and Dr. Valdez was shocked over the sallow, wicked-looking woman.

"This mold is effecting everyone, and I was wondering if you..."

"Yes," Fadul said with uncharacteristic enthusiasm.

He wasn't sure what she was agreeing to but seized the entire anyway.

"First thing, you need fresh air in here," he said, and despite her protest, opened each of the windows a crack, a more difficult choice than it seemed, since the air inside was filled with fumes and the air outside was filled with mold. He chose not to ask the reason for the heavy smell of ink: discretion was required in his profession and a man of his stature who was so easily misunderstood and targeted knew to make as few enemies as possible.

Fadul frantically ran to each of the windows to make sure the birds couldn't enter, and Valdez was disquieted by her fear.

"If you'd sit here, I'd like to take a look at you."

She sat and put her gnarled, ink-stained hands into the incandescent palms of the doctor.

4

WHEN THE NEW SCHOOL YEAR began, just weeks after the twins' arrival, a dozen children of school age walked to Araca with frizzy hair and rings of wet at armpits and waistbands, green mold darkening the seams of their book bags and shoes. Though the school was on the far south side separated from the town square, it was the first time any of them had crossed into Araca, and they were led by a mother who was stiff and nervous.

The twins seemed as united as the day they were born, but life (or is it love?) won't allow two people on the same path at the same time for very long, and one day shortly after the beginning of the school year, a boy from a wealthy family in Araca singled out Maria and began to court her. Maria blushed when he spoke to her, smiled at him across the room, and the next day, for the first time in their joined lives, Maria purposely wore a coat that didn't match her sister's, and the boy, in patent leather shoes and a well-fitting coat, held her left hand in the schoolyard, while Magdela held Maria's right. This spurred the interest of other boys and they washed their hands and tucked in their shirts to crowd around Maria, competing for her attention.

At Maria's side, Magdela became gloomier with every quip her sister was told, and as the days went on, with every flower that was plucked from the roadside and presented to her, with every suggestion by the patent-leather boy of a late-night rendezvous. Magdela stewed in her resentment, deaf to the jokes the boys hoped were amusing, and her initial reaction to them was so hostile that the circle of boys shied away from her, then excluded her altogether. No point trying your luck with a girl so glum.

For the first time in their lives, the sisters were differentiated, and their reactions were so extreme that within a month they didn't look identical but like the comedy and tragedy masks of theater. Monday morning, they walked to school hand-in-hand as always, but Maria was lost in a reverie of romance, and Magdela floundered in her gloom.

As there were no other twins in town, the symbiosis of the newcomers had not been something anyone in

Tartatenango had seen before, so the sudden rupture of it didn't register either. Paloma, who had experience with the sudden disappearance of a twin, struggled with feeling Magdela's pain of loss while also vehemently defending Maria's right to be her own person. She and Jade heard the story of Maria's admirer over dinner in the bar, told in snippets by Maria with her eyes averted, details emerging between sips of guava juice.

The following morning, Paloma set her coffee cup down with a thud and, thinking of Gabriel, resolved to help the girl find love. She negotiated a return to her little house but insisted that Old Man Orjuela continue to live there, and the Saturday after setting the furniture right again, Paloma took off her apron, combed her hair and invited Maria to accompany her to the seamstress in the hopes a few hair ribbons could be brought out of the protective rice bags.

While they were away, Magdela locked herself in a closet to weep.

THE CONVICTION THAT THESE WERE Paloma's daughters, whispered at night despite all evidence to the contrary, was heightened when Magdela, after school, was drawn to the sound of the smithy, as Paloma had been. The girl paced toward the swish, the ping, the enormous fire.

Whippet the blacksmith watched all the comings and goings of Caketown and knew what he was looking at when Magdela became increasingly dejected, walking slump-shouldered to and from school. Seeing her pacing toward him, he tossed a metal file into a bin with pity. Back in the capital, Heroica, he had younger, twin brothers and had seen the sorrow on the one boy's face as the other moved off, this first abandonment, unmatched in its impact.

He gestured her forward and held out a leather apron and gloves. "Industry is the best healer. And I could use an apprentice."

Within a week, Whippet and Magdela faced each other at the forge every day after school. They crashed successive hammers on the hot steel and Magdela felt every blow reverberating up her spine. All her anger and confusion went into the hammer.

Every evening Magdela came home sooty and dirty. Her biceps were increasingly muscular, and she was surprised when she walked down the street that no one pointed out what felt like nakedness: the deformity of a twin alone. They had gone everywhere together, no event started without the arrival of the other; no meal began until the sisters were both holding forks. All books were read by both, gossip and news were shared. They had been pump and pump handle: there was no purpose for one without the other. Now, every smudge of soot, every burn on her arms from flying embers made Magdela feel worse. They were marks of difference, of a girl who had become superfluous as a sister.

Entering the little house, Magdela smelled like iron and sweat, which Paloma inhaled and overcome by the memory of Gabriel, took to her bed weeping.

MAGDELA FELT THAT HER NEW family was draining away like water from a broken bucket, and she redoubled her work with Whippet, shoeing horses even on Sunday. The hiss of hot steel plunged into cold water accompanied the morning cock's crow and she worked with feverish intensity until long after the marsh insects' serenade. She dragged herself to school in the morning, exhausted.

The sisters hardly spoke, and Paloma seemed to live at the Caketown Bar which brought in less, now that so many of the young men who had spent their evenings drinking and brawling in Paloma's establishment had been conscripted with Gabriel or were in hiding from the police, and the mold had all but closed the wedding business.

A silence descended on the little house. The lace curtains, growing a spider-web of mold, and the delicate furniture seemed less and less appropriate, as if Paloma had gone feral again.

Just before Easter, Maria wept over dinner that the patent-leather boy had refused to speak to her, and the conclave of boys deserted the twins to let them walk home alone.

Maria, who had spent the time that Magdela was in

the blacksmith shop sitting on a park bench waiting for the patent-leather boy, took a job after school as a baker's lass. In the evening after a meager dinner, something left over from the kitchen at the Caketown Bar, day-old bread, supplemented by sausages or a piece of cheese Magdela exchanged for a shoeing job, Maria would clear the dishes and Paloma would bring out a jar and together they would count the little piles of coins, especially meager compared to the hoards she used to hide in the vine house.

But they were together, the sisters reunited and though Magdela had the more dirty, dangerous and physically demanding job, both sisters returned home in the evenings sweaty and tired from physical labor, Magdela covered with soot and Maria covered with flour.

IN THE FIRST WEEK OF August, when the noon sun was as hot as the smithy's furnace but could not burn off the moss chewing through Caketown roofs, Maria came home from work with a spring in her step. A chuckwagon cook, young and hungry for women, stopped into the bakery to buy a sack of flour, and Maria, standing at least a head taller than all the other girls in the bakery, caught his eye. For the first time since the disappearance of the patent-leather boy, Maria was up lit up with possibilities and she wanted to share it with her sister, so she stopped by the blacksmith shop on the way home.

She stood close to her sister so she could be heard over the roar of the furnace as she gushed over the potential for a new beau, his hair, his strong arms, the spurs on his boots, describing the same all-consuming chipper daydream she had skipped through for the patent leather boy.

"He thinks I'm pretty," she said.

Magdela whirled around in anger.

"Of course he does! You're beautiful!"

But Magdela misjudged how close Maria was and the red-hot horseshoe she was holding in long tongs brushed against Maria's dress. Perhaps because of the butter in the seams or the flour caked on the skirt, the dress burst into flames.

To Paloma, the bridesmaids shrieking about a twin who had been injured by her sister and the frantic run of the dwarf doctor convinced her once and for all that it was pointless to struggle against the bad fortune that befalls divided twins. There was no outrunning it: it was the natural order that tragedy followed a bifurcated twin. Death had been stalking her and now others were being injured because of her cat-and-mouse game with her specter-sister, Camilla. Other twins were being separated and injured because she was flaunting the natural order. This tragedy surpassed her interest in her bar, her devotion to the bridesmaids, her intentions on the next big sale.

There was only one way to fix it: It was time to join her sister.

Tossing down the dishrag she paced toward the river to plunge into the swift-moving current.

# Chapter 11

1

Dr. Valdez used vinegar-soaked cloths to treat the burn that ran from Maria's thigh to her forehead.

Magdela had thrown her to the ground and, when the flames were out, had torn at the hot fabric with her work-hardened hands. But it exposed Maria just as villagers were running to assist them and, as there was nothing with which to cover her, Maria ran toward her home weeping with the left side of her body naked and fire-red.

Magdela sat in a heap by Maria's bed, weeping into her hands, while her sister writhed in pain.

Unlike any other event in Caketown's history – not

the knife fights between the muleteers or the battles over Romani turf -- the police arrived to investigate the incident. Chief Sanz dismounted as if stepping into offal and demanded to be told the location of the burn victim.

With his shiny boot, Sanz pushed aside the kneeling Dr. Valdez, but when the officer looked at Maria's half-naked body, Magdela scrambled from the floor to her feet and protectively stepped between them to block his view.

Chief Sanz stepped to within an inch of her nose, but Magdela set her feet wide and crossed her sooty arms over her chest. Valdez covered the injured girl with a light sheet.

"Who is responsible for this?" Sanz glared at Magdela while gripping the head of the truncheon on his belt.

"I am." Her fury was directed at the policeman, but he heard it as malice toward her sister and he grabbed her arm to jail her for assault.

He dragged Magdela outside, but she fought him off and, surrounded by angry bridesmaids and pleading mothers, he let her go, warned them all while sputtering and looking around himself in surprise at the women's response. He was outnumbered.

"Bring my horse," he ordered, though it was just steps away, and he fumbled to make an excuse to return to the mayor.

(As the years went on, the struggle between the

officer and Magdela was embellished, of course. By the time the story had been retold around the fires of the muleteers a dozen times, she had not only freed herself but had stripped the officer of his rusty weapons and chased him out of town; and by the time she died, an old woman in a rocker on the edge of the dancefloor clutching a cameo of her sister's likeness that contained a lock of her hair, she was a legendary warrior who had fought off a squadron and taught them all the meaning of resistance.)

When it happened, however, Sanz reported to the mayor that the injury was a result of a smithing accident and that he had wisely chosen to take no action.

"They're just a bunch of whores and old women," he said.

Mayor Cardoso frantically paced his office. "But what men intervened?"

"No men, sir. Unless you call the dwarf a man."

Cardoso slammed his fist on his desk and bellowed. "Who is in charge over there? I've seen his operation and there's a man getting rich from vodka. I want to know who he is! I will not be usurped in my own town!"

"I'm not aware of any..."

"Get out!" he ordered.

2

No one had seen Paloma walk into the river and, besides, they were immediately preoccupied by the noon sun that burned the green moss into a powder so thick that it blew through Tartatenango like dried pea soup.

That night, though, a rare type of black locust descended, and in the villagers' dreams, their scratching feet were mistaken for rustling branches or nagging ancestors, and the groggy early risers thought in passing that the black-backed bugs were buds on the trees. It wasn't until the children, shuffled outside to give their parents a little morning peace, arrived at their front doors squealing and covered in bugs, that the residents realized that their town was being smothered. Fathers who took brooms to wipe them off the front of their houses soon ducked back inside, unnerved that their hair was now so entangled with bugs that it looked like it was moving of its own accord. When squished, the bugs exuded a pungent orange smear that, by noon, grew so thick with the bugs' efforts to enter the houses that it blocked the sunlight from the windows.

The bugs stripped the trees, ate the molded crops, gnawed on the waterlogged fence posts until they were sharp points, drove the mangy dogs to hide deep under the houses again with their noses covered by their paws, and the cats, who pranced out to do battle, soon turned tail and ran under the beds of children. Doors were black with them; the sky was dark and roiling. Farmers looked at their naked fields with the chagrin of a swimmer whose clothes have been taken from the riverbank. The bugs competed with the debilitated chickens for the last morsel of grain, then carried the newborn chicks away which made an entire generation of Caketown children insist that chickens could fly.

The insects drank all the water in the dogs' bowls, the horses' troughs, and then amassed over the spring and dove on its source until their crushed bodies plugged the opening and stopped the water altogether.

The compound of the Caketown Bar was now void of its inspiring leader, sheltering ivy and gentle arbors, reduced to a perimeter of exposed logs and gnawed branches. The windows and doors of Fadul's house were sealed shut with dead bugs and Magdela tended to Maria in a darkened room.

Jade clambered out of a cupboard with orange bug goo down the front of her blouse and the sling in which she carried Jewel. She stood with her hands on her hips in the middle of the dance floor, astounded: it had taken a single day to strip the village of a half year's growth, already reduced by the mold. Kitchen gardens were twigs in the dirt and maize had been stripped from its stalk.

Cosimo took buckets down to the pool at the base of the spring to gather the fish flopping among the newly exposed rocks, though he was impeded by young girls who hung over the rim to reclaim the pendants, coins and saint's medals that they had thrown into the water with their wishes. The plug in the spring was so dense that he put the word out for pickaxes and chisels.

There was no water for tea or tortillas or soup, but there was wine, rum and a little fish so Jade, assuming authority without knowing Paloma's whereabouts, offered the Caketown Bar for a potluck. She called to the villagers by rousting the itinerant musicians who were huddled together on the far side of the kitchen, their instruments covered in whatever cloth they could find. They struck up a happy song but hit sour notes when a bug that had flown into one end of a horn shot into the musician's mouth at the other.

The dressmaker arrived with chorizo made by her mother in the country. The tanner offered hot pickled beans. A hanging ham, glazed with the yellow goo of bugs killing each other to get at the flesh, was declared a loss. Traumatized cows wouldn't give milk and the few chickens that had survived knew better than to lay eggs in a world like that.

The musicians couldn't muster the enthusiasm to play jaunty tunes, and sorrowful dirges seemed cruel so Jade, the bridesmaids, Old Man Orjuela, the doctor and Cosimo stared into their cups of rum until long after the moon rose, wondering where Paloma was, and shuffled to bed in a silence more acute for the lack of the cicadas' serenade.

The next day, Cosimo and a few hearty souls collected into great canvas sacks the dead bugs that had crashed into the buildings and fed them to bewildered pigs.

IT SEEMED AS IF THE bugs had taken the clouds with them as well when a scorching drought descended on the town. Fruit trees that had been denuded of their leaves now shriveled in the noonday sun. Heat vapors could be seen rising from the road and the roofs immediately after sunrise; young children crawled under the house into the dark back corner with their dogs as the older children dragged themselves to school. As the bugs had taken all the water, there were no cooling showers or overflowing rain barrels, just endless days of torpor and sweat, lying in a hammock, or crouched in the shade, worried and parched. Those who worked in the distillery worried about what part of their feeble garden would be dead when they returned. Doris wouldn't bring her accordion out for fear the bellows would dry and crack. Customers for the wedding business who came from places less parched turned their carriages around and went home. The Rebel soldiers, arriving to collect more bonds, donated a dozen casks of water but were called away to a skirmish in the south. Jade and Cosimo organized a bucket brigade to haul water from the river but though many had replanted after the ooze had washed their seeds away, there weren't enough crops left to tend. Exhausted by the heat, they strained and boiled the river water but could only produce enough for baby bottles, coffee and a glass of water apiece for the villagers. Valdez made sure Fadul received some as she sweated and worked in her imprisonment.

## 3

A WEEK AFTER THE BUG attack, which had spared the town of Araca because of its lack of gardens and livestock, and three days into the drought that also seemed to pinpoint the southside, Orietta received a double dose of bad news.

During Rodrigo Cardoso's campaign for mayor, when he had dragged Orietta around like a show animal, she had had to develop a way to run the business without being there. Wearing her cassock, she met every morning with Juan, her second in command, at a tree stump on the edge of the Cardoso property and exchanged a packet of receipts and correspondence for an envelope of instructions and responses.

That morning, Juan arrived at the tree stump sputtering about orange glop and blackened windows, no water, the Jaguar gone, the spring plugged with golden sap, and it required Orietta to grab him by his shoulders before he collected himself and announced that the water in the cistern at the distillery, fed by pipes from the spring, was nearly empty, and that the spring that supplied it was ruined.

"The Jaguar's gone?" Orietta asked. "Gone where?"

"Disappeared."

As Orietta dropped her hands and considered what Juan was saying, she heard her bellowing husband calling for her from inside the house. Juan disappeared into a cluster of trees.

Orietta slipped into the house, exchanged her kaftan for a frilly bathrobe, and glided into the room with a smile, though forced, that washed over Rodrigo like warm buttermilk on the throat. His ire softened slightly as he waited for the maid to leave the room and close the door.

"I will not be a cuckhold," he said sternly, though without the rage he had directed at the officer.

Orietta's eyes widened. She hadn't thought his suspicions had taken him in that direction. "Of course not! Nor will I be a wife whose husband keeps mistresses and visits whores."

He gripped the back of his chair. "I forbid you to be the bookkeeper for that...operation. You're the mayor's wife now. You have other duties. Your boss, whoever he is, will have to do without you." Without a professional connection, any contact she had would prove her romantic involvement. Any siting would be a tryst, not a business meeting.

"Surely combining bookkeeper and mayor's wife is..."

"I won't have it. Do you hear me?"

"Any more of this outburst and the entire house will hear you."

He glowered, unmoved.

"As you wish, my dear," she said flatly. "I'll inform them today. If you could just have your staff draw up a final list of all the deposits and the balance, I can turn it over."

He rolled up his sleeves as distraction. "That won't be necessary. It's none of your concern any longer. Write a note of resignation and I'll have it carried there."

Orietta pivoted on her heels and returned to the kitchen just as a dowdy woman with protruding teeth knocked at the back door and announced herself as the new house manager.

Orietta stormed back to her husband.

"Manager? There are only the two of us here. What could possibly need to be managed, Rodrigo?"

"She's here to accompany you," he said darkly, not looking up from his papers.

A cold chill went down Orietta's spine. Orietta's beauty engendered two types of reactions: enchantment, which is how most in her life currently reacted; or loathing, a jealous disapproval that sought her downfall. She had seen it among the housewives plotting to run her out of town. Orietta could tell from the scowl on this woman's face that she fell into the second category.

Orietta had been able to run the business through her dual identity and the ruse of her minor bookkeeper role, but Rodrigo would have an impact on the business other than the inefficiency and distraction of her charade if The Warden, as Orietta considered this woman, accompanied her everywhere she went.

But it was imperative that she get to Tartatenango and find out what happened to the water, and Emu.

She retired early after dinner and when The Warden was convinced that she was asleep, Orietta slipped out of the house in her rough-hewn clothing with her invisibility bucket, to return for the first time, to Caketown.

## 4

THE MINUTE ORIETTA WALKED THROUGH the arch to the Caketown Bar, Jade threw her little arms as far around her as they would go. The bridesmaids shrieked and rushed to her side to welcome her back.

"Where have you been?" they said, pulling at her sleeve, and Orietta realized her dual identity was intact.

"She's been working," Doris said. "Practically lives at the distillery I hear. But we've missed you."

"Thank you," Orietta said quietly. She felt bad about not being entirely truthful.

They pulled at her arms to get her onto the dancefloor, but Orietta laughed and extricated herself, pacing back to The Hummingbird.

"What has happened here, little bird?" Orietta asked after kissing the tiny woman's head. "What happened to the trees and the crops? Where's Emu?"

"No one has seen her."

A dozen times a day, villagers wondered if she had gone off with a mule train, rode with a shipment to the coast and would be heading back. No one knew. It had been nearly two weeks. The villagers refused to consider that she might have left them permanently, or that she was so despondent as to kill herself: she was Jaguar Paloma, after all, the reincarnation of a puma that had survived three months in the parched marsh, and who was their fearless leader. The rumors that she had fallen into the water didn't frighten them. No one other than Orietta knew the story of her sister's drowning and the specter's call to join her in death. It had been a secret told late at night in the first days of the strangler fig tree house, just Orietta and Paloma.

Jade took Orietta by the hand and sat her down, explained the insects, the blistering sun that punished Tartatenango. Paloma had not been gone long. She would return, no doubt. Jade poured them tall glasses of rum with mango juice.

Orietta shook her head with resignation. Araca had water but Orietta had imported the water from Paloma's special spring, and it gave the vodka a taste like no other.

"I prefer Paloma's spring water, but I can tap into

Araca's. If we have no water, we have no distillery. Without the distillery..."

"Half of Caketown has no job," Jade said.

"I'm afraid the distillery is doomed no matter what," Orietta said. "The banker..."

"Who is now the mayor?"

"Yes, that's him." She felt bad that she couldn't be honest with Jade but hiding had become a reflex. "He's charging the company all kinds of fees and fines. He thinks it's run by a man."

Jade looked at her with amusement.

Orietta knew it would be impossible to explain without revealing the wedding and the subterfuge.

"Well," Jade said, "if he thinks it's run by a man, let's give him a man."

"I will not give up my business!"

"Of course not! But this sounds like you need a front man, a stand-in, and I know just the person," Jade said, and touched Orietta's hand before running off. She returned holding Cosimo by the elbow.

Orietta chuckled as the big man sat down, a commanding presence that she knew would make her husband wither in his trousers.

"I'm afraid he'll be intimidated by just one glance at you."

Cosimo sat back with a small smile and wide arms. "Who better to bring low than a man this big? In my experience, men bent on another man's destruction only continue if they think it's not working. The trick is to make them think that they're successful, that you're in terrible pain, dire straights. Once you appear vanquished, they keep you around for comparison. A tree is only tall when growing by a shrub."

The women laughed but Orietta shook her head. "He's already stealing from this so-called man for being more prosperous and successful than he."

"Is he more successful?" Cosimo asked.

"Yes, I am," she said firmly, and reached out a hand to shake with Cosimo, who only vaguely knew of a shrouded woman who owned the distillery. She had been heads-down with her work and he hadn't really paid much attention to her.

Jade introduced them more formally. "This is Orietta Becerra, the owner of Magdalena Elixirs. She employs half the village. One of the founders of Tartatenango."

"The mayor doesn't know any of that," Orietta said, sighing over her foolishness. "For the sake of the village he probably shouldn't. It's just that he refuses to believe that a woman could run the distillery. He's angry enough that there's a prosperous man here, he would be livid to know it was a woman."

Cosimo put his hands behind his head to consider. Ordinarily, he would ask what was in it for him: they needed a man, he had leverage. But Jade was there, and for some reason it seemed crass to ask.

"Perhaps his prosperity should be tied to it," Cosimo

said. "A cut of the profits? Like a bribe. Your success is his success."

Orietta turned to Jade. "He's a wise one." The little mother blushed.

Cosimo sat forward and thought, again, of how beautiful the little Hummingbird mother was. "How can I help?"

5

Cosimo wore the suit he bought for the bond scam but arrived at the bank with a hang-dog expression, his tie askew, his sleeves half rolled up, and the sweat from the drought looked like anxiety. He asked for a private meeting with the manager and asked that the company records of Magdalena Elixirs be brought to him.

Rodrigo, working in a back room with an accountant, lit up when he was told of the arrival of the owner of Magdalena Elixirs. Finally. Finally! He would meet his rival in person! Rodrigo pulled his shirt and vest down and tried in vain to button his collar as he paced toward his office. He stopped in the doorframe, though, when he saw the stature of the man sitting in front of his desk.

Rodrigo, half as tall as Cosimo, squeezed behind his desk and felt hostility building until he saw the look on Cosimo's face and the stumbling way he rose, to shake hands with the banker but not meet his gaze.

"Cosimo Carrasquilla. I appreciate your taking time from your demanding duties to see me."

"You own Magdalena Elixirs?"

"For now," he said softly, waving his hand over the ledger. While he wanted to point out the number of fees and fines levied by the bank that had the pages awash in red, he kept to the plan. "I'm not a very good businessman," he whispered.

"But your business is quite large," Rodrigo said, surprised by the big man's humility.

"Sales driven by people's thirst for liquor, that's all. And now I find myself in need of...more sophisticated advice."

"Yes, a good man knows his limits," Rodrigo said.

"I was wondering...if you might...of course you have other tasks, but if you might see your way to advising me."

"Good man, I'm the Mayor! I have...important issues to attend to."

"I could give you, say, two percent of the profits? After all, Mayor Cardoso, any advancements from today would be due to your wisdom."

Rodrigo calculated: two percent of total profits going to him personally was greater than the sum of the fees and fines to the bank.

They shook on the deal, arranging to meet monthly, and Cosimo returned to Caketown certain of victory.

When Orietta sat down for dinner that evening, though, there was a large velvet box beside her plate. She looked at Rodrigo suspiciously. She had had a difficult day trying to find where there was an extra two percent to give to her scheming husband.

"What's this?" she asked, then opened the box. An emerald necklace glittered against the black velvet.

"Surely the mayor's wife should display his magnificence," Rodrigo said as he paced to her side, picked it up and fastened the necklace on her. "My God you're beautiful."

Orietta turned away. Always just the bauble. Decoration as a woman's only revenge.

On the other hand, she reasoned late that night staring at the ceiling, he was draining her account into his and the bank's. If she bought jewels, she could drain his account – which was their account – and be accompanied by The Warden while she did it. That was some level of recompense, at least.

THE FOLLOWING MORNING, ORIETTA SLIPPED out hours before Rodrigo headed for the bank. She had spent a sleepless night, and just before dawn, decided that if profits were going to be siphoned off and given to Rodrigo, she would spend it before it got to him. Donning her scarf and hat in her office and walking onto the production floor, she announced that everyone in the distillery would be given a raise. The cheer that shook the rafters was the best sound she had ever heard.

The next day she purchased a wagon and a team of horses to collect the men and women from Tartatenango, so they didn't have to walk to work and back, especially in the rain. Later in the week she distributed gloves embossed with the company name and a likeness of the Virgin. She had four shirts made for each employee, two linen ones for the heat, two heavy ones for when the weather turned, and bought canvas work aprons for everyone.

As a result, the policeman who now rode through Tartatenango every day on patrol noticed the overwhelming presence of Magdalena Elixirs. The south-side of town was now inextricably linked to the mystery man and his business.

THE MORNING AFTER THE PROFIT-sharing meeting, however, a roadblock was set up with such flimsy reasoning that even the police officers poking between the crates, barrels and bales leaving Tartatenango didn't know what they were looking for. The foolishness delayed the morning's shipment of spirits until it missed the boat to La Ceiba Grande, and, caught without procedures to guard it, half of it was stolen or shattered before it was loaded the next day.

Two days later, three yuca fields in different areas burst into flame.

The mayor in his office sat with his fingers in a steeple in front of his lips, immovable, hiding his pleasure at the news.

"Two percent," he scoffed at the wall. "Leaving ninety-eight for him. I'll show him what two percent looks like."

He called in the loan officer and had him draw up papers to call in all of the loans that had been given to the distillery, with all the payments against the principle reassigned to administrative fees and the two percent given to Rodrigo directly. Rodrigo sent it over to the distillery in the hands of a young clerk.

Orietta, reading it at her desk, shuddered when she realized that the demand was not only for more than all of the deposits remaining in the account of Magdalena Elixirs and the gold in the safe as well as in her safe deposit box, it would also require the liquidation of assets, the sale of equipment, and the end of the business.

ORIETTA WAS SO ENRAGED THAT during a night-time visit with Jade the two women were afraid she would wake little Jewel sleeping in a sling against Jade's chest.

For once, Orietta fumed, she wanted to be valued for her capabilities, not her looks. For the first time in her life, she *had* capabilities, she realized. It had been a surprising joy to watch the old recipe work at scale, be improved by Paloma's spring water, and then to see each of her ideas for bottle design and production actually work. Best of all was to see Caketown women and men hold their heads high after a job well done, and to relax a little knowing that there would be food on the table for their children. Her determination to make the business work wasn't from confidence, it was from desperation: to protect her friends, the villagers. She realized that it had a wonderful truth in it: they were her friends. The first she had ever known. Kind and respectful. Fun. Even though she wasn't living in Caketown now, she had known of their children and the antics of their dogs, of the ailments of their old mothers. She cared. They brought her fruit from their gardens which she ate hungrily on the way home from work, never sharing it with Rodrigo.

"I will not be run out of my own business! I was run out of town because of the greed of a man; I won't be destroyed by another."

## 6

THE WORKERS OF MAGDALENA ELIXIRS didn't understand the sudden absence of Orietta who had always been the first to arrive and last to leave. Nor did they understand why Cosimo was suddenly sitting behind her desk when a scrawny clerk from the bank arrived and departed. But they gathered at the Caketown Bar that night as they heard she had requested.

With Cosimo and Jade flanking her, she wanted to shout about the banker's treachery, to point out the blame so the business's demise wasn't a result of her mismanagement, but it was her mismanagement: failure to see the truth of a man she had thought was harmless.

Suddenly she was like the rest of the landlords, overlords and employers: willing to sacrifice the villagers for themselves. The looks on her workers' faces devastated her. The women on the bottling line were saving for shoes for their children. Carlos was trying to re-roof his mother's house. Jorge had three young sisters and a widowed mother to support. The black women from French-speaking lands needed their jobs to keep out of whorehouses on the north side of Araca, and several of her employees who had just one hand or walked with a crutch would find it hard to be taken on elsewhere.

"The bank..." she struggled not to cry. Jade put an arm around her waist, and Cosimo around her shoulder. "The bank has called in our loan and we have no other option...than to close." She covered her eyes with her hand and wept. "I'm so sorry."

She bought mugs of rum and bowls of soup for everyone gathered but they clustered away from her and grumbled as they straggled back to their homes.

Orietta was so lost in thought as she trudged back to her house that night that the bucket left bruises on her leg. Where was Emu, she wondered? She could be strong if Emu were here.

THAT SUNDAY AFTER CHURCH RODRIGO was in fine spirits, welcoming his cadre with jovial slaps on their backs, hearty handshakes and overflowing glasses. He even waved to Pablo on duty in front of the house, who doffed his hat and grunted.

Orietta heard their chortling and pounding on the table while she fiddled with needlework she didn't know how to do, under the watchful eye of The Warden.

"It's fiscal responsibility," Rodrigo pronounced drunkenly as he showed them out.

They chuckled to themselves and congratulated his genius. "I hear one of them nearly burned her sister to death. Can't have our children with the likes of those."

Pablo sauntered over to them. "Burn it down, I say."

"Yes! Good idea," Rodrigo said, stumbling toward him. "I'll give that order for sure! You mark my words!"

Rodrigo's compatriots laughed at his excess but spun around and gave him a drunken salute.

Hearing them, Orietta closed her eyes and ground her teeth.

MONDAY MORNING, CHIEF SANZ AND both mounted policemen blocked the path of the children who were setting off to school.

Two mothers who accompanied the smallest children stood between the chests of the horses and their charges.

Sanz picked his teeth and made his pronouncement. "Araca resources are for Araca residents."

8

AT THE DISTILLERY, THE SAD dismantling began. The last cases were shipped out, the remaining yuca was pulped and brewed. Juan was sent off to barter for the return of the empty bottles. Slowly, sadly, the best of the massive copper pots was taken apart and loaded onto a wagon to sell on the coast. Line workers were given brooms that they glumly dragged across the floor and the brewers lovingly polished the brass piping now laid out on the floor to be loaded for scrap metal an hour later. They sold the windows and doors, the knobs and racks, took hatchets to the crates, stripped the tin from the roof until the building was derelict and started to lean. As much as Orietta wanted to give all the horses and wagons to her staff, she could only afford to give the oldest mare to Jorge in the hopes that he could farm.

More than ever, Orietta wanted to tell Rodrigo that the business had been hers, to snarl into his face, but his rage was frightening, and she worried that he would lock Cosimo up for fraud. At dinner she pushed food around her plate and started to cry. Men have genuine enemies, she thought. Clear vendettas and animosity that is carried for generations. But here she sits at his dinner table, dressing as he expects, wearing his grandmother's ring. Her tears dripped onto her plate.

"I knew it," he snarled at her. "Let me remind you: until you have my son, there will be no other man but me."

WITH THE DEMISE OF THE distillery and the banishing of the children, the unemployed men languished in the blistering heat, occasionally bursting into fights like irritated dogs. Valdez spent his time bandaging faces and splinting arms, applying compresses to black eyes and administering to Fadul who had developed a litany of complaints that disappeared when she put her hands into his. The birds not on duty at Fadul's house had flown away into the marsh; the monkeys sat with their feet in the river and splashed water to cool the Antoinette wigs they cradled in their arms. The unschooled children swung in hammocks with no sense of time. With the wedding business closed and without the factory there were no parties, just sad drinking. The Wheel of Chance, now run by Sister Agnes, sat idle.

Where was Paloma, they asked themselves as the sun beat down on them. Despite asking every mule driver and tinker if they had seen her, there had been no sign of her, and it had been too long for even a complex trade involving a trip to the coast. Her disappearance added to their woes: rain was a distant memory, crops had died, their leader had deserted them. A search party was called but the prospect of venturing out in the heat and the cataclysmic sunshine, even to find their leader, held little appeal. Three men who knew of Paloma's legend but, like everyone else, not where she had been raised or whether she had family, volunteered to head out to find her. Their plan was to go into the marsh: she had gotten lost there before so maybe she was struggling there again.

Orietta resolved to spend her days as far away from Rodrigo's house as possible and rode with The Warden to Le Ceiba Grande to buy emerald necklaces and ruby earrings. At each stop, Orietta insisted that The Warden model the jewels while she kept herself behind a heavy veil, and she smiled as the jewelers complimented The Warden preening in front of the mirror. Orietta was sure she had seen The Warden smile a bit at the seductive flattery and the sparkle of jewels almost too heavy to wear. After their purchase, they ate heavily, and Orietta insisted that she nap in the carriage before leaving, which made The Warden sleep with ragged snores. Orietta slipped out of the carriage into the National Bank of Calexicobia where she filled a safety deposit box with the jewels but not the cases. Soon, The Warden brightened when Orietta suggested another trip out of town. The bills were sent to Rodrigo at the bank and when he protested, Orietta chided him quietly.

"Displaying the mayor's magnificence," she said.

He grunted and returned to the newspaper, not registering the sarcasm in her voice.

9

THE SKIN ON THE RIGHT side of Maria's face, arm and chest healed with the look of white lava. The chuckwagon cook moved on without a word to her.

The sisters were inseparable once again, but Magdela, without Paloma to protest, and to escape the heat, spent her nights in the blacksmith shop where the ping of her hammer could be heard until it was almost dawn.

Maria refused to leave the little house that Gabriel had built. She tended a small, shriveled garden under an awning behind the house where she couldn't be seen, chattering and indecisive, picking flowers that had already died, switching the vase several times before she was satisfied, asking the air what she should cook for dinner and when she got no answer, asking again.

Maria's chatter turned into an incessant flow. Though alone, she described everything in her garden and how it was grown, inventing the genus and family of each bud, tree and flower she had planted after the bugs, though almost all had died in the drought. She talked about the fairies and goblins that are believed to live in gardens and the history of the country but jumbled them until, in her stories, the goblins played major roles in distant wars and the fairies had plans to take her to Paris. She started wearing odd hats and a single shoe, a belt that she festooned with dried flowers and vegetable peels. She started talking as soon as she opened her eyes and she wove increasingly fantastical stories until Magdela went to work to escape the onslaught of words, only returning when her sister had fallen asleep sweaty and exhausted by her own chatter.

To Magdela, life was as hard as the iron she hammered. Loneliness doubled back on itself: both her parents were dead and her sister, whose love was as necessary as her own lungs, had nearly deserted her for love, been brought close again by tragedy, but had now escaped into a world of fantasy. And since the accident, Magdela's guilt was between them like four panes of glass. It hurt to look at her sister. Any time she wasn't working, Magdela combed the streets of Tartatenango for ribbons and porcelain figurines that

Maria had requested, chasing down a hard-to-find fruit, a special chocolate delicacy that had to be delivered to the village in a small crate filled with straw. Maria just had to make quick mention of a trinket before Magdela would spend her free time looking for it, sending telegrams in pursuit of it, entrusting money to charlatans who too frequently took the coins and disappeared. She brought Maria quinoa pudding and churros, special cakes thin and crisp slathered with dulce de leche. She brought home coconut cookies and flan. Magdela was a regular at the bakery but only bought a single serving and breathed a little sigh of relief when watching her sister eat.

## 10

ARRIVING LATE AT NIGHT TO meet with Cosimo and Jade, Orietta was distressed over the state of the heat stroked Caketown. Men who had been conscientious workers now slumped under the tree passed out with a bottle. Women who had been chipper and hard-working despondently fanned themselves and their sweaty, crying children. Orietta had almost enough jewelry to finance a smaller distillery, and that was heartening. Build it further away, under another name. She wanted to grab the hands of her former employees and reassure them that she would think of something, but Orietta sighed. Chances were slim: the rejection of the children from the school had made it clear that Rodrigo didn't want to just ruin the business, he wanted to destroy Cosimo's lineage, and that any business associated with him would be doomed to failure again.

Orietta looked over the table at Cosimo and Jade who were holding their tiny children in their arms.

"Please be careful," Orietta said to Cosimo. "I thought he was just interested in the money, but it's clear that Rodrigo is bent on destroying you. Destroying the village. And he has succeeded! Look! There's no work. No money."

"There is another option," Cosimo said obliquely, as he looked to Jade for her opinion.

"Absolutely," Jade said, with a hardness and anger Cosimo had never seen on her face before.

Cosimo leaned in and described the government bond operation.

"A cut could go to the villagers."

Orietta downed the remainder of her rum and sighed deeply. It was the best she had felt in nearly a year. Since before she left Tartatenango, she realized.

"Sell Rodrigo the bonds. Appeal to his arrogance," she said. "To his love of power."

She looked into the bottom of her glass. "Any word from the search party for Emu?"

Jade shook her head sadly.

"Where did they go to look?" Orietta asked.

"Into the marsh, thinking that maybe she had lost her way again."

Orietta shook her head. "She would never, ever, head toward the marsh. Where was she last seen?"

"On the riverbank."

Orietta closed her eyes, laid her head and forearms on the table, and wept.

# Chapter 12

1

The river beckoned Paloma with its promise of finality and, standing between the breast-rocks, she had fallen into the water like a great tree downed in the woods. Eyes closed, rolling face to the sky, she had chanted her sister's name, Camilla, as the current turned her toward the ocean and bore her rapidly out of sight. Fighting the insistent call of her sister was futile. Paloma surrendered.

Water plants grabbed for her but missed, overhanging branches stretched out but couldn't harm her, and it seemed to Paloma, silently chanting the mantra of her sister's name, that time had lost its boundaries, as if time was slowing so it could consider her sacrifice, as if it needed a moment to right the wrong of years ago and alter time enough to reunite the twins.

Eyes closed, arms at her side and legs motionless, she was flotsam, oblivious to the sun at its zenith blistering her lips and burning her forehead, trying to pierce through her eyelids. As jetsam, she was not aware of whole flocks of birds that lifted from the trees at the sight of her; or swarms of river snakes that swam beside her but wouldn't approach. Fish collected under her as thick as a raft as she continued to be pulled by the current like an eel or a captive mermaid, abandoning herself to it, as if she could enter another realm through force of will.

Death was her destination, oblivion its gift. She had surrendered her legendary fighting spirit as if it had been an insult to her sister and to the natural order of twins. Floating or submerged, she couldn't tell and didn't care. Would Camilla's specter pull her under, or just greet her after she had settled to the bottom? Would Gabriel be there as well? They were fleeting thoughts before she returned to the darkness of her mantra. Had the sun gone down, or had she just floated through a patch of cold water in the shade of a tree? Had days passed? She didn't know or care.

Nor did she care that after what seemed like a week, her back scraped across pebbles and she landed on a sandbar at a bend in the river. She lay with the back of her head and her shoulders against the cool sand, feet and ankles still in the water. She had hoped for a quiet death by drowning but if Camilla insisted that she be a caiman's dinner there was no fighting it. The inevitability of her death, and the method of her demise, were both beyond her control and her comprehension. So, when she heard a rustling in the weeds behind her, she chanted her sister's name in double-time, then stopped abruptly as she felt a velvety warmth press into her shoulder and arm. Was she to be devoured by a jaguar? How appropriate, she thought. Surprised enough to finally open her eyes, she looked up at a golden Mastiff dog who had taken up a position as a sentry. A futile task, she thought, but just before she dropped off to sleep, she noted the comfort of his solid muscles and soft fur as he crouched against her length. She heard him growling in the night, pacing the shoreline, and felt him resettle himself. His strength was a comfort and, when he finally slept, she turned and curled into him, her arm under his front leg to lie on the velvet expanse of his chest. In the morning, he turned, laid his heavy head on her shoulder, and gently nudged her chin.

But the dog's devotion engendered gratitude and gratitude implies obligation, which requires a future. Paloma sighed deeply and sat up, a bit renewed by the tenderness of the animal, and bewildered by the inability of her sister to make good on her life-long threat. If not now, when, she wondered? Had it all been a ruse? Had her sister been toying with her all these years? Had it been a plague that she had visited upon herself? She brushed the sand from her dress, her arms, the side of her face.

As Paloma surveyed her location and draped her arm over the Mastiff sitting at her side, she saw a man gliding down the river toward her, standing, staff in his hand as if he were a saint walking on water. He was tall and slender, like a willow branch, and as surprising as his movement was his halo of copper hair. He pulled his shallow, flat-bottom boat onto the sand beside her and the Mastiff sprinted forward, wagging his tail. The man drove his staff into the sand, patted the dog, picked up a line of fish from the bottom of his boat, and began talking to Paloma in a language she had never heard. Lilting and musical, it rose and fell more sonorous than bird song; it was complex, orchestral. She had no idea what he was saying, and he didn't explain through gestures, check to see if she understood him, or slow down so she could catch a word or two. The words spun around her like the woven harmony of birds and insects as night descended on a jungle. It was a weaverbird nest of sound.

They were on a tiny island sandbar near the crook of the broad Magdalena River, and Ian McAllister, his moss green eyes twinkling as he continued his incomprehensible narrative, ducked into thin willow shrubbery. The dog wouldn't follow until Paloma had struggled to her feet, brushed off her legs and agreed to follow, which she did just to please the dog.

The island reminded her of her first strangler fig tree house with Orietta: it was barely as long as her compound in Caketown and only twenty paces wide. To boaters sailing past it was a clump of marsh trees with no sign of humans, but Ian had cut a small clearing in the middle for his encampment, with log barriers on the shoreline to keep out the caimans.

Ian squatted in the clearing, his hair the same blazing color as the fire now jumping around his skillet. He was an Irish conscript in the British Navy who had jumped ship in La Ceiba Grande, leaving behind his beloved violin to prove that he had fallen to his death. All knew that he would never set foot on land without it. He had traveled upstream in much the eel-like manner of Paloma, and he had escaped detection because he never went into town, traded only with locals, and bought no more than he needed.

He poured Paloma a mug of clear water without interrupting his harmonic monologue. The Mastiff sat at attention on a low wooden platform and, as Paloma was more trusting of the dog than the man, she sat down beside him and draped her arm over the dog's back again.

Ian prattled on about a place called Donegal and his mother's soda bread, told long, involved stories without mimicry of raising sails, bailing water, or constructing something of many parts. He talked as he scaled the trout and threw the dog a fish-head. He talked to her as he cooked. At a break in the onslaught of words, as he flipped over the trout in the pan, he set the skillet down and spun his hands around with an emphatic shrug of disbelief, then smiled broadly as if understood by a soul mate. He launched into a new story as he dug an extra blanket out of a rucksack hanging from a branch and when he went down to the riverbank to wash, his words trailed off for the first time: Paloma and the Mastiff, whose heads were at the same level, turned eye to eye in surprise at the silence.

She ate his fish and drank his coffee, helped him gut and dry his catch. She slept with his extra blanket on the platform curled into the dog and woke in the night to an offered glass of rum, slept spooning with the dog and woke to the aroma of flapjacks.

It took a week of lying in the hammock to stop thinking of her sister, and even harder to stop thinking of polishing tables and calculating business, then another week to stop strategies for the shipping business. It took an additional two weeks to stop dreaming of the injured twins, and to dampen the voice inside that reminded her of her responsibilities in Caketown.

Ian demanded nothing from her except to allow her to be awash in the sound of his voice, which after four days, Paloma decided was the sound of an oven making love to a pie. She lay there as the sun warmed the pebbles, baked the sand, dried her rope of hair. And as her body warmed, she relaxed, surprising herself that even her sorrow was a tense, rigid emotion that could loosen.

She wanted to empty her mind, to live without goals or plans. To defy time. Why shouldn't she sleep, eat, gut fish, sleep? Here on this little island, there was nothing to do and no reason to do it, which turned from the forlorn surrender that had made her plunge into the water but morphed into a freedom. Just as she became hot, a sudden mist off the river would cool her skin and after a shudder the sun would bake her again. She heard nothing but bird song, leaves in a breeze, the contented snoring of the Mastiff, and twice a day, the shush of Ian's boat on the sand, then the relentless but tender storytelling.

TIME STOOD STILL. HER LIFE was reduced to a dog's existence: relaxing and blessedly pointless, enveloped in complex language she was not required to understand.

So, after what felt like a month in his enclave, when she straddled his hammock and made love to him, they went from a mysterious monologue to a wordless conversation.

ONE MORNING, (SHE COULD DISTINGUISH time of day if

not day of week or month) she lay in the hammock listening to the sound of Ian's shallow boat pushing off the sand, when the canopy of trees bloomed with bright red flowers. It could be seen from miles above in the mountains, like a red umbrella suddenly unfurled in a green jungle. By the afternoon, the flowers had enticed butterflies and the butterflies brought birds until the little hide-out, which had been safe because of its camouflage, was now a bullseye for wildlife. As she drifted in and out of sleep, wild ducks swam to shore and built nests of reeds and feathers.

The emptier Paloma became and the deeper her sleep or the quieter her gestures, the more the trees filled with nesting birds. Snakes burrowed their eggs in the mud; the ducks laid twice a day. Fish spawned near the shore until the water was the color of milk.

The following morning, after Ian had gone off and the Mastiff was patrolling the perimeter, Paloma heard singing.

She listened intently: it wasn't bird song. It wasn't a woman across the river. It wasn't a snippet of a tune playing in her head.

It was from her stomach.

But it wasn't indigestion. It wasn't wheezing or rumbling in her gut.

It was a tune, with a pattern, and she dropped her hands to her belly.

She was pregnant.

The Mastiff returned from his patrol and put his nose against her stomach, snorting, inhaling, then waging his tail and looking in her eyes.

Being pregnant was surprise enough, after being married to Gabriel without children, but pregnant with a singer? Impossible.

She didn't say anything about it to Ian in case it was her imagination gone feral in this idyllic place, and because she didn't speak his language anyway. What if he thought she was crazy? Ian curled into the hammock with her, unaware of her pregnancy, and his chatter drowned out the soft song of her baby. The symphony of his voice filled the clearing to the canopy.

But while Ian was oblivious the animals responded to her pregnancy. Flocks of ducks ringed the island with little yellow chicks. The boughs above her bent heavily with nests now raucous with newborns. There were so many butterflies on the branches that the tree changed color when they flapped their wings.

Ian was flummoxed by the sudden bounty. Now he had duck eggs to sell, and the fish were so thick that he could scoop them into a bucket with his hands. With so much extra food to trade he set off in the morning, boated further and returned later.

Eight weeks after she first heard the singing, Paloma and the dog were sitting on the pallet shoulder to shoulder watching dragonflies zooming back and forth, when they both heard something and turned sharply toward each other. The Mastiff's ears pitched toward her as Paloma looked at her belly.

Harmony.

She had conceived twins, and they were singing in harmony.

As SHE SWUNG IN THE afternoon breeze floating on the harmony from her belly, the duck eggs piled up in bright white pyramids, like the antithesis of cannon balls; the snake eggs mounded under the sand like a flounce all around the island. Butterflies hung in writhing clusters on a branch at the far end.

She rose only to pick a mango from the overhang or eat one of the eggs that the mother duck almost rolled into her hand as an offering. She snagged a fish, mostly for Mastiff, though most days he just stood in the shallows and fished for himself. A month of stars and cicadas went by, another month of breezes of jasmine, two weeks when she could hear the fish gulping on the water's surface or turning with a splash. The world was so quiet there was no reason to not close her eyes. She swung in the hammock, hands on her belly, lost in a dimension that had a smell but not a texture, a movement but not a surface.

But the animals' fecundity made Ian nervous, and his language took a harder edge. He paced their little enclave and as he walked the perimeter, he started seeing the eggs as money that should not be wasted. He gathered a few into his pockets and cast off his boat, returned with a basket and bright eyes to scurry around with an industriousness that she had never seen. Running around trying to catch the chicks, he disturbed all the birds in the trees; the other mother ducks squawked and hustled their brood away from him.

"Stop!" Paloma said, launching herself out of the hammock and grabbing him by the shoulders. "Just because it's here doesn't mean you have to take them."

He, of course, had no idea what she was saying.

"Just leave them be."

He touched her cheek and smiled but continued his harvest, with a compulsive need to gather it all up and cash it all in.

She tried to step between him and the bounty, but the cornucopia drove him to distraction. Now he hardly sat. He had baskets to gather, and enclosures to build. He grew dirty and gritty from exertion.

And the caimans, who knew that the ducks and birds would light off and so were a long shot, now saw them penned up, and they woke Paloma in the night with the sound of splintering wood and screaming chicks.

She made another attempt to stop him, shaking the wood splints in his face, then begging him.

Still, Ian gathered the bounty, stepping around the increasingly furious Paloma. A few more transactions wouldn't hurt, he tried to explain. A few coins hidden in the mud at the base of the tree wouldn't jeopardize them. A few ducklings traded wouldn't draw attention.

But Ian had strayed far from the island, away from the quick, innocuous trade or the hidden fishing hole, and had begun to hawk his wares at the village market. He covered his hair with a hat, turned away from police officers and authorities who paced the gathering, and confined himself to working on the side streets, but one morning Ian decided to buy Paloma a bracelet, and he paced into the center of the square, determined, negotiating, jubilant, hat off, until the eye of the British patrol leader was caught by Ian's long arm sweeping up to look through the gem to test its clarity: the sparkling shot of emerald shone like a brief beacon.

They chased him to his boat, and he tried to dodge into little-known estuaries, but his small flat-bottom canoe and a pole were no match for the crafts of the British Navy. They dragged him away as he was beaching the boat and Paloma shrunk into the shadows to restrain the frantic Mastiff but stayed there rather than assist Ian. Now that she was pregnant, it wouldn't do to be arrested, or to let the dog be killed. And he wouldn't have understood her endearing words of farewell, anyway. But there was a reticence that surprised her, a passivity. When Gabriel was carried away, she had charged into the street and threatened to fight all the soldiers, and though Ian was the father of her children, she hid herself.

Having just lost a second lover to the demand for cannon fodder -- Gabriel to the civil war and Ian to the voracious British Empire -- Paloma was reminded that women only borrowed men; the war machine claimed them like no woman ever could, against their will, without question or protest, used for purposes not of their choosing. One could never really be certain with men, one didn't *have* men, possess men. As a result, the world had relegated her heart to fleeting encounters with men, like a man would take a favorite in a whorehouse and forget her name when she moved on.

HOT ON THE HEELS OF the British were the locals who swooped in to steal what she had. They robbed the duck nests and beat the branches of the trees to dislodge the birds. With enormous shovels they unearthed the snake eggs and danced in the sand. They stripped the fruit that was being eaten by the butterflies.

Just as four men – each twice as wide as Paloma -- walked determinedly into the river to get to her, she grabbed the Mastiff by the collar and dragged him into Ian's boat: the dog would be shot dead in an instant defending her.

She pushed off the shore, standing ramrod straight, glaring at the four intruders. It was bravado, she knew, as she clearly would have lost the fight even if she hadn't been pregnant.

The current picked up as soon as she sat at the

rudder, as if the river resolved to spirit her away. And as Paloma glided away with the Mastiff, digging the pole into the increasingly turbulent Magdalena River, the red tree blossoms on the ring of her compound all lifted into the air, not blossoms at all, but birds with four young ones each who took to the sky and flew above her canoe in a chevron before veering up into the clouds.

There was no doubt, though, that the river would widen and deepen further, and without oars she could be adrift without water or food, unable to dodge the increasing boat traffic. She had floated here without knowing where she was, and the unknown jungle continued on both sides of her. And now pregnant with twins, she couldn't endanger them by putting herself through privations. She thought with a shudder of the difficulties she had faced in the marsh. She needed to come ashore where she could rent a wagon or find a bus. And ride on credit? At this point she didn't look like a successful trader or bar owner, just a feral woman, more hugely pregnant than time would explain, without a coin to her name. She steered near the shore across the river as best she could but couldn't fight the current to land. She leaned on the rudder, but the current responded with more force and increased her pace downstream.

"You had your chance to claim me," she shouted into the air. "Camilla, do you hear me?" Birds lifted off the tree branches. "You had your chance, and you spit me back. Go! Be dead!" She cupped her hand under her belly. "You can't have me now!"

Her rantings frightened the iguanas off the rocks. Vultures circled but thought better of it and flew away. And the commotion brought a man out of the jungle to ride his horse along the shoreline for a moment, then spur his horse back into the jungle.

Paloma leaned against the rudder with all her strength to battle the current that rushed the boat toward the choppy middle of the river. She was whipped by low-hanging branches, and a mother caiman with her young brood swam stealthily behind her. Water splashed into the bottom of the boat as she steered around eddies and rocks. Mastiff steadied himself on the bottom of the boat as best he could.

"You can't have me!" she shouted again into the air, just as a man rode out of the jungle and paced beside her.

It was Gonzago, alerted by the rider who then took his place at the head of the mule train so Gonzago could ride back to Paloma.

"Beloved," he called to her. "Paloma!"

She turned to him, startled and then relieved.

Gonzago lassoed the rudder and hauled the boat ashore.

Despite her height, he lifted her from the boat and carried her in his arms to a mossy spot under a tree.

After introducing himself to Mastiff, he sat in front of Paloma, straddling her with his long dusty legs.

"How did you know?" she asked breathlessly.

"Orietta." She had sent word to the mule trains to look for Paloma, hired runners to inquire at docks and boat launches, asked the bargemen, the anglers, finally paid Juan to discretely take out a boat and look for bits of her in caiman's nests.

Gonzago took her hands and kissed them with relief.

Seeing Gonzago with his long black hair now coiled in a leather thong but the same warming eyes the color of beef broth, she touched his cheeks and rode on waves of conflicting emotion: he had been her first love, her first loss and she was grateful for the rescue, but she felt like a curse. Every man she cared for had been taken. Her feelings, his feelings, were immaterial when the meatgrinder of fate started in on them. Whether it was rooted in beloved conversations with Gabriel or the wordless connection with Ian, the world wrestled love away from her, ripped it from her arms. And her love for women, too, she thought mournfully, thinking of Orietta. As much as she wanted to wrap herself inside Gonzago's oversized leather jacket, whose long fringe was almost like a curtain as he sat with his big hands on her shoulders, life would take him from her, no doubt.

As soon as Gonzago wrapped her in a blanket, he heard the singing. He cupped her belly, looked at her with wide eyes and smiled.

"So, your magic continues," he said, as he slid his scratchy beard across her face and kissed her cheek.

"I don't know what you're talking about," she said mournfully.

"Jaguar Paloma, rainmaker, bringer of blue fog and odd flowers, and now mother of a *cantante*, a singer. You are so precious."

"Fables," she said, and dropped her head to his shoulder. For his sake, he should leave her here in the shade and escape before a government claimed him, but she was pregnant and had others to think of.

Gonzago whistled for a rider and sent him to return with Gonzago's wagon.

"Precious to me," he said, close to her ear.

2

It would be several months before Gonzago's mule train would be anywhere near Caketown, and he was in no hurry to return her. They resumed their lovemaking as if he had never left, as if years had not gone by, and the twins were silent until Paloma fell satisfied onto the pillows. She didn't ask about their destination or request transport to Tartatenango, too confused to make plans, too uncertain.

Their love made Gonzago chipper, which heartened the muleteers, and the developments since she stepped into his wagon buoyed spirits as well. It had been a dusty trail to that point, and their casks of drinking water were getting low and spoiled. Though the muleteers were surprised, Gonzago knew it was no coincidence that they found a spring where none had existed on their previous loop through the territory, and that the fishing and game were so plentiful the muleteers joked that the rabbit had walked up and put its own head in the loop. All the dogs abandoned their posts and walked with Mastiff; the goats refused to be herded at the end and clustered around Paloma as she walked beside the wagon. The chuck wagon chickens laid double-yoked eggs every day.

The mule train wound through the mountains, across the high plains, down a treacherous pass, stopping twice a day to load and unload goods, then setting up camp before dusk.

The more pregnant she looked, the more of the muleteers acted like magi, bringing her the best blanket, the cloak they had bought for their girlfriend back home, extra biscuits or jerky they wanted her to keep in her pocket in case she got hungry. In the evenings, they sat cross-legged in the soft dust at her feet with their ears cocked, cradling an unlit pipe or a rosary, listening to the twins.

Several months into the journey, though, one of the muleteers attending church in a village en route told a priest in passing about the miracle in Paloma's womb. The priest grew red-faced and apoplectic, railing about the Devil, the sorcery of evil women, that only Mary's womb had produced a miracle.

The priest's words wended their way through the encampment and there were hostile, late-night gatherings. Sides were taken. Strong words mixed with strong drinks until those who adored Paloma were set upon by those who thought she should be abandoned at the next trading post. Late night skirmishes soured the atmosphere and became noon dustups. The foreman of the second line was forced to use a bull whip on a three-way knife fight.

But word got around, and at the next village they pulled into they were met with a phalanx of nuns, a gnarled priest, and hostile women with rosaries. Gonzago insisted that Paloma, quite big now, stay in the wagon, and he shut Mastiff in with her for fear the dog's protectiveness would be mistaken for rabies and he would be shot. It was the encounter that changed everything. It was no longer business as usual. Their arrival heralded more than a bath and a bottle of rum. After the third village where they were met with clubs and rosaries, this one high in the hills, followed by another late-night drunken brawl among his own men, Gonzago called a morning meeting with his foremen and, reluctantly, gave three mules as severance for six men whom he banished from the train.

THAT NIGHT, WITH GONZAGO ASLEEP but not yet snoring, Paloma touched the head of Mastiff by the bed, settled into her pillow, cocked her ear and listened. One melody. One voice, not two. A stronger voice, clearer, but alone. No harmony.

It had been two voices.

"Oh God, no!" She sat bolt upright and clutched her belly. Gonzago pulled himself up beside her.

"No, Gonzago, it can't be another twin...injured!" Or dead, she thought. "Can you hear it?"

Gonzago pushed his long hair back behind his ears and listened, leaned to put his ear to her belly. The look on his face as he sat upright make Paloma cover her mouth and start weeping. They were right to shake their rosaries at her, she thought, she was cursed. She had left Caketown to protect the injured twins, but the curse had followed her.

"We need to get you home," he said, and struggled back into his pants and boots. It didn't matter what the calendar said regarding Paloma's pregnancy: she was much further along than was normal, but what is normal when it came to his giantess?

Gonzago spent the night in conference with his foremen, shifting cargo, reallocating the already-reduced staff of muleteers, dragging the goats from the side of the wagon, and ordering the dogs to return to their posts. At first light, with Paloma still in bed, Gonzago mounted his horse and rode in front of their wagon toward Tartatenango over a risky path that was almost straight downhill, leaving the rest of the mule train to follow the established route and continue business. But as Paloma's wagon pulled out, all the goats broke out of their makeshift pen and the dogs barked in protest at being left.

"They won't let her leave without them!" Gonzago shook his head, but in the midst of the chaos, reorganized the entourage to include a hay wagon for the animals, and drove Paloma's wagon himself with his horse tethered to the back so the wagon driver could drive the hay wagon. He turned on his seat to see the muleteers throwing their hands up at the desertion of their dogs and shouting out the names of customers who were waiting for goats. Gonzago sighed but drove the mules onward.

"We'll sell them in Caketown," he muttered. "At least the chickens are caged."

It seemed that daybreak never arrived because dark clouds amassed over the wagon train and its posse of animals who jostled with each other to be closest to the wagon door and Paloma. Thunder rumbled in the distance and then rain fell on them like a bucketful thrown out a door. Within minutes, the road was muddy, and the bleating goats struggled to keep up. The route was treacherous on a dry day, with a sheer cliff on one side and a granite wall on the other but the rain, now sluicing off the hills and cutting a gully on one side, made the wagons skid. When three goats slipped and fell to their deaths screaming like women, Gonzago stopped the train at the next level ground and not bothering to shake the rain off his coat, threw open the door to the wagon.

"Paloma! You must calm down."

She was weeping into her pillow. He sat on the bed and grabbed her face between his hands.

"Beloved." The rain dripped off his hair and down his face. "The goats are dying from the rain. If it continues like this, we'll all be washed downhill."

"I don't know what you're talking about," she said tearfully. "Rain is rain."

Gonzago shook his head as he had when the goats insisted on following. He didn't need to convince her, just calm her, he reasoned. He put his hand on her belly and felt the baby kick. "Feel," he said. "Get this one home safely."

He stroked her hair like he was talking to a skittish mare. "Easy. Nice and easy, now. Make her feel safe."

Great rumbling thunder rolled across the sky and made the goats bleat with fear, but the rain pelting the roof slowed. Gonzago considered whether he could soothe her enough to make the rain stop, or whether he should make headway in the reduced rain. Most important was to get Paloma to a midwife or doctor: who knows what kind of downpour she would create if the second baby died.

He clambered onto his seat and resumed the treacherous descent. The road was slick, and two more goats stumbled but recovered. After an hour, the rain stopped, and Gonzago assumed that Paloma had fallen asleep, but the rumbling clouds reminded him that a nightmare for Paloma would be a nightmare for them all.

## Chapter 13

1

Tartatenango, scorching hot and nearly barren, looked like the pampas. Leaves had wilted and turned to leathery underbrush; the jungle had degraded into brittle duff and the dirt was a sterile yellow. Exoskeletons of the bugs that had stripped the place lay wedged between rocks and fenceposts. There was less dancing at the Caketown Bar and more fighting, which Jade didn't have the energy to stop; four men in a brawl knocked each other's teeth out and the chickens ate the molars in the morning.

The search party looking for Paloma returned emaciated and shaken by the immensity of the marsh.

The games of chance had been shut down and sat

dusty and forlorn at the far end of the compound. Mice ran up the bumpers of the craps table and the roulette wheel could be heard creaking when the wind picked up. At least once a week a bird would perch on one of the numbers on the big wheel, setting it into motion and, as the bird flew off, the villagers gathered, buckets, baskets and shovels in hand, to wait with expectation over the final resting number, though there was no game and no gain to be had.

The heat had turned the noon siesta into day-long torpor and the somnolence made the villagers slow to notice the menacing cloud that was approaching. When they did, they debated whether it was the return of the black bugs, but made no provisions, as it was too hot to work, and they had nothing left to protect anyway.

They thought the bells on the mule train, the bleating of the goats, and even an enormous thunderclap was a trick of the heat. It did not convince them, until a covered wagon pulled up surrounded by goats and dogs, and Gonzago helped Paloma to get down, belly first.

THE VILLAGERS WERE SHOCKED AT her return, at her arrival in a carriage, not from the marsh at all. But the joy of seeing her, and the shock of her enormous pregnancy, made them roar. Those who believed she had left them had been hurt; others worried that she had been carried off by the government for challenging Gabriel's abduction; Jade was frightened by vague sightings of her falling into the water but tried to keep the faith as she kept the bar's business together. Only Orietta knew of the lengths to which she had gone to find Paloma. Today, the villagers were jubilant, until they saw the look on her face.

"Get a doctor," Gonzago said as she leaned heavily on his arm.

The rest of the jubilation and well-wishes were drowned out by a rolling thunderclap and pelting rain. The villagers bent double, shrieking, then stood up with relief and even more joy than over the return of their leader. They opened rain barrels, brought out buckets, and dragged their children from under their houses where they were no longer safe. They clawed away the dead leaves from their pots of vegetables and flowers so the soil could absorb the water. Cosimo, handing Matias off to Jade, walked through the compound with a shovel, quickly digging troughs and run-offs, scraping out the mass of dead vegetation as the rain soaked his shirt to his chest. Sister Agnes and the Drunken Monk crawled from under a bush where they had passed out and knelt on the dancefloor in prayers of thanks, circled by the bridesmaids who swept the floor laughing while the rain poured off their hair and soaked their dresses. Mothers, in the middle of hauling river water to be boiled, jubilantly threw the buckets on the ground. Children jumped in the puddles that quickly formed but slipped and fell in the ensuing rush of water and had to be rescued by the groomsmen as they were swept toward the river. The Romani, who usually positioned their wagons away from each other for greatest privacy now circled their wagons and erected a canvas roof covering the space between them.

DR. VALDEZ HAD BEEN ALERTED to Paloma's arrival and had been organizing his office for a delivery but was shocked by the sight of Paloma anyway. At six foot five, she had always towered over him, but standing in front of her today and looking up, Valdez couldn't see her face for her enormous belly.

"Let's get you comfortable," he said, resorting to his standard patter. "There's nothing to worry about."

The steely look Paloma gave him chilled him, but he scurried around the office so quickly that his iridescent hands left a visible trail of white.

"Are you staying?" he asked Gonzago, who was holding her hand. "If not, find Jade and send one other."

Gonzago squeezed Paloma's hand and ducked out of the tent, shouting for Jade over the roar of the rain.

"Doctor, they sing," Paloma said with fear. "I can't hear them singing."

"Can't hear anything with this rain."

"No. There were two, and they sang."

He looked at her with an indulgent smile,

accustomed to superstition, the delirium of pain, the plaintive pleas of mothers.

"In your heart, no doubt." Valdez guided her to the birthing table.

Paloma gave him a withering stare that turned into a shriek of pain, and ten minutes into her labor, the rain turned to hail.

THE VILLAGERS OF TARTATENANGO HAD never seen hail, never heard of it, and they were bewildered as they were pelted by the tiny white balls that bounced off the dancefloor and collected like white lace over the rotting leaves. Dogs ducked under the houses again and cats under beds while the monkeys shrieked and huddled in a circle to protect the Antoinette wigs. The bridesmaids chased the little hailstones, laughing, while Sister Agnes and the Drunken Monk lay in full prostration, switching from prayers of gratitude for the rain to pleas against the End of Days. The Romani stripped the hail from the manes of the mules and rolled the balls between their fingers. Little girls watched in amazement as the balls fell into the buckets of water and disappeared.

Fadul's birds, frightened by the pelting hail, flew off and the sudden light in her house made her turn away, then bolt out the door and let the hail gather in her hair. It was the first time anyone had seen her smile.

Cosimo leaned on his shovel laughing as the

hailstones collected on his broad shoulders. Jade ran toward him with both children in her arms, hail gathering in the folds of the blankets.

"What is it?" she asked with fear.

He chuckled and shook his head in amazement.

"Ice."

To Valdez, the birth of Paloma's daughter, Valeria Marti, was flawless. Quick, with very little blood loss, a robust baby who lie in his glowing hands as if encased in a halo.

Paloma, however, took a cursory look at her and turned to the doctor. "Twins. They are twins."

The doctor scurried for his Pinard horn, listened to her belly, shook his head but said nothing until Paloma had delivered the afterbirth and he was able to search through the tissue.

"I'm sorry but there is no twin."

"But there was!"

Valdez considered, stroking his beard. "Perhaps early on. It's not uncommon for a twin to be... subsumed by the other."

"Subsumed?"

He didn't want to say eaten. Or consumed. "One becomes... incorporated into the other. The two become one. Nothing to worry about."

Paloma looked at him with a sorrow he hadn't expected.

"The most important thing, now, though," he said, "is to get this precious one to the breast."

He handed the baby over and she latched on well, nursing as Valdez cleaned the room. Paloma was able to relax a bit and smile down at her little one. As the sole survivor of a pair, she was more Paloma's daughter than others realized. But it wasn't until the baby started to hum that Paloma cradled her and was convinced that all was well.

"Time to get you cleaned up and resting," the doctor said, and moved the baby to a crib.

Then Valdez did a double take. He had assumed that the clear voice he had heard was Paloma, but the sound now came from the crib.

Paloma noticed his surprise. "She's been singing like that for months." It hurt too much to mention the harmony and the twin now disappeared.

The doctor was completely flummoxed. "That's impossible," he said. "A baby is incapable of understanding the patterns that are required for song. Or the... vocal control needed even to hum." He sniffed, peered into the crib, stroked his beard. "Their first pattern is, perhaps, circadian rhythms of the day, but the skill to..." he struggled to describe it. "To perceive and replicate a vocal pattern is... unheard of. Unprecedented. Inexplicable."

Simon Bolivar Valdez had traveled the known world, had delivered a tribal chief of conjoined triplets, cut a snake from inside a man's leg, sewed up wounds of all shapes and sizes, battled parasites with hooks that left slime trails in the lungs; he had severed a man's ear and attached it to the man's son; banished an ant colony from a woman's kneecap but he had never, ever, heard a newborn sing.

2

THE BIRTH OF VALERIA THE singer, or the *Infante Cantante*, caused pandemonium in Caketown.

The baby was long like Paloma was tall, pale with a golden halo of hair like her father.

For the first week of her life, she could make haunting sounds like the love songs of mermaids. Unlike in other locales where they had been chased out of town, Caketown villagers sat mesmerized as the baby dozed, suckled, sang, slept. By the third week she could do trilling scales.

News of Paloma's return and the birth of the child reached Orietta when the baker delivered guava roll cakes to the cook who told the maid while she stirred an enormous pot of soup and Orietta was within earshot.

That night, Orietta hurried to Caketown with her bucket and set it just inside the gate.

Paloma and Gonzago were dancing slowly, with little Valeria sleeping between them. The blue mist that had been seen only when Gonzago was in Paloma's bed had returned and was pooling at the base of her little house.

Orietta stood at the edge of the dancefloor quietly weeping with relief. Her friend's opinion had meant so much that she had allowed it to completely derail her life. She owed Paloma an apology like none she had ever given.

Paloma did a double take upon seeing her, transferred Valeria to Gonzago and hurried to take Orietta's hand.

"I'm so sorry," Paloma said, as the two women scurried to a small table by the bar. She wanted it said immediately in case things were derailed again.

"No, I've been a fool," Orietta said tearfully.

"I never should have said anything. I had no right."

"I've made a total mess of things, Emu!"

"But the distillery was a great thing for Tartatenango!"

"And I married the monster who destroyed it," she whispered.

They sat silently with their hands clasped, breathing in the solace of their reunion.

"I'm so sorry about Gabriel," Orietta said. "I came to the memorial."

"You did?"

"I stood in the back. I... couldn't bear to see you that way. And your wedding... I'm so sorry." She thought of the massive loan and how she had traded on her looks to get it. "You were right. About everything."

WITH THE BABY ON PALOMA'S knee, the bridesmaids treated their leader as if she was the Virgin Mary, especially when a new devotee gave Paloma a turquoise cloak. When she rested her hand on the head of Mastiff, they likened Paloma to a Paleolithic queen in command of lions.

To Paloma, motherhood was a transformation like no other. She understood, now, how the women of Tartatenango could walk across mountain ranges to get here, do battle with foes twice their size. How the prospect of separation could drive a woman to murder or madness. The whole world consolidated into the tiny package that was her swaddled daughter. And at the same time that she was ferociously protective, she felt more vulnerable than she ever had, more so than even during her ordeal in the swamp, more connected than during the most intimate nights of her marriage.

GONZAGO HAD SENT HIS MULE train on ahead so he could keep an eye on Paloma and the baby but couldn't stay any longer without losing his business to mutiny. He had promised protection if Paloma and child joined him, tried to seduce her, cajole her, beg her but she was renewed and strengthened by her motherhood, and so refused.

"Return," she whispered to him in bed that night, and laid the sleeping baby on his chest until he thought he would break open from her fragility and her trust.

Over coffee in the morning, still shirtless and unwashed, Gonzago laid maps across a table in the bar and planned a smaller route within his current plans so he could swoop back to his beloved rainmaker and her golden-throated child.

PALOMA, PREVIOUSLY KNOWN AS A shrewd but honest trader, then as a jaguar transformed, as founder of the town and tavern owner, was now Mother of the Singing Baby, *Madre del Infante Cantante*. Women in Tartatenango brought their newborns, even toddlers, and begged Paloma to be their wet-nurse, even for a single suckling. Thankfully, Paloma's milk was so plentiful that her breasts were three times their normal size and when Valeria nursed at one the other leaked enough milk to run down the front of Paloma and puddle for lapping dogs and monkeys at her feet. It all seemed a lot of fuss to Paloma, but she was willing to oblige and could be seen at all hours with Valeria and babies of all colors and ages at her breasts, chuckling over the looks on their faces and flushed by the sensuous pleasure of nursing. In return, villagers brought her flowers, cakes with dried fruit, candles of supplication. Old women were praying at their feet, and men removed their hats before laying out flowers and newborn chicks.

By two months old Valeria would sing herself to sleep, by three months her voice was loud enough to soothe the entire nursery of babies.

Sister Agnes was perhaps the most transformed by the *Infante Cantante*. Still a little delirious from the previous night's drinking, she rubbed the sleep from her eyes, adjusted a small rum cask under her arm, and saw from across the compound the serene Paloma in a blue cape with an adored child on her knee, so biblical, like the statue that had set Sister Agnes on her initial path of destruction.

Then the baby sang, a sound that made birds fill the trees above her, and the birds who had returned to trap Fadul shake their wings. Dogs sat in rapt attention lined up like sentries beside Mastiff, with the monkeys aligned above them in the trees. Sister Agnes set the rum cask down and fell to her knees in front of Paloma and child.

Paloma looked at her suspiciously, but she had seen the haggard nun passed out under the bushes and staggering the streets frequently enough that Paloma had stopped thinking of Sister Agnes as the swindler who had chased her out of the floating village. There was no need to punish her further.

After two hours of prayer Sister Agnes cut her hair down to the scalp, washed herself and her clothing in the river, found her wimple in a rag bag in the costume room and dedicated herself to silent, sober, obeisance to the child.

Paloma did her best to keep the deification in check. Thanksgiving for the lovely music was one thing, but the opposition they had faced on the road had taught her that bringing heaven and hell into the discussion was dangerous, and while Sister Agnes' assistance (and especially her silence) were welcome, it all made Paloma uncomfortable. She refused to allow people to call Valeria a miracle, slapped away the hands of anyone who thought the baby's touch had healing powers. But she had indulged them all with her breast milk which looked like complicity, so a cottage industry sprung up of carved medallions of the *Infante Cantante* as a saint, and tea towels painted with her likeness.

THE NUNS BY THE SIDE of the road, who now sat under the shaded porch of a cottage that the villagers had built for them, were awestruck by the baby. The local priest, fueled by stories of the protests on Paloma's journey, stormed to Caketown to denounce it all, but by that time, the nuns had heard too many stories of boys and girls abused by priests, and had recalled the injustices done to each of them. They blocked his entrance to Tartatenango as they had blocked others in the past but stood with their arms crossed, hostile and unapologetic.

"One can pray *for* the baby without praying *to* the baby," the head nun said and glared until he pivoted in retreat.

WHEN WORD OF THE BABY'S music got out via the mule train, so many people arrived that impromptu concerts were organized just to control the crowds. A delegation from the floating village brought dried fish and bouquets of water lilies. Romani flocked from all over the country, and hermits came down from the mountains. Everyone who had had a faux wedding booked a return to walk down the aisle to what was called angelic music, with the faux couple kneeling in front of the baby who was propped up in a hand-carved throne. The seamstresses competed to sew Valeria the most cherubic dress. The field behind the bar was filled with wagons packed so closely that their sides rubbed. The bakeries produced little hand pies with a musical note on the crust and worked around the clock. The florist was able to revive trade after the drought, and boys and girls got jobs hawking skewers of meat from the street corners. The lace and beading workshop burned candles like never before; the bridesmaids and groomsmen cleaned themselves up and got back on the dancefloor. Magdela made a habit of being a stand-in groom, sending away to Heroica for her own tuxedo and when not booked as a groom, she and another woman in a tux danced all evening in each other's arms.

Tartatenango was no longer a settlement, but a full-blown town, with all the smells of horse sweat, spilled beer, laundry soap and leather, the sounds of guitars and accordions in the night, and children who ran wild down the lanes until their little feet remembered the location of every protruding root and wagon track, every spot of shade on an overhang at the river, every bend in the jungle where a fruit tree grew.

A sister and brother team carved statues, headstones, and hearths, the wood chips fragrant and reassuring. Women wove belts and knitted hats, made lace gloves and thin veils, their hands incessantly busy, fingers flying, unlike the town to the north where the women sat idly in the gloves, their soft hands motionless in their laps.

Tartatenango developed its own unique communication network when a woman walked into town pulling a small wagon, doves covering her head, shoulders and her arms, as thick a white blanket of birds on the wagon top as the birds were thick and black on Fadul's house. She had set the birds quietly in a row by the road and assembled a dovecote from ornately carved wooden slats. For a small coin, she would send one of her doves to deliver a message, and every morning as the sun rose, birds would fly off carrying birth announcements and pleas for reunification. The bridesmaids and mothers clustered there in the evening in hopes of a response, and soon the Rebels used the doves to coordinate bond sales and battles.

That month on the full moon there was no wedding, so the dancing women were especially drunk and staggered around the dancefloor to the obscene songs of the groomsmen. Old Man Orjuela was shuffling jauntily, his arms around Doris who snapped her fingers in time to the music.

The allure of the baby even coaxed Maria from her hiding place in the covered garden. She arrived in a plain black dress and a veiled hat, and Jade, overjoyed that Maria had found a way to rejoin life, wrapped her in her arms. Soon Maria caught the spirit of the festivities and constructed a large collection of hats with veils that she then matched with flowing robes and feathered scarves, her costumes becoming more outrageous every week, while still hiding her face, until she moved through the Caketown Bar like a Merlin-figure, genderless, passing herself off as a soothsayer from Madagascar, then a duchess from Poland, a cloaked and reclusive magician from Ecuador.

Magdela wept with relief the first time she saw her on the dancefloor and, in her tuxedo, accompanied her to the bar every evening thereafter.

Having been in hiding for so long, Maria was wild

and unhinged at the Caketown Bar, inappropriately butting into people's conversations, sitting on men's laps, singing at the top of her lungs, and as an inexperienced drinker, waking up on the floor with a hangover.

PALOMA, WHO REASSUMED THE CASINO operation from the newly devout Sister Agnes, finished handing out the night's game of chance winnings to an old couple who cautiously listed the culverts and gardens, fences and chicken coops that could now be repaired or restored or expanded, a litany so forlorn, so filled with tentative hope, that Paloma was tempted to double their earnings right there. A few people won big and put new roofs on their houses and Paloma forgave debts and sometimes slipped a few chips into the apron pockets of wives who came to collect wayward husbands on the verge of losing too much.

IT SEEMED AS IF EVERYTHING had been put right: their founder was home, temperatures were balmy, the wedding business booked up as fast as Jade could make the appointments, and the ceaseless stream of visitors brought the village almost back to full employment. Two of the youngest protesting nuns traveled back to their nunnery on the far side of the swamp and returned with the wedding dresses they had worn to marry Christ, which they gleefully donated to the wedding business. Paloma had had buckets of boiling water carried to the spring which melted the bug goo when pickaxes and shovels had failed. It resumed its flow. Every night from 3 a.m. until 5 a.m., it rained enough to fill the cisterns and water the crops, stopping in time for the air to be fresh and gentle as the Caketowners woke for coffee and *aromatica*.

A request came in for the Valeria to sing in concerts as part of a traveling circus. A preacher with a tent revival tried to bamboozle Paloma into signing Valeria. Even the rodeo on the other side of town, whose riders added to the population of cast-off women every year, sent word of their interest. Paloma refused. Again, the road held no appeal, especially now that it had shown its dangerous side. The only enticement was the prospect of a life with Gonzago, which promised a solace she hadn't known since Gabriel. Even his silly belief that she controlled the weather could be forgiven as romantic excess.

3

ONE SUNDAY MORNING A CARRIAGE for hire pulled up and an old woman named Consuela Gracia made a beeline for Old Man Orjuela. A month ago, she had come with her niece who had wanted a raucous party, but Consuela had been so struck by the tenderness of Senor Orjuela as he comforted her niece before her faux wedding, that Consuela had thought of nothing since. She had seen that his kindness healed even the most wounded, that people traveled for hours to receive his absolution.

If his love could melt your heart when he didn't know you, imagine the feeling if he actually loved you, she thought. Two days ago, she had made up her mind:

legal or not, she wanted this heart-melting Senor Orjuela on her arm.

At first, he was befuddled by her proposal, but Jade caught on and explained.

"Marry *me*?" he blustered. "No one wants to..."

The bridesmaids sent up a chorus and the groomsmen insisted.

Magdela fought hard to be best man.

They scrubbed Orjuela red, called in a barber, and put their coins together to have the best costumes tailored for him. The entire costume closet was emptied by all the groomsmen and bridesmaids who volunteered to be in the wedding for free. Mostly, they were excited over the chance to sit him down and form a semi-circle around him.

"No one could have asked for a better father," one of the groomsmen said, and Old Man Orjuela choked up.

"You've always been there for me, Dad." They went around the circle, extolling his virtues, his sacrifices, retelling outings in the jungle and times he had saved them from a rabid dog, stuck up for them in the face of teachers and police. They loved his funny jokes, they said, and still had the little toy he had carved for their crib. They reminded him of how he had taught them to fish, how he held them when they cried.

"We're all so lucky you're our father."

The wedding was delayed by more than an hour, as

Old Man Orjuela wept over their hands as others had his.

Dancing with Consuela, though, he was conflicted.

"It's all make-believe," he said to her.

She smiled and put her hand against his smooth cheek. "But your tenderness is not."

It had been years, perhaps decades, since he had been touched with such affection, and he turned his face and kissed her palm, gathered her hand in his and held it against his heart.

They became inseparable.

4

THE INCREASED WEDDING BUSINESS AND musical events
helped the coffers of some but not all. The burly man
who could not pass for a groomsman, the hunch
shouldered, the toothless, all had a place at the distillery
but not at the wedding party. Cosimo saw the brooding
unhappiness and the suspicion of worthlessness that
drove men to violence and also saw himself in many of
them when they postured, chest out with pride but
stumbling from drink. Unwilling to be the only rough
and ready man to be included in the parties, he
sheltered a glass of vodka against his chest and
returned to his sheep wagon. He had long given up the
guilt that he had felt in his early years as a man unable

to live up to the expectations of the father who named his only son after the great Venetian trader. But he wanted a profession to be proud of. He wanted to teach his son to be honest, but more than that, to be capable and lucky and courageous enough to make a success great enough that he didn't have to resort to thievery, for him to have enough money to never resort to a swindle again. And while Fadul was hard at work in her bird-encrusted house printing bonds that he could sell in quantity to the banker, Cosimo was losing interest.

He pulled out his pipe and sat on the front porch after putting Matias to bed. Jade was out walking Jewel to get her to sleep and she and Cosimo had long ago stopped pretending it was an accident that Jade always wound up at his steps. She climbed onto the porch and put Jewel in the crib with Matias. She settled herself into a large rocker made to fit her by great mounds of pillows that Cosimo would put out every evening.

"I want to do something for Matias," he said, his head hung but looking in her direction. She would have put her hand on his shoulder if she could have reached, but she settled for the crook of his elbow.

"Something to be proud of," he continued. "Something genuine. Legal," he said it like it was an odd concept. "Something legal. It's why I haven't sold the mayor the bonds yet. I keep asking myself: which ledge am I going to back away from?"

Jade got onto her knees in her chair so that her eyes

were at Cosimo's level and, putting her tiny hands on his cheeks, smiled with relief and joy. She kissed him and he scooped her up and brought her to his lap. They rubbed their cheeks against each other like puppies, kissed temples, necks, and palms of hands, sunk their noses into fragrant hair. There was lust, but even more powerful, there was homecoming, recognition, a private camaraderie as they moved the babies indoors and spent the night nurturing their love.

## Chapter 14

1

Rodrigo Cardoso's desire to punish the distillery owner dissipated when the last bin and bolt of Magdalena Elixirs was carted away, and he spent his days in the bank as he had before, silently reading, while the teller watched the dust motes in the sun beams and the loan officer dreamed of Orietta.

His quietude ended, however, when he strode late into his businessman's meeting and the village priest, having already riled the men up, turned on him. Utter blasphemy on the south side of town. A baby, deified. Fallen women, drunken men. Rumors of Rebel sympathizers. What was he going to do about it? Had he no control? They encircled him, punching an accusatory finger into his chest, making demands, muttering under their breath as they turned away.

By the end of the luncheon, Rodrigo had a seething, vicious determination to purge the land of anyone who could or would challenge him. Starting with the southside of his own town. Riffraff anyway. Unsanitary. Drunkards and thieves. Bastards and women with no morals. He could not have it on the edge of his town.

To rid an area of inhabitants, make the area uninhabitable, he resolved, as he grabbed his coat, and headed out the door.

TWO NIGHTS LATER, PABLO ORGANIZED five men with vats of herbicide strapped to their backs to spray a billowing fog of arsenic, mercury and lead over an area south of Araca. Unfortunately for the mayor, however, the men Pablo hired were grifters who had no knowledge of Tartatenango and so assumed that the target was a huge gathering of Romani who had set up between the city limits of Araca and the beginning of Caketown.

The toxic fog killed all of the Romani's chickens and cats, three dogs, and an old woman sleeping in the hedgerow because she had gone out in the night to pee and lost her way. Every one of the Romani woke with a splitting headache.

Over morning coffee, they keened for the old woman

but silently struggled to place how they knew her. The coyotes had already carried off the cats and the chickens and while they bemoaned the loss of the dogs, they realized they could not remember whose dogs they had been. By noon, the grass and shrubs had turned brown and died, even the centuries-old trees seemed to be struggling, while the Romani sheepishly admitted that they didn't recognize each other. Standing around the communal fire, they turned in circles, unable to definitely claim their wagons and by three in the afternoon the women weren't certain that they were even married.

They quickly buried the old woman and the dogs together, thinking perhaps they were a foursome who had died in a love pact, and turned their back on the whole thing since they knew that Romani plus a mysterious death spelled trouble for them all.

BY THE EVENING, THE ROMANI wandered into relationships that seemed better at the time; children followed the wrong woman home because they like the way she smelled.

The meek had a vague memory of an act of heroism and energized by the false remembrance of bravery, set about their projects with new vigor and confidence. Women who had lived under the cloud of loneliness for years were heartened by a nagging conviction that they had had a great love in the past.

The Romani chief could not remember who had been married to whom nor where he had put the registry, so he had no choice but to declare everyone single. What God has joined, apparently only God knows, he announced.

New love was discovered, and abusive men and angry women found themselves alone without remembering their crimes. The men who had sprayed the herbicide lost their memories as well but, based on a vague feeling that they were somehow attached to the Romani, they pitched their tents with them and stayed.

Mostly, though, the Romani were elated, experiencing as if for the first time a warm tortilla, convinced that flan was a new invention, that fried *arepa* with its soft cheese was an amazing development, their taste buds and imaginations lit up like those of curious children.

It was that sense of wonder that made Paloma suspicious: while these Romani had never come through town before, a 70-year-old man sitting in the bar who was baffled by a mango meant something was going on. She put Jade in charge of the bar and set out for the Romani camp.

When Paloma saw the devastation, she suspected the mayor right away: the swath of dead vegetation was too precise to be natural, and it was so clearly on the boundary between Araca and Tartatenango that she took it personally. It chilled her blood and she slowly walked back to the bar, frightened for Orietta, frightened for them all with a man that vicious on their outskirts.

But the Romani were buoyed up by the lightness of life without the memory of tragedy or heartache; they were ebullient over the sudden freedom to follow their heart and their impulses. Suddenly single, they danced and kissed and begged Paloma to let them use the corner of her compound to make love in their new life with an unknown partner.

The Romani began to be driven by their true callings: the tinsmith discovered the joy of writing poetry; the goatherd became a dancer; the pickle merchant built herself a grinding wheel for knives. Women took over their husbands' businesses and the wheelwright picked up an embroidery hoop. Forgetting the family trade, people chose the profession that intrigued them and in the first weeks, before they wrote procedures down, they would wake up in the morning not having remembered the new profession they had chosen yesterday let alone all of the skills that were required to practice it. People grew wary of the tarot-reader and the apothecary, wondering if the day before the two had been the mule trainer and the tanner. The cook had to pin to the wall the most basic recipes that her three young workers usually used as a matter of course, and then to double her exasperation they arrived each morning requiring instruction again and she had no choice but to train them since she couldn't remember if they were the women who had worked there the day before.

The traders among the Romani, however, had the most difficult time of it, not able to remember the relative value of things or what they had initially paid, which is key to trading. They lost all cunning and guile. Old debts were forgotten, generations-long disputes were finally solved.

People forgot which of their belongings were valuable and which key fit into which door so the whole enclave went unlocked and was easy prey to the first band of Romani teenagers who cleaned them out in a single evening but then forgot the road out of town. They were easily corralled in the morning, and all the goods were redistributed, though this time more evenly since no one could remember whose silver jewelry and tarnished spoons belonged to whom.

The next week, the Drunken Monk conducted a group wedding for the Romani in Paloma's compound; 20 couples including the grifters brought suckling pigs, roasted capon and cake, so the whole village was in a frenzy of dancing and happiness, the white skirts of the brides flashing as they danced through the night.

THE MAYOR, WITHOUT EXPLANATION, HAD ordered Orietta to stay at home during the Romani's difficulties and it wasn't until they had packed up and the last bell on the last wagon was heard leaving Caketown that she was able to slip past The Warden and arrive at the bar.

Her route took her through the moonscape caused by the herbicide and when Orietta arrived, the reception was far less cordial than the last time.

"I know he did this," Paloma hissed at her. "It could have been us, Orietta. It could have killed Valeria, and Jade and little Jewel. All of us." She waved in the direction of the retreating Romani. "They're not right in the head anymore!"

Orietta sat down and held her head in her hands. She had watched Rodrigo's rage increasing and had considered the banishment of the school children to be a hateful act, but she had never thought that he would be intent on Caketown's annihilation. Or that he would order it done in such a vicious way. The rage that had been building, then bottled up when her business was ruined, bubbled to the surface.

Paloma, pacing, lunged across the table at Orietta. "This man must be stopped."

Orietta stood with a venomous look in her eye, their faces inches apart. Paying off the loans had taken every bit the distillery had ever earned, the proceeds from the sale of every bit of copper and unused bottle. He had taken the finest thing she had ever been involved with. "We're just the ones to stop him."

Paloma went back to pacing, slower, with less anger. Orietta hailed a waitress for more rum.

"Cosimo was going to sell him bonds but has had second thoughts even though a new batch is nearly ready," Paloma said.

Orietta shook her head. "It's not enough to just take his money. Not now. Not after that." She gestured to the destruction just north of the bar.

## 2

COSIMO DROVE A BUGGY IN a wide circle on the outskirts of Araca, steeling his nerve before arriving at the bank. He was disheveled, his collar open and his cuffs undone; he smelled of drink and his hair was wild, the picture of panic. He tucked a black satin envelope under his arm and nervously requested a private meeting with the manager.

Facing Rodrigo, Cosimo used his best techniques: the bonds were given to him by his father, the last thing he owned, he said. He had meant these for his son. He agonized over his decision, looked away in shame, tried to hide his embarrassment by not looking Rodrigo in the eye. That part of the charade was real, at least: it had taken a lot to get him to take on this one last scam. He ran his hands through his hair in anxiety; 'changed his mind.' No, no, he couldn't sell. He put the bonds back into their envelope and made ready to leave.

Rodrigo took the bait. To take the last thing this lummox owned would be sweet. Beautiful revenge to see him grovel like this. He bought them all.

"Thank you, sir," Cosimo said, as he tucked far less than the bonds were worth into his vest pocket. "You now control a bit of the federal government." He said it as an off-hand remark but knew its impact, and slowly buttoned his cuffs as the idea sank into Rodrigo's mind.

The mayor let the bank ledger fall open again. "The federal government?"

"Yes. Bonds are loans, of course, and they afford you a tiny voice in the government. I have known men who gathered a stack of them and marched into the capital to be heard. As you know," Cosimo said, leaning forward, "the man with the money is always heard."

A voice in the government? Rodrigo rolled the idea in his mouth like hard candy. The real government, not just this little backwater town. He chuckled nonchalantly. "What an interesting idea. The government certainly could use some advice these days." He fiddled with a pen, laid it in a straight line beside a stack of paper. "You have more?" Rodrigo hoped he sounded disinterested.

"I could look. I think my father has a few more. And I have...contacts."

"I'm always happy to help. Money is tight everywhere and it is a pity about...your distillery. Why don't you bring me the bonds you have?"

COSIMO, NOW MORE WILLING TO participate since the mayor had used Cosimo's desperation to undercut the price, returned after two days and sold him two more. After the first half-dozen purchases, the bonds became Rodrigo's new obsession. He made doodles of the scroll-work border during bank meetings, made love to the embossing when he was alone with them, touched the sharp corners as if they were the pure edges of God's wrath.

His obsession made him drop weight, shrinking inside his clothing, which Orietta thought made him look more like a child pretending to be a man. His pant cuffs dragged on the floor as he paced his office rolling up the sleeves of his jacket.

After two weeks of frenzied buying, the certificates filled a deposit box. The two percent of the profits from Magdalena Elixirs that he kept in a separate account was gone within days.

Every night before heading home, after the teller and loan officer had donned their coats and left, Rodrigo opened the growing number of deposit boxes filled to the brim with bonds and ran his hand over them, not calculating their financial value but imagining the day that he could carry them to the capital, set them down on a desk and demand a position in the government. Chancellor of the Exchequer? An ambassadorship to Paris? Head of the Department of Commerce? Late at night, sipping a glass of port, he would envision himself leaning forward and advising the Prime Minister on tactics for the war.

One month after Cosimo crossed the threshold of the bank with the bonds, Rodrigo's personal fortune was gone, and he began embezzling the bank's money.

3

IF ANYONE IN ARACA HAD been paying attention to Caketown they would have seen the effects of an influx of money. The Rebels still got the proceeds from the original process with the bonds secreted and moved around the country, but Tartatenango used the bank's money to help those displaced by the distillery's demise. Valdez restocked his supplies and gave free exams. The streets were made level and a repair team reinforced the shanties of the old folks. A dentist arrived; small packets of meat were handed out each Sunday and all the children were given shoes. Jade bought better blankets for the women's dormitory, cribs for every child, and bought carved animals and puzzles from a woodworker on the far side of town. Doris was able to build a wooden floor beneath her clothes lines and after another month, set up vats for dying cloth.

Two months into Tartatenango's revival, a teacher turned up at the gate. Disillusioned by the bustle of city life and the way parents treated him like a servant, he came to Caketown and set up a school in an abandoned corn crib where, despite weeks of scrubbing, the occasional bit of silk still fell onto a lucky child's notebook.

He was a lithe black man from Curacao who, with great flair and enthusiasm, danced the lessons more than lectured. The expanses of the ocean, soaring bird migrations, swirling fishes, the rise and fall of emotions in great pieces of literature, all flowed through him as he stood in front of the students in his tight shiny pants and crisp shirt, seeming more prepared for a dance floor than a classroom.

When the children ran home after class, he spent early evenings teaching Doris to read.

MAGDELA'S BLACKSMITHING WORK FOR WHIPPET expanded to include ornate hinges and locks. Horses were better cared for and shoed on time. The shop's output improved, and they moved into iron work for rigs, hitches and latches. Whippet repaired wagons, built contraptions for wells, could be called upon to ingeniously forge an intricate lever or moving part and they couldn't keep up with the demand for spikes and nails.

Orietta, Paloma, Cosimo and Jade toasted with rum late at night. Time for the second part of the plan.

Sunday after church, Fadul, temporarily liberated by Paloma from her imprisonment-by-bird, drove Caketown's finest wood-paneled wagon to Araca's main square where she set up her tintype camera on the pavilion Rodrigo had built during his campaign. Doris started up a tune on her accordion, grabbing the attention of the families on promenade who clustered around the tintypes of the butcher's boy dressed in a tuxedo and top hat, the family of the plowman in the best regalia that they had in the costume cupboard. She called to them.

"Stand for a minute, wait for three, have a portrait for life! Step this way, folks, bring the kids."

Unbeknownst to its residents, Arca was increasingly cut off from the rest of the world and had taken on a dusty somnambulance, with quaint ways and old-fashioned clothing, a pace of life from several lifetimes ago. The invention seemed shocking, and the opportunity to preen for it, irresistible.

"Oh Rodrigo," Orietta whispered and clutched his arm. "A portrait of you. To hang in the bank."

Rodrigo tilted his head, smoothed the front of his vest that ballooned out on each side of the thin man.

"Or the mayor's office," he said. "A portrait. Of their leader."

"Yes," she said as if it had been his idea. "What are they called again?" feigning a girlish confusion.

"Tintypes." He watched the couples laughing, inspecting the samples, digging in their pockets and queuing up, mothers straightening the clothing of their children.

"I'll bet they don't have them in the provincial capital," Orietta said haughtily.

He studied his wife like there was a sea-change going on in his mind.

"Imagine," she said, "my husband's likeness hanging in every post office and government storefront from here to the capital." She fanned her face with her lace-covered hand.

THEY ARRANGED A SPECIAL SITTING, just for the mayor, and Fadul, who seemed to have aged a decade since her imprisonment and was more grizzled, grey and sallow than before, ordered him around like he was a muleteer.

"A portrait-sized tintype for a man of your stature, not a little one to slip in a pocket and be disregarded," she mumbled.

"Yes, of course," he agreed.

"Framed and hung over a mantle."

"Yes, yes. And the frames need brass plaques. Rodrigo Cardoso, Mayor of Araca."

"Don't forget the bank," Orietta prompted.

"Good thinking. Rodrigo Cardoso, Mayor of Araca, President of Araca Bank and Trust."

Orietta declined to be included in the portraits, and Fadul, who didn't know the mayor's wife was Orietta-the-shrouded, secretly rolled her eyes over Orietta's faux-demure protests that her beauty belonged only to him. The mayor easily settled into an emperor-like portrait in his best suit, now festooned with medals and pins that Orietta had never seen. He stood on the top two steps of the pavilion with his shoulders back and had Orietta vote: top hat on or off, sword or no sword, walking stick or not. He settled on top hat, sword, hand in jacket like Napoleon and Orietta applauded quietly, while laughing inside.

A dozen tintypes were laid out on the floor of the pavilion and Rodrigo inspected them as a general would troops. He chose one for his home, one for the bank, one for the mayor's office, and ordered Fadul to ship the rest to post offices around the province. Good advance work for his rise up the political ladder, he concluded.

They had made a special batch of bonds to be sent out: bonds that were clearly wrong, with an error so glaring that Fadul protested, stormed around the place, a black-clad, angry woman lashing out at Cosimo and Orietta like the black crows pacing across her roof. But she made them, muttering about the danger.

The hyper-flawed bonds in the frames of the Cardoso

portraits fanned out across the province the way a good labyrinth works: a trusted friend who knows a dodgy man putting the screws to a hungry policeman in cahoots with a jewel thief who knew a postman; and a naive teacher behind in rent who sends an unwitting child with an envelope of money to a muleteer with a grudge who made an arrangement with a young man who will stop at nothing, each unaware of each other and so lost like a spiderweb in a wind storm.

One of the tintypes of Rodrigo hung on the wall of the post office in the capital. They planned the reveal of the flawed bonds and Cardoso's culpability for a day when the magistrate and the head of the Treasury Department were both walking through the corridor for their luncheon with the postmaster. A swindler in Cosimo's employ inspected the tintype but quickly slit the paper at the back of the frame with a pen knife secreted in his hand.

"Whoa," he said, stepping back as the counterfeit bonds spilled out from behind the frame and slid onto the floor.

A junior clerk, also on the take, gathered them for the blustering magistrate and stood back as all hell broke loose.

Cardoso and counterfeit bonds! What is he playing at? With indignation and harrumphing, the machinery of justice and revenge began to turn.

Three days later, unannounced, the Treasury

Investigator, backed by four men on horseback, walked into the bank flanked by soldiers.

The Treasury Investigator whistled for an officer to bring in the evidence and put it on top of the ledgers and ink pots on the banker's desk.

"Is this your portrait?"

"Yes," Rodrigo said proudly.

"And you arranged for them to be hung in post offices around the province?"

"I did." He threw his shoulders back and raised his chin. "Perhaps a bit presumptuous I admit but I have political ambitions beyond this little town."

"And what are these?" the Investigator demanded as he revealed the government bonds behind the torn brown paper.

"I have no idea why they would be there..." he stammered.

"No knowledge of government bonds?

"Well yes, I have quite a bit of knowledge," Rodrigo said, puffing out his chest as if about to lay down his trump card and demand his say in government that very instant. He would show them, he reasoned. Power is to be wielded.

He opened seven rows of deposit boxes deep inside the safe. "I would imagine," he said, presenting them with a wave of his hand, "that I control several of your salaries with this level of investment in the government."

"They're counterfeit!" the Investigator shouted into his face. "Arrest him," he ordered. "And seize the bonds."

"No, you misunderstand!" he shouted, struggling against the officers. "I'm a gentleman, and the mayor of the town." They tightened their grip on him.

With his hands in front of him in shackles, Rodrigo was walked out of the bank weeping for himself, alternately stamping the ground and then bending double while screaming for Cosimo.

He struggled to get close to the Investigator and whispered. "You don't want bedlam. Allow me to get my affairs and those of the city in order or you'll have your hands full. We have a south end that's very dangerous."

The policeman tightened his grip on Rodrigo's arm.

Cardoso shook his head as if dispelling a bad dream and called to his political sycophants. "Pablo!"

Pablo stepped from the side of the bank where he waited for orders, and grinned. Rodrigo twisted and struggled, sputtering, waving his arms in the direction of Tartatenango. What Pablo heard was the order he had been waiting for since the first time Rodrigo had drunkenly promised to issue it: to burn the place down. He and his two cohorts hustled to the wagon and set out for Caketown.

THE POLICE HAD FIRST COME to the house to find Rodrigo, so Orietta had followed them to the bank, partly to make sure the plan worked, partly to enjoy her husband's demise, but she had heard his drunken plan to burn Tartatenango and now saw his henchmen spring in action.

"No! You can't!" Orietta screamed at him as she looked southward and understood what was intended. "No!" She lifted her skirts and started running toward Tartatenango.

Pablo's underlings, no smarter than the grifters, lit the devastated Romani campground on fire with oil-soaked torches Pablo kept in the wagon with the cudgels and knives. The herbicide, though, acted as a propellant and flames shot out from the edge of the road through the entire field of the Romani, then jumped across the bushes to the first houses of Caketown.

"Fire!" Orietta screamed as she ran down the backstreets of Tartatenango. "Run! They're coming for you! Fire!"

The residents of Caketown threw down baskets of laundry, shovels, and hoes. The muleteers ran to the nursery with Paloma and mothers to save the babies while the villagers untied their horses, unlocked their chickens and pigs, abandoned their cats and called for their dogs. Fire, they shouted to one another. Drivers put old folk into the space in their half-loaded wagons and called for the bridesmaids. Dr. Valdez ran on his short legs with his big bag until he was picked up by a muleteer who leaned over on his horse and hoisted him one-handed onto the back.

Most ran screaming into the jungle, followed by the monkeys with their wigs, the birds, the livestock. Doris' laundry line caught fire, the shirts and dresses shriveling and falling in an instant. Houses toppled and the dormitory was lit from within by tall red flames. Tin roofs crashed to the ground and shanties pitched over from the heat. The bar burned down completely, except for the dancefloor that held back a fringe of flame on its edges.

At the smell of the first house bursting into flame, Maria screamed and ran toward the river, reliving the day of her disfigurement. She plunged into the river and waded to a flat rock with Magdela at her heels. Jade, the seamstress, the nuns, and other women with their swaddled babies in their arms, ran into the river and clung to the shrubs and grasses.

Those in the jungle were cut off from the river, so a bucket brigade was useless, and they could only stand by and watch everything they had worked for and everything they had engulfed in flame.

THE MULETEERS RODE THROUGH EACH of the streets and had dropped off Old Man Orjuela and Sister Agnes before returning to look for any stragglers. Orietta ran holding her skirts up above her knees through the backstreets and alleys of Tartatenango shouting at the top of her lungs and dodging falling timbers. She stood in an intersection, turning in every direction to be sure all were gone, as the muleteers surveyed the scene on their nervous horses. Then both the riders and Orietta realized that the flames surrounded her, with the muleteers and villagers on the other side of the wall of flame.

Orietta took her hat off, her hair cascaded to her shoulders, and the beauty of her caught the muleteers' breath in their chests. They had no idea who she was, but she seemed like a specter. She was their Joan of Arc, but so beautiful that she was surely an angel. A beam of light seemed to radiate heavenward, where she would ascend any moment, they were sure. They didn't worry for her safety, and as the smoke thickened around her, they were certain that she had risen.

All exits cut off by the flames, Orietta ran into the labyrinth of the strangler fig tree, curling up as the fire roared around her. Billowing smoke filled the maze of the tree, but the fire burned around it, as she curled up behind the silver vines in the deepest part of her first home and slipped away from smoke inhalation.

As the flames took down the last building and the rest of Tartatenango was a silver pile of ash, Paloma walked through the crowd in the jungle with Valeria and three other children in her arms, taking a head count, orchestrating tearful reunions, gathering those with burns and calling for Valdez. Three men restrained

Cosimo as he roared about returning to find Jade. Paloma heard snatches from the muleteers.

"Thank God we were warned by that lady..."

"I swore she rose into the clouds."

"Beautiful. An angel. Couldn't have been real."

"A lady..." Paloma started. "Orietta!"

Paloma pushed Valeria into Cosimo's arms, already full of Matias and Jewel. She ran in her longest stride back into Tartatenango, with Cosimo on her heels. Word went out among the villagers, but they were looking for the simple, shrouded Orietta.

Without hesitation, Paloma returned to the strangler-fig tree, calling to Orietta. Their house was gone except for a tilting chimney, the bar was nowhere to be seen, the dancefloor was a black-edged jigsaw puzzle piece. Paloma fell to her knees in the ash in front of the charred strangler-figure tree, blackened everywhere except in one spot: the vine tendrils, usually a silver grey, formed a bright green cage for Orietta, who lay curled in her sky-blue silk dress untouched by flame.

Paloma crawled through the ash to reach her, burning her knees and shoulders but she pulled Orietta out and cradled her in her arms, rocking and weeping with Mastiff howling at her side. The muleteers fell to their knees and covered their faces with guilt at having left her. Cosimo found Jade and others coming out of the river and he roared again, this time with relief.

THEY LAID ORIETTA ON THE side of a door that hadn't been charred and propped it on four barrels. People filed by, shocked and heartbroken, as no one in Tartatenango had ever seen Orietta except in her sack dress and hiding hat, had never seen the perfect symmetry of her face, the thick and lustrous hair, flawless skin. Those who had thought Orietta-the-shrouded was dowdy were now cut to the quick. The women and men who had worked for her were devastated: beautiful on the inside, generous and kind, she was also beautiful on the outside, and they felt petty for having been angry when the distillery closed.

The bridesmaids sobbed: their whole lives had been spent pretending to be someone this beautiful, while the old women cried into their handkerchiefs. They wept for the loss of one so beautiful, for the world's loss now that the beauty would decay; and as Paloma spun the story of her disguise and her marriage, they wept for being deprived of her beauty while their enemies in Araca had basked in its glow. They wept for the torment of one so blessed with beauty that she was forced to hide it for fear of abuse.

And when they heard that the mayor was to blame for the fire, their grief turned to rage.

At the first smell of fire, the townspeople of Araca had gathered their children and fled. Chief Sanz, pressed into service by the Treasury Investigator, chained Rodrigo to one of the posts of the Victorian pavilion, and joined the effort to evacuate the city. The buggies and coaches streamed out of town, abandoning everything to the flames, with no plan to return. The keening for Orietta was so loud and plaintive that the fleeing townspeople thought it was the horn of a ship run aground; some said banshees announcing the death of their queen, and the old women twisting in their seats as the little city receded were convinced it was an upending of the town's cemetery whose spirits now charged them with brutal neglect.

When those who had stayed behind saw the soot-covered villagers of Tartatenango marching en masse into Araca in pursuit of Rodrigo, the ash of their homes blackening their pant legs and hems, with their beloved Orietta carried on the door, even the biggest men went pale with fear and fled.

THE NORTHERN-MOST SEAMSTRESS RUSHED toward Paloma with the turquoise cloak that she had been mending at the time of the fire and had carried into the river where she had fled. She reached up to drape it over Paloma's shoulders.

Paloma, in her turquoise cape with Valeria on her arm and Mastiff by her side, lead the procession, flanked by dogs, sheep, goats, all the townspeople, while the monkeys in the wigs brachiated through the trees above them, and the black crows that had trapped Fadul flew above them in the formation of an ebony chuppah. The groomsmen wept unapologetically, while Magdela and Whippet menacingly slapped wrought-iron pokers into their palms.

At the sight of Orietta's pallet, Rodrigo's knees buckled. "My wife!" The police directing traffic out of town were aghast. Young men from Araca who had been driven to be worthy of her without acknowledging it, had taken out loans and started shops and services, finished their schooling, studied for the captain's exam, painted their houses more often. Seeing her laid out, they wept like children.

"Murderer!" the Tartatenangans shouted as Rodrigo came into view, and while he had been struggling against their grip, he now called to the police for protection.

"Mur-dur-er!" the crowd chanted. The black crows settled on the pavilion above the chained Rodrigo.

Cosimo, with both babies cradled in his arms and a weeping Jade clinging to his elbow, stepped forward, his eyes burning like a bull when he saw Rodrigo.

Rodrigo shouted at the policeman who was nowhere to be seen. "Sanz, you have to get me out of here!"

The banshee wailing of the women reached a fever pitch and then baby Valeria, who sat on Paloma's arm with her pudgy hand on the side of Paloma's breast in a mudra, began to sing.

The crowd quieted as the silver thread of her voice

rose into the air. Unlike her other singing that reminded them of happy newborn lambs on unsteady feet, of the joy of a first flower above the ground, this song was in a minor key, so mournful that rage was turned back to sorrow. The song of a leaf fallen into a deep well, of a hawk finding her chick at the bottom of the tree. Any who weren't weeping for Orietta wept from the mournful song of heartbreak coming from the baby.

Rodrigo, the music enveloping him, hung his shoulders but lifted his head when he thought he saw his own mother in the crowd. Though she had been dead for more than a decade, he saw her there. These people could have included his mother. And him; it had been him and his mother, struggling, just the two of them, his mother work weary and abandoned by love. These were his mother's people, and the full weight of what he had done struck him, as the Treasury Investigator returned and charged him with his crimes.

"Forgery, arson, treason, murder," he intoned as he put Rodrigo into the paddy wagon, and all rode away chased by a mob of Tartatenangan men and the screaming crows.

A brutal hot noon sun broke through the clouds as the crowd came into the deserted center of Araca.

Just as Araca chose to be unaware of Tartatenango, the Caketown villagers had not ventured into Araca further than the back doors, out sheds, or coal shoots, had never seen firsthand the front of the houses or the town square, and they looked with surprise at the whitewashed buildings, the decorative, carved scrollwork and the clean glass windows of the storefronts. No rough boards on sawhorses here, there were display cases with little signs, and curtains, shelves in straight rows rising from straight and level floors. Wooden sidewalks, well-tended streets.

The cook from the Caketown Bar was the first to take over a kitchen in an Araca restaurant, striding in and stirring a pot of soup that had only just now gone cold. She stoked the fire and checked the supply of dishes (matching, without chips!), donned an apron and began feeding the sad crowd. Doris drew baths in the biggest house while the bridesmaids went house to house gathering clean clothing for the soot-covered villagers.

Cosimo and a friend who had gone foraging returned with a coffin and Orietta was set on sawhorses in the pavilion where devotees filed past her day and night while Mastiff sat beneath the coffin and Paloma sat by its side, Sister Agnes and the protesting nuns praying at its foot.

Gonzago and the mule train, alerted by a weeping tinker, turned around in the middle of the mountains and returned in time for the funeral, though it meant goods were spoiled and supplies undelivered. Every woman and man who had worked at Magdalena Elixirs, every patron of the Caketown Bar, every trader, angler, farmer, boatman and shepherd poured into the city and pitched their tents on the village green. Esteban the boatman brought a dozen people from the floating village. All the Romani who had come through town set up their wagons on the north side, including those Romani whose sense of wonder had been rebooted when their memories were erased. The Rebel soldiers laid down their rifles for the day and said the rosary on their knees.

They buried her in the middle of the town square with Old Man Orjuela and the Drunken Monk officiating, Sister Agnes in full prostration, and Simon Bolivar Valdez touching foreheads with his incandescent hands.

Within a month, Tartatenango had overtaken Araca. A mountain man came down from the hills and carved a six-foot statue on a gothic pedestal. On one side he fashioned the shrouded Orietta, an enormous radiating heart filling her chest, and on the other, the elegant beauty Orietta, rays of light shooting from the top of her head. Fresh flowers were found there every morning, even when the great-grandchild of the youngest Tartatenangan was an old woman.

Dr. Valdez turned one of the big houses into a hospital and the lithe teacher designated another as a school. The baker from Caketown took over the ovens, the butcher stepped into the gleaming tile store. Paloma, tenderly going through Orietta's house, found the recipe for her remarkable vodka and gave it to Cosimo and Jade, who rebuilt and reopened the distillery, employing every able-bodied woman and man, reinstating the kitchen garden, the transport wagons, the aprons and gloves. The Warden had snatched Orietta's jewelry box at the first smell of smoke but finding the cases empty next to a single key, figured out Orietta's strategy, rode to Le Ceiba Grande and withdrew the jewels from the bank deposit box without being questioned. She bought a steamer ticket to Spain. Maria could not be cajoled off the rock so Magdela built a hut over her as shelter from the rain and set up a pully system to float a basket of food to her three times a day. Maria spent the rest of her life there.

Fadul had run into the jungle as soon as the fire made the birds flee and she never stopped: there were sightings of her more than 500 miles away, a woman in black who walked bent double, ducking invisible birds, writhing as if she had developed a tic or was being pecked at by crow-demons of R Johnson tintype man and ghost.

Paloma relaunched the Caketown Bar in an indoor market with one side open to the square that, remarkably, never had to close its doors to inclement weather. Matias, son of Cosimo, grew up to be a rodeo clown, perhaps having learned as an infant at the fence post that staring down a deadly animal was somehow followed by life's joy. Valeria's concerts were conducted on the dais built by Rodrigo until they financed a grand concert hall and, though she was no longer a baby, her skill improved, and people flocked to see a ten-year-old who sang opera. Children abandoned at the city gate were taught violin and French horn, finally making up a children's orchestra that toured with Valeria throughout Calexicobia, to Paris and back. Sister Agnes renounced the cloth, the bottle, and her vow of silence, traveling with the orchestra and running the orphanage with a jubilation and tenderness that she never knew she possessed. The wedding business flourished and hosted the genuine unions of Cosimo and Jade, Paloma and Gonzago, Doris and the lithe teacher, Consuelo and Old Man Orjuela, as well as the faux weddings of a stream of pregnant women, young mothers, and lonely men, who wept over the wrinkled hands of the Orjuelas as they whispered of their pride in the courageous and honorable people they had become.

## About the Author

 JESS WELLS LOVES MAGICAL REALISM because it "celebrates the delightful oddities of life." The author of six novels and five books of short stories, Wells is a winner of a Foreword Indies Book Award, a four-time finalist for the Lambda Literary Award, a recipient of a San Francisco Arts Commission Grant for Literature, and a member of the Saints and Sinners Literary Festival Hall of Fame. Her work has been republished in Britain and translated into Dutch and Italian. Follow her on social media and at www.jesswells.com where she blogs regularly on un-sung women and the writing life.

Please follow her on:

Facebook

Instagram

Goodreads

BookBub

## Discussion Guide

1.   What are your favorite images in this highly visual book?

2.   If you could have a faux wedding like the ones offered in Caketown, what would it be like? How many would you have? If you had it to do again, what would you change about your own wedding?

3.   Would you want Old Man Orjuela at your wedding, or in your life? What would he say?

4.   Do the consequences of Orietta's beauty still exist today?

5.   Who are your favorites among Paloma's lovers and why?

6.   Discuss the social situation of single mothers. Have you had any similar experiences? What do you think of the idea of 'paper and cake'?

7.   The story dramatizes the links between twins and the strong connections between women. Have there been any examples of this in your life?

8.   Have you read other writers in the magical realism genre?

9.    The author imagines this, in part, as an homage to Gabriel Garcia Marquez and the women of *One Hundred Years of Solitude*. What parallels can you draw between the two works?